4/14

GRAPES OF DEATH

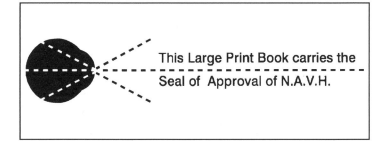

This Large Print Book carries the
Seal of Approval of N.A.V.H.

A TANGLED VINES MYSTERY

GRAPES OF DEATH

JONI FOLGER

THORNDIKE PRESS
A part of Gale, Cengage Learning

GALE
CENGAGE Learning·

Farmington Hills, Mich • San Francisco • New York • Waterville, Maine
Meriden, Conn • Mason, Ohio • Chicago

GALE
CENGAGE Learning·

LIBRARY OF CONGRESS CATALOGING-IN-PUBLICATION DATA

Folger, Joni.
    Grapes of death : a Tangled Vines mystery / by Joni Folger. — Large print edition.
        pages ; cm. — (Thorndike Press large print mystery)
        ISBN 978-1-4104-6661-7 (hardcover) — ISBN 1-4104-6661-2 (hardcover)
        1. Vineyards—Fiction. 2. Murder—Investigation—Fiction. 3. Large type books. I. Title.
    PS3606.O44G73 2014
    813'.6—dc23   2013042500

Published in 2014 by arrangement with Midnight Ink, an imprint of Llewellyn Publications, Woodbury, MN 55125-2989 USA

Printed in the United States of America
1 2 3 4 5 6 7 18 17 16 15 14

This first book is dedicated to all my Texas pals, especially those in Bastrop County. Yes, I took some liberties and made up some stuff, but I promise the names were changed to protect the innocent, so I know you'll forgive me. I miss you . . .

ONE

The sun was riding low in the sky, painting a dazzling array of orange, pink, and lavender on the horizon as the little red sports car zipped along Highway 290. At Elgin, thirty minutes east of Austin, Elise Beckett quickly signaled, turning onto the Farm-to-Market road that would take her home to River Bend, her family's vineyard.

The late July weather had been truly heinous over the last couple of weeks, with temperatures hovering in the triple digits for fifteen days straight. When you added humidity into the mix, it could really put a dent in your day. So Elise had done the only thing a homegrown Texas girl *could* do — put down the rag top, drop the pedal, and let the wind blow.

Normally she drove to Austin Bergstrom Airport and flew to Big D, but late Friday afternoon she'd instead made the five-hour drive from River Bend. She'd had a case of wine from the vineyard to schlep with her and would never have gotten it through airport security without a fight.

It seemed no matter how hard Elise tried, she was always running late for something, and today was no exception. She'd planned to leave Dallas and head for home much earlier, in hopes of beating the Sunday traffic. Unfortunately, thanks to Stuart, that was not to be. By the time she'd finally hit the road for the drive south, she was resigned to the fact that she'd probably be late for Sunday family dinner. Again.

Elise and Stuart Jenkins had met through his work with the TOGRF, the Texas Organic Garden and Research Foundation. She'd been doing the preliminary work on the hybrid vines she was developing for her family's vineyard, and they'd hit it off immediately. Stuart was attractive, stable, and brilliant — everything she thought she wanted in a partner.

They'd been dating for just over six months, and for the most part it had been fine. But lately Elise was starting to feel like something was missing — though, for the life of her, she couldn't put a finger on what was lacking.

All she knew for certain was this long-distance relationship was starting to wear thin, mostly because Stuart expected her to be the one to get on a plane to Dallas every free weekend. He, on the other hand, had come down to Bastrop County on only a handful of occasions during the entire time they'd been dating.

As if reading her thoughts, Stuart picked that moment to call her cell phone. She tapped her earpiece and answered with, "Miss me already?"

"Of course I miss you," he replied, chuckling over the line. "But I forgot to tell you that Charles and Teresa invited us to a dinner party they're hosting next Friday evening. Do you think you could come up a little earlier next week?"

"Stuart, I haven't even gotten back home yet."

Charles and Teresa Davenport were close friends, but more importantly, Charles was Stuart's immediate boss. Naturally Stuart would want to attend, but it annoyed Elise all the same.

"Now, see? Think about how much more convenient this would be if you lived in Dallas and didn't have to drive back to the boondocks of Delphine every Sunday afternoon."

"Stuart!"

"I'm just saying . . ."

"Well, don't." Elise took a deep breath and, after counting to ten, let it out slowly. "It's just shy of four o'clock and I'll be lucky if I make the family dinner on time. Pointing out what a pain the drive can be is not helping at the moment."

This was something else that was beginning to grate on her nerves: Stuart had started to nag her about moving to Dallas. Not that she was opposed to the idea of living in the city, but she loved working for the family vineyard. And Elise was nothing if not loyal. She was also finding that she was a hometown girl at heart.

"Okay, we'll let that go for now. Have you come to any decisions about the job?"

Incredibly, Stuart had sprung a job offer practically as she was heading out the door a few hours previously, which was one of the reasons she'd been late heading for home.

And not just *any* job either.

The TOGRF was expanding outside of Dallas. A benefactor had donated a large chunk of land for an organic research facility. The organization intended to break ground within the next few months and was looking for the brightest horticulturists and botanists in their respective fields. Stuart had been chosen to head up the project —

which was an amazing honor in itself — and he was now in the process of assembling the team.

"Stuart, you said you would give me time to think about it. I don't consider a few hours adequate time for a decision of this magnitude, do you?"

"I know, sweetheart. I'm sorry, but with your Master's degree in horticulture and the hybrid work you've done for the vineyard, it makes you a perfect candidate to fill one of the positions! Then there's the added bonus of us being together here in Dallas. And you have to admit, the wage and benefit package that comes with the job is amazing."

"Yes, and the work that will be done there is very exciting. The project will be on the cutting edge of organics. You don't have to remind me that this is the chance of a lifetime, Stuart, but I still need time to think about it. It would be a big change for me."

"And you're worried about your family."

"Of course I'm worried about them."

Duh! What if she decided to take this job? How would she break the news to them? When her father had his fatal heart attack two years back, he'd left the twelve-hundred-acre vineyard in its entirety to her mother. Laura Beckett depended on her

11

three children to help run the business.

Her older brother, Ross, was business manager for the vineyard and lived in the guest house with his wife, Caroline, and their two boys, Caleb and Ethan.

Her sister, Madison, who was two years younger than Elise, lived in the family residence and was in charge of all bookings at Lodge Merlot, the property's special events facility. She also assisted at The Wine Barrel, the vineyard's retail outlet.

Elise was the middle child. She'd inherited her father's passion for the land and with her education in horticulture, she was at home in charge of the vineyard's growth and development. At twenty-eight, she chose to live in the nearby town of Delphine these days, but River Bend would always remain home.

Would her family understand if she decided to take the incredible opportunity Stuart was offering?

"Look, I can't talk about this right now. I'm almost home. I'll call you in a day or two."

She knew she was being short with Stuart, but it was all so overwhelming she worried her brain may explode. This discussion was something that would have to be put on the back burner for the moment, because she'd be damned if she was going to be late for yet another family function.

Her maternal grandmother was always riding her about her lack of punctuality and would have her hide. Abigail DeVries, Miss Abby to everyone in the county, might be seventy-two years old, but she was not to be messed with — especially when she was cooking.

Elise's smile spread as she glanced over at the acres of grape vines she was now passing, knowing the rows of various varieties ran right down to the banks of the Colorado River.

Though her family had farmed the land for over a century, the vineyard was relatively new. It had been her father's idea nearly three decades ago and was a thriving business today. She felt blessed to be a part of that heritage. That she got to work for River Bend as well had been the icing on the proverbial cake. Would she really be able to turn her back on this place, even with the tempting offer Stuart had thrown at her?

Rounding the next curve, Elise flipped on her blinker as the stone gates that marked the vineyard's entrance came into view. She'd been so engrossed in her own thoughts that the sudden single *whoop* of a police siren from behind startled her.

13

Looking in her rearview mirror, she was annoyed to see the sheriff's car turn through the gates after her. If he wanted to ticket her, he was going to have to do it up at the house, because she wasn't about to be any later than she was already. She'd rather face the entire Bastrop County police force than her grandmother's ire.

As if reading her mind, the car followed her past The Wine Barrel, past Lodge Merlot, and right up to the sprawling stone ranch house of the family residence.

Pulling the cruiser in next to Elise's sports car, Deputy Jackson Landry climbed out of his vehicle and scowled at her over the hood. Like most of the folks in Delphine, she'd known Jackson all her life. At four years her senior, he was her brother's best friend.

Growing up, the boys had been inseparable and mostly a nuisance to her and Madison. She had to admit, though, she'd harbored a crush on Jackson for a time, and he could still scramble her pulse with a look. It was a shame that their timing had been so poor. It seemed that whenever he was dating someone, she was free. Then, the minute he was free, she was dating again. At the moment, they were both in relationships.

Elise sat in her car and watched Jackson stalk toward her. She admired the way the light breeze ruffled his sun-streaked, chestnut hair and how handsomely he filled out his uniform. *Fate could be a cruel bitch,* she thought with a sigh, letting her thoughts run.

He used to bug the livin' daylights out of me . . . oh my how things change. I'd like to have a taste of all that yumminess, maybe show him a few new uses for those handcuffs. Too bad he's dating Maelene McKinney. That woman has no imagination. And, of course, there's Stuart . . .

"Ms. Beckett, do you have any idea how fast you were going?" he asked.

Leaning down on the car door, he was close enough for her to see her own reflection in his mirrored sunglasses.

"Nope. But I'm sure you're gonna tell me."

He opened her car door and gave her a stern look. "Too damn fast — as usual."

Climbing out of the car, Elise held out her wrists and batted her eyelashes. "You gonna arrest me, sir?"

"Don't tempt me. Seriously, El, you drive like you're running at Daytona. You're gonna kill yourself and maybe someone else one of these days."

She made a face. "You know Gram will ban you from the dinner table if you give me a ticket."

After a brief stare off, he broke first. His warm, rich laughter poured over her, and she smiled in return.

"I doubt that very much. Miss Abby loves me cause I'm so pretty."

She gave him a smirk. Though he was probably right, she couldn't help taking him down a peg. "Yeah, you keep tellin' yourself that, pal."

She leaned back into the car for her briefcase and purse. When she straightened, she could have sworn he'd been checking her out. Of course, with those damn mirrored sunglasses, she couldn't be sure.

"Were you just lookin' at my ass?"

He took her arm as they started up the sidewalk toward the porch, and a wicked grin eased across his handsome face. "Well, if you're gonna put it out there, darlin', yeah, I'm gonna look," he drawled. "Geez, El, get a grip. I'm a *guy.*"

"In other words, you're a pig," she answered with a grin. "No pun intended, Officer. Just don't let Maelene hear you say that."

"Wouldn't make any difference," he said under his breath.

As they climbed the stone steps and crossed the porch to the massive oak entry, she shot him a look and wondered what he'd meant. Then Jackson opened the door — and they were greeted by shouting.

"Oh, goodie," Elise muttered, unable to hide the sarcasm in her voice. "Uncle Edmond is here."

From the sound of the argument, he was in the study with her mother. The door was closed, but they were obviously covering old ground, though his was the only voice loud enough to be heard clearly in the foyer. This was not the first time her dad's only brother had caused a ruckus at the farm. He'd always been a bother, but in the two years since her dad's passing, her uncle's tirades had become more frequent.

"Jacob had no damn business leaving you land that's been in my family for generations! You're not even a Beckett."

"Well, at least he's consistent." Elise glanced up at Jackson — who'd taken off the hated mirrored sunglasses — and she was surprised by the intensity in his bright green eyes and the hard look on his face. "Jax?"

"He shouldn't talk to Miss Laura like that."

"Why, Deputy Landry. What a master of

the obvious you are," she said, trying to elicit a smile. When that didn't work, she sighed. "Look, it's not like this is the first time, Jackson. And Mom can take care of herself. Come on," she said, taking *his* arm this time. "Let's go see what Gram's got going on in the kitchen. Uncle Edmond will wind down and leave soon enough. Then we can sit down to dinner in peace."

She had to fairly drag him down the hall, but he went. Once they neared the kitchen, the tantalizing aroma coming from the huge pot her grandmother was stirring took over, and Elise thought they were out of the woods.

"Mmm, something smells yummy in here. What are we having for dinner, Gram?"

"Beef stew, cornbread, and salad, with pecan pie and ice cream for dessert," Abigail said, then turned and saw Jackson. She immediately broke into a beaming smile. "Jackson! Oh, honey child, I'm so glad you could make it."

Jackson flashed Elise an *I-told-you-so* look as she watched her grandmother grab him and pull him in for a hug.

"Miss Abby, your tasty meals are the highlight of my week. Sorry I've missed the last two Sundays. You know crime waits for no man."

"Oh brother! What a suck-up," Elise said, rolling her eyes.

"Jealous much?" Jackson made a show of hugging Abigail back. "I told you, El, I'm just so danged pretty."

Elise scrunched up her nose as if smelling something rotten. "Careful, Gram. His head gets any bigger it just might explode. Trust me; you do *not* want to get any of *that* on you."

Jackson burst out laughing, just as Ross stormed through the back door with Madison on his heels.

"Maddy said Uncle Edmond is here causing trouble again."

Elise frowned at Madison. "Did she now?"

Yep. *That's* what they needed this afternoon — someone to stir the crazy pot.

Her sister at least had the good grace to look sheepish. "Sorry, but there was something different about Uncle Edmond this time, and it scared me. So I went and got Ross."

"I told Caroline to stay up at the house with the boys until he's gone," Ross grumbled. "I don't want my kids exposed to any more of his crap. Seriously, this has to stop."

"I agree," Jackson put in.

"Geez, Jackson, don't fan the flames,"

Elise said, but he ignored her.

"Has your mom thought about that restraining order we talked about last month?"

Ross snorted. "She won't even discuss it, but clearly something needs to be done."

"Okay, let's just calm down," Elise said, stepping into the fray. "You have to look at it from Mom's point of view, Ross. She doesn't want to be the one to ban the surviving Beckett brother from land that's been in his family forever."

"That's just bull, El," Ross returned. "Uncle Edmond has never been interested in working the land, and you know it. He's only concerned with what the winery can give him. He's always looked for an easy buck, a free ride. He would have run it into the ground in short order, and Grandpa Beckett knew it. That's why he left it to Daddy."

"Your dad was the one with the passion for it, anyway," Jackson added. "Jacob loved the land and growing grapes."

"Hello?" Elise said, waving a hand in front of Ross's face. "Do you both think I just crawled out from underneath a rock? I don't need a history lesson! But last time I checked, Mom was the owner of record for River Bend, and the fact remains that she's the one who will ultimately have to deal with Uncle Edmond. So take it down a notch, will you?"

"Elise's right, you two. It's Laura's decision and you need to respect that." Having cast her vote, Abigail turned back to her stew but added over her shoulder, "However, she is going to have to deal with that man soon enough, cause his threats are gettin' worse — and he's gettin' meaner about 'em."

As if to emphasize her grandmother's last comment, the conversation in the kitchen was interrupted by the sound of a commotion in the front of the house, along with more raised voices. Ross, Elise, and Jackson headed in the direction of the shouting, followed closely by Madison and Abigail. There they found Edmond nose to nose with Neil Paige, the property foreman, while Laura and Carlos Madera, one of the vineyard employees, watched with concerned faces. Her uncle's features were contorted with anger along with his signature sneer.

When Edmond had moved back to Delphine after her father's passing two years ago, Elise had begun to notice startling differences between the brothers. Her father, Jacob, had been a gentle man, rarely even raising his voice. Her uncle was a different story, and she'd always found it disconcerting to see her father's familiar image shadowed with such hostility in Edmond's face.

"I don't hold with bullying a woman for any reason," Neil was saying. "You need to leave before this gets out of control."

"Yeah? And who's gonna make me? You?"

"If need be, but I'd rather not dirty my hands with the likes of you. If you don't leave now, I'll just call the police."

Edmond blustered at that. "You're not part of the family. You're just an *employee*. That's not your call to make."

"No," Laura spoke up with quiet intensity. "It's mine. And I've had enough, Edmond. I've tried to find a solution to this situation that would satisfy both of us, but that hasn't materialized. I think I've been more than patient with your horrible behavior and outrageous demands since Jacob's passing, but I'm done."

"*You're* done? Lady, this isn't over till I say it's over."

"You're wrong, Edmond." With a sad look for her brother-in-law, Laura glanced at Jackson and then shook her head. "You can leave on your own or with the help of Deputy Landry. It's your choice. But you *will* leave now."

"You may think you've won, but I'm not going down without a fight. And I'm not afraid to get down in the mud with a gold digger like you."

"How dare you talk to her that way?" Ross stepped forward and positioned himself between them. "What's *wrong* with you? This is *not* the way you treat family."

"Ross —"

"No, Mom," he said, cutting her off. "I'm tired of his crap and so is everyone else. He needs to hear this, because everyone here sees him for what he is."

"What I am is the rightful owner of this vineyard!"

"Oh, please. This isn't about River Bend. If Dad would have left it to you, you'd have sold it in a heartbeat for what you could get out of it. You're nothing but a money-grubbing loser looking for a way to cash in on something others have built."

"Ross Alexander! That's enough!" Laura grabbed his arm and pulled him back before things could escalate further. "Edmond, please don't make this harder than it has to be."

"Oh, I'll go . . . for now. But this isn't over, Laura, not by a long stretch. This proposal would have solved your problems *and* mine, and you know it. You're gonna be sorry you didn't play ball." He looked around the foyer at the faces looking back.

23

"You're all going to pay. Big time."

With that, Edmond turned and came face to face with the foreman. They stared at each other for a good ten seconds. Silently observing, Elise held her breath, thinking they might come to blows. But then Neil stepped aside and her uncle stormed out, slamming the door behind him.

An uncomfortable silence reigned for a few moments with nobody knowing what to say or do.

"Well, that was fun," Elise said, trying to defuse the tension. All she got for her efforts was a stern look from her mother.

Then Ross spoke up in a quiet voice. "Someday somebody's going to take him out, and no one will shed a tear." A chill went down Elise's spine.

"Ross, you don't mean that," Laura said.

Ross glanced up at his mother, and the look of resolve on his face gave Elise another chill. "Don't I?" With that, he turned and went down the hall toward the kitchen.

"I'll go talk to him, try and calm him down," Abigail said with a sigh and followed Ross.

"I'll help," Madison said, hurrying after her.

Jackson glanced at Elise. "I think I'm going to go out and make sure Edmond is gone before sitting down to dinner. I'll be back in a minute. Come on, Carlos. You can help me."

Elise nodded absently as she watched the farm foreman cross to her mother. "You okay?"

"Yes, I'm fine, Neil. Thanks so much for coming over. I thought that whole thing might go sideways for a minute."

He chuckled. "Not a problem. You know anytime you need backup, I'm right over at the bunkhouse."

"Have you had your dinner?" When he shook his head, she nodded toward the kitchen. "Why don't you stay and have dinner with us? Go on back with the others. I'll be along in a few minutes."

When he'd gone, her mother turned to Elise with a look of tired concern. "Something is going to have to be done about Edmond. Ross is right. This can't continue."

Elise went to her then and gave her a hug. "I know you didn't want it to come to this, but he's really left you no choice, Mom."

"I thought he would get tired of arguing and finally work with me on some kind of compromise, but clearly *that's* not going to happen."

Elise frowned. "What did Uncle Edmond mean when he said his proposal would have solved your problems as well as his?"

"Oh, don't worry about it. That's just Edmond trying to start something." Her mother waved a hand in the air and tried to laugh it off, but Elise got the distinct impression there was more to it then she was letting on — a whole lot more.

"What are you going to do?"

"Let's not worry about that tonight, honey. We'll have a family meeting tomorrow. That's soon enough to make a decision. For now, let's go have dinner."

At that moment the door opened and Jackson came back in without Carlos.

"Is everything okay, Jackson?" Laura asked.

"Yes, ma'am. The coast is clear."

"Good," she said with a nod and slipped an arm through his. "Then let's go eat. I'm starving."

Elise followed them down the hallway with her uncle's comments playing over in her mind. What problems could her mother possibly have that one of Edmond's wild schemes could fix?

TWO

Morning dawned as sticky and humid as a sports club steam room. Dragging herself out of bed, Elise felt like someone had drained her blood and replaced it with some kind of low-energy sludge during the night. She would definitely need about a gallon of diet cola to get her motor running smoothly again.

She'd slept in fits and starts, unable to get Stuart's job proposal out of her head. Between that dilemma and her uncle's cryptic remarks about making trouble for the vineyard — as well as her mother's lame explanation of why there was nothing to worry about — she'd had a terrible night.

Fortunately, she didn't have much time to dwell on either issue this morning. Her mom had called a family meeting for eleven o'clock, and she needed to get moving if she was going to make a run by the greenhouse to check on her hybrid vines beforehand.

By the time Elise got out of the shower, you could cut the air in the bathroom with a machete — which did nothing to improve her mood. Why this room didn't have an exhaust fan, she would never know.

When she'd originally left the security of her family's home and moved out on her own, she'd thought the apartment above the Delphine Drug Store in town was quaint, with sort of an old-world charm. The owners, Avery and Lila Parker, ran the pharmacy downstairs and were the best landlords ever. They never even complained when she ran a few days late with the rent — which happened more often than she'd like to admit.

It was a plus that they'd given her free rein with decorating, and she'd taken full advantage of their generosity in that area. While she'd loved the apartment's original wallpaper, it was too far gone to save. So she'd meticulously removed every scrap and painted each room in a soft pastel color scheme.

Having a passion for old-fashioned linen and just about anything antique, she had run across some really fabulous lace curtains at one of the shops on Main Street. Between her collection of porcelain pitchers and the Pop Art that adorned the walls, her apartment may be eclectic, even unconventional, but it was bright and fresh and suited her perfectly.

However, on the minus side, the old radiators took forever to come up in the winter, then blasted you out with heat once they did. And the two window air conditioners worked off and on at best. More off than on, truth be told. With the heat wave they'd been having, this was *not* a good thing. She found a hammer worked well with the radiators and a few good whacks with a shoe did wonders for the air conditioning units.

Speaking of shoes, what the hell did that big, fat blob of a cat do with her other sandal?

"Chunk!" she hollered, then muttered under her breath, "Where are you, you little spawn of Satan?"

Of course, she'd named him Chunk for a reason — and the word *little* had nothing to do with it. Her Snowshoe Siamese was eighteen pounds and, for reasons known only to him, had developed a penchant for hiding her shoes. Problem was, he usually only took one of a pair, so she had a plethora of mismatched shoes in her closet at any given time.

Stomping into the living room, she found his royal highness lounging in the Papasan chair like the king of the world. He looked up and lazily yawned as she approached.

"Where is my other sandal, mister?" she asked, brandishing the lone shoe she'd found. The cat blinked and began to bathe, obviously unconcerned with her wardrobe issues. "Seriously, Chunk, I don't have time for your shenanigans today. I'm already running late!"

Dear God, I'm talking to my cat like I expect him to answer, she thought, and then grumbled aloud. "I *so* haven't had enough caffeine for the way this day is starting out."

Throwing on a different — and matching — pair of sandals, Elise grabbed her purse and briefcase, and then headed for the door.

"I'm going now, twerp," she said over her shoulder. "Please don't destroy the apartment or any of my footwear while I'm gone."

In her haste to find more caffeine, she failed to don her sunglasses. Racing down the stairs, she nearly blinded herself when she stumbled out into the bright, early morning sunlight. Luckily the need to pay rent saved her from permanent damage. She ducked into the drug store in search of her landlord.

"Well, good morning, Elise," Mrs. Parker greeted her with a cheerful smile. "How was your trip to Dallas?"

"Long and eventful, Mrs. P.," she answered with a snort. "Like I need to add anything more to my already overflowing plate."

She would have laughed, but she wasn't really finding any humor in the situation at the moment. If anything, her weekend trip and Stuart's offer had only added a layer of stress to her life that hadn't existed before.

"That sounds ominous, dear. Anything you want to share?"

Elise sighed. "Oh, don't mind me. I didn't sleep well. And it seems I've gotten up on the wrong side of the bed." She grabbed a diet soda out of the refrigerated unit by the counter and pulled a couple dollars from her purse. "A little caffeine and I'll be right as rain."

Mrs. Parker shook her head and made a tsking sound. "You know that stuff is terrible for you. It'll eat holes right through your stomach."

Elise laughed and gave the older woman a look of mock horror. "Please, Mrs. P., don't ruin it for me!"

Mrs. Parker chuckled along with her. "Heading out to the vineyard this morning?"

"Yep," she replied with a nod and handed over her rent check. "But I wanted to drop this off before I forgot again."

"Oh posh, we never worry about you. You're a good girl, Elise, even if you're not always prompt with your rent."

Opening her cola, Elise took a couple swigs and then smiled. "Thanks, Mrs. P."

The older woman frowned then and leaned on the counter. "Is everything all right out at the vineyard?"

The tone in Mrs. Parker's voice gave Elise pause. She re-capped her soda and slid it into her briefcase. "Of course," she replied slowly. "Why do you ask?"

"Oh, it's probably nothing," she said with a shake of her head. "Small towns, you know. Just something Avery said last night."

"Oh? What was that?"

"Well, he ran into Pam Dawson over at Pit Barbeque, and she told him things would be changing out at the vineyard very soon. He thought she was acting peculiar, ranting about how Edmond would be coming into a whole lot of money one minute, the next how he was a screw-up who'd ruined her life. But then, that's Pam," she said, rolling her eyes. "She's nothing if not a trifle odd. Personally, I think she may be a touch bipolar."

Elise tried to smile but felt a sudden chill at the older woman's words. Pam Dawson was her Uncle Edmond's on again-off again girlfriend and a terrible gossip. Since her uncle had spread all kinds of unfounded rumors around town in the two years he'd been back in the area, Elise felt certain Pam was only repeating more of the same here. Still, it was disconcerting.

"I can safely say that I haven't heard of any major upcoming changes," she said, digging into her purse for her car keys. *Haven't heard of any, but that doesn't mean something's not afoot,* she thought.

"I guess you'd know," Mrs. Parker replied. "Probably just talk anyway."

"I would hope so." Again, Elise tried to laugh it off, but the look on her mother's face the previous night when she'd questioned her about Edmond's comments popped into her head. Surely Laura would tell the family if a major change was coming, right? But what if it wasn't just talk?

Mrs. Parker reached out and put a hand over hers, snapping her out of her thoughts. "I know he's kin and all, Elise, but I'd keep an eye on your Uncle Edmond all the same. Your daddy was a good man, but that Edmond has been trouble his whole life. I wouldn't trust him any farther than I could see him."

"I'll keep that in mind, Mrs. P." Shaking

off the sense of gloom that permeated the air, Elise grabbed her purse and briefcase and headed for the door. "Gotta run or I'll be even later than I already am. Have a nice day."

This time she slipped on her sunglasses before heading out into the sunshine — and literally ran into another piece of bad news in the form of Deputy Darrell Yancy.

"Whoa, where's the fire, El?" he asked, taking her by the shoulders to steady her when she stumbled.

"Sorry, Darrell. I didn't see you."

Having graduated with her brother, Yancy was the mayor's nephew and never missed an opportunity to throw around *that* connection whenever and wherever he could. He'd also been sweet on a certain Miss Caroline Wilcox before she'd become Mrs. Ross Beckett. That Caroline had picked Ross over him was something Darrell had never forgotten — and he blamed Ross to this day.

"How are the plans for Cousin Deana's wedding coming along? They're still having it out at the vineyard, right? Or is that going to change too?" he added with an oily smile.

"That's Madison's project, so I'm a bit out of the loop on details." She sidestepped and tried to disengage herself from the deputy when he held on just a bit too long for comfort. "But everything is right on schedule."

Hosting the wedding for the mayor's daughter was a big deal in the county and would bring in a good chunk of change for the vineyard. But she frowned as Darrell's last words sank in. "What do you mean, 'is that going to change too'? What else has changed, Darrell?"

"I don't know." The look he gave her was sly, as if he knew something she didn't. "I've just been hearing scuttlebutt. A little birdie told me some big changes were coming for River Bend."

Elise sighed. "Let me guess — a little birdie named Pam Dawson? Or maybe a big rat named Edmond Beckett? You should know better than to listen to the garbage either of those two spread."

"We'll see," Darrell said. Turning, he slithered up the street but threw a parting shot over his shoulder. "Save a dance for me at the reception, *Ms.* Beckett."

Elise gave a noncommittal smile and turned away. *In your dreams, Creepy McCreeperson.* Shaking her head, she headed for her car.

If she thought she'd put her worries out of her mind, her little chat with Mrs. Parker and the unpleasant run-in with Darrell had brought them all back with a vengeance. By the time she arrived at the vineyard, Elise was mentally freaking out and hoped ten minutes in the greenhouse would calm her nerves and help her put things in perspective.

She found her grandmother in the greenhouse tending her vegetables.

"Morning, Gram."

"Hey, baby girl. Back for more fun?"

"Yes, ma'am. I figure I've got maybe ten minutes to play in here before the meeting. Do you know what Mom wants to discuss — besides the obvious problem with Uncle Edmond?"

Abigail shook her head. "There's something going on, that's for sure. But every time I ask, Laura puts me off. And I can't tell you how annoying that is."

"You, too?" Elise chuckled. She put her bags down on the potting table and then turned to her grandmother. "Last night I asked her what Uncle Edmond meant with that odd remark about his scheme 'fixing her problem', but she denied anything was wrong."

"She's never deliberately tried to hide anything from me before, not even when she was a little girl," Abigail said with a note of sadness in her voice. "It may be annoying, but I have to say, it's got me a bit worried as well."

Elise nodded. "I know what you mean, Gram. She's always been honest with us, especially about anything involving the vineyard. But last night . . . I can't say she out and out lied to me, but I got the distinct feeling she wasn't being completely honest, either."

"I'm hopin' she'll come clean with whatever's going on in this meeting."

Elise turned to the young vines in large clay pots sitting under lamps on the tiered table along the wall. She examined the starts for indications of potential problems and trimmed them as she spoke. "I've been hearing rumors in town, Gram. Pam and Uncle Edmond have been pretty busy."

"I wouldn't worry about it, sweet pea." Abigail put her tools away and took off her gardening gloves. "Those two are just as worthless as teats on a bull. Nobody with a lick of sense will listen to their prattle." She sighed. "Caroline's opening the shop this morning so I can attend this family conference. I guess I better head up to the house and put on the kettle. I made scones for us to snack on during the meeting."

"Mmm, love your scones. I'll be up in a bit."

After her grandmother walked away, Elise thought about what she'd said. If her mom wasn't even confiding in her own mother, maybe there really was something to worry about. But what?

As she went about checking her hybrid starts, she pondered different scenarios. Her mother was healthy, at least as far as she knew. *Oh my gosh!* What if her mother had been diagnosed with some kind of deadly disease?

Okay, take a breath, chicken little, she thought. That was something her mother would *never* keep to herself.

Could it be something to do with the vineyard itself? Sure, things had been tight for a few months with the recent drought conditions. But they went through this every year.

This second batch of hybrid vines she'd been working on was coming along nicely and would soon be ready for transplanting alongside the first wave. They would be much more drought-tolerant, reducing the cost of extensive watering during stressful weather situations like they'd had this summer. It was a step that would eventually give River Bend an edge over their competition.

Of course, the new vines wouldn't bear a full crop of fruit for a number of seasons to come, and they wouldn't produce a profit for several years after that. With the economy in a downswing, it had been a tough year, but every vineyard along the Colorado River was in the same boat. She felt certain that things would turn around. They always did.

Stop projecting, Elise, and wait for the meeting, she mentally admonished herself. *You really don't need to borrow trouble.*

As she fussed with her starts and documented their growth, she lost track of time. When she finally checked her watch, she had to run to the house to avoid being late again. All family gatherings took place in the spacious dining room, and she was out of breath when she arrived just as the meeting began.

Ross fairly scowled as she sat down at the table next to him. "Nice of you to join us, El."

"Sorry, got held up in the greenhouse." She shot him a sour look. "Sounds like I'm not the only one who got up on the wrong side of the bed this morning."

"No, I'm sorry." Ross gave her a sheepish grin. "Caroline and I fought last night. We both went to bed angry, which is something we swore we'd never do."

"Oh, Ross." Elise rubbed his shoulder. "You guys talked it out though, right?"

Ross shook his head. "Didn't have a chance. She's covering for Gram and Madison at the shop during the meeting and was up and out the door before I got out of the shower."

"Sancia's at the house with the boys?" Elise asked. Sancia Madera and her husband, Carlos, both worked for the vineyard and she was happy to watch Ross's sons when needed.

At her brother's nod, Elise continued. "Then the minute this meeting is over, you high-tail your sad self down to the shop and straighten things out."

Ross laughed at that. "Yes, ma'am."

"Let's get this meeting started," Laura announced as she breezed into the room. "I've got a full schedule today, and it's already quarter after, so I can't waste any time."

"What's on the agenda?" Abigail asked as she set out two plates of scones and poured a pot of tea to steep. "I'm assuming Edmond and his nonsense is one topic."

Laura nodded. "Yes, I need to make a decision about that, and I want everyone's input."

"You know where I stand," Ross spoke up.

40

"I say put the restraining order that Jackson mentioned into place. And that's just for starters. Uncle Edmond has threatened to take legal steps, and even though that will get him nowhere, perhaps we should fire the first shot."

Surprised at his venomous reaction, Elise glanced over at her brother. "Wow. When did you become so hateful toward Uncle Edmond? I mean, he's been a pain lately, but he's still family, Ross."

Ross threw her an angry look. "You wouldn't know it by his actions. He's made it clear he has no use for this family." He shrugged and continued with a bit more calm. "I simply have no use for him. Let him live with his choices."

"Sadly, I've begun to feel the same way," Laura put in. "I've tried to be reasonable and fair with Edmond and told him on many occasions we would welcome him moving onto the vineyard and working with us. I would gladly share everything with him in that way. But he's refused the offer each time it's been extended."

"I love Uncle Edmond," Madison offered. "I mean, like you said, El, he *is* family." She glanced up from the doodling she'd been doing in her event planner and smoothed her French braid with a free hand. When

41

her sister was creating an event at Lodge Merlot, Elise knew she hated for anything to disturb her focus. And her next sentence emphasized that irritation. "With the Adams-Wilkinson wedding coming up, his behavior is unacceptable. It could affect our bookings at the lodge and spoil the whole affair for our client."

Laura nodded. "That's a real possibility. The mayor could have gone to half a dozen other places, but she chose Lodge Merlot for her daughter's big day. We need to make sure it goes off without a hitch; Edmond could be a very *big* hitch."

"So, what *does* Uncle Edmond want?" Madison asked.

"He wants everything handed to him on a silver platter," Ross spat.

"Ross, you're not helping," Laura admonished and then turned to Madison. "He made a new proposal last night that is as unacceptable as all his schemes have been in the past."

"And that is . . . ?" Abigail asked.

"It started out basically the same as the others. He wanted me to deed him six hundred acres — half of the vineyard — free and clear. Which of course, he would then sell."

Ross barked out a laugh. "What a

42

shocker."

"All right," Elise said, with a frown. "But what's different about this new proposal? Sounds like the same old song and dance as before."

Laura sat back in her chair. "The difference this time is that he's got a buyer lined up, though he wouldn't say who." She took a deep breath and let it out. "And he wants a specific six hundred acres . . . in the south quadrant."

"*What?*" Elise jumped up so quickly that she knocked her chair over backward. "But that's where the first batch of my hybrid vines is planted!"

THREE

"He can't be serious!" Elise shouted. "I've spent the last few *years* working on those hybrids. They were designed to give River Bend an edge over other wineries. How could he think this would be acceptable?"

"Well, golly, El, let's just think about that for a minute," Ross said sarcastically. "Oh, wait — this is Uncle Edmond we're talking about."

Laura frowned. "That's enough, Ross."

"But this makes no sense," Elise insisted. "I understand Uncle Edmond's motivation, I do, but what could possibly be the incentive for us to agree to something like this?"

Laura put up a hand. "Calm down, Elise. I realize this is disturbing, but at least now you can understand why I was so troubled last night."

Abigail poured herself a cup of tea and chose a scone from the plate. "I'm with Elise. That deal makes no sense, even for a nutjob like Edmond."

Elise righted her chair and sat down. There was something missing, something her mother wasn't saying — but what? "Mom, last night I asked you what Uncle Edmond meant when he said his plan would solve your problems as well as his own. You told me then that it was all just talk, but that's not the truth, is it?"

Laura sighed. "No, sweetheart, I'm afraid not." She shifted a glance to Ross before continuing. "I know I should have called this meeting sooner, explained the situation long before this, but we felt it would just upset y'all prematurely."

Elise looked back and forth between Ross and her mother. She was starting to understand why her brother hadn't seemed the least bit surprised by this development. "So you two decided to keep something from the rest of us? Is that it?"

"Sweetheart, Ross is the business manager for the vineyard, after all. We were only trying to protect you, but I realize now that was a bad call. We should have discussed the problem as a family."

"You think?" Abigail gave a disgusted grunt. "Well, we're all here now." Folding her arms, she spared her daughter a narrow glance. "Spit it out while we're all still

45

breathin'."

Clearly displeased, Laura shot her mother a you're-not-helping glare. "The vineyard has a balloon payment coming due on the loan we took out when we built Lodge Merlot."

Ross finished the bad news. "Unfortunately, with sales down like they have been, we might not have the money to make the full payment by the date required."

"What the heck does that mean?" Madison asked. "If we default on the loan we could lose the vineyard?"

"No, we won't." Ross shook his head. "It would never come to that, sis. We do have some reserves, and if need be, we can make up the difference there. But with the overly dry conditions requiring more extensive irrigation, and the crops yielding less than we'd previously forecasted, it means more dollars going out than coming in."

"That's what Edmond was talking about last night," Laura explained. "I gathered from our conversation — or should I say his hollering and carrying on — that he owes money somewhere. And I mean a whole lot of money. He told me that if I agreed to deed him half the vineyard, his portion of the sale would get him out of hot water."

"Well, why in the world would he think

you would ever agree to a stupid idea like deeding him half the vineyard?" Abigail asked. "Even his own brother knew the folly of *that*. No, that man had his chance when you proposed a partnership early on, Laura, and if memory serves, he thumbed his nose at the offer."

"Yeah, so why go back to that now?" Elise asked, unable to put the thought of losing her hybrids out of her mind.

"Somehow he found out about our upcoming loan payment and thought to capitalize on that information," Ross said, then snorted. "In his twisted way of thinking, he assumed we would jump at the chance to pay off the loan — even at the expense of losing half the vineyard."

"And giving away a lion's share of my research and development to the buyer in the process," Elise snapped.

It was all so sordid and disappointing. How could Edmond even *think* about doing this to them? And there she'd been, defending him at every turn, because he was her uncle. What a fool she'd been. Well, no more. Ross was right, the man had made his choices and now he'd have to live with the consequences.

"As much as I hate the thought of barring a family member from the property, I say we implement the restraining order for now. Then see how it goes from there," Elise said at length.

Laura ran a hand through her short, dark crop of curls. "Then I want a show of hands. If you disagree, now's the time to speak up. Is everyone on board with this first step?"

Elise looked around the table at her family members as each in turn raised a hand.

"Then it's settled," Laura said with a quick nod. "Ross will call Jackson and have him come out first thing in the morning. I'd like everyone on site for that, so we all hear it at once and are on the same page. Now, if there's no other business to discuss . . ."

Stuart's offer popped into Elise's head. A life change of that magnitude was something she would normally discuss with those closest to her before making any decision, but now was definitely not the time. With the vineyard facing these new issues, Stuart would just have to wait for his answer. No way was she going to add to her mother's stress level by suggesting she might be jumping ship.

When nobody spoke up with any new business, Laura blew out a breath. "Then we're done. I have a mountain of paperwork to tackle, so I'd better get to it. Ross, when you have some time, I need help with that new accounting program you installed on my laptop."

"Sure, Mom." Ross shot a glance at Elise before turning back to his mother. "Uh, I need to run down to the shop for a few minutes, but hopefully it won't take long. I'll help you with that as soon as I'm finished there."

Elise watched him go as the wheels turned in her head. She thought perhaps a trip out to the Pit Barbeque for a late lunch and a chat with Pam Dawson might be enlightening. If she could run down her uncle in the process, even better.

The rest of the family would probably think she was crazy — heck, she probably was — but before she completely wrote off her uncle, she wanted to hear his betrayal from his own lips.

My timing is impeccable, Elise thought as she drove into the parking lot at Pam's restaurant just after one o'clock. A pulled pork sandwich would be the perfect excuse to surprise her uncle's girlfriend and have that friendly chat.

But it seemed that the surprise was on her. When Elise went inside to order, she found Pam was sitting at a booth in the corner having what looked to be a very chummy conversation with Henry Kohler. Henry owned the Kohler Winery, and though his vineyard was smaller than River Bend, he was one of their biggest competitors.

Delphine might be a small town, but this appeared to be more than a chance encounter.

When Henry looked up, Elise thought he looked a bit guilty before he smiled and waved her over. "Hello, Elise. How are things at River Bend?"

"Aside from a little dry, just fine, Henry. How are you faring out your way?"

The older man chuckled. "Oh, we're getting by. Although the extra irrigation has added more expense than I'd like. But we'll all manage, right?"

Elise laughed. "Do we have any other choice?"

"I've found there's always another choice," Pam added with more than a touch of sarcasm.

Elise was sure she would say something more, but Henry quickly put a hand over the Pit owner's forearm, and she clammed right up.

What is up with that?

"Well, I should be getting back," he said. Standing, he leaned heavily on his ornate oak cane. "We'll talk later, Pam. And quit worrying; it will all work out. You'll see. Elise, it was a pleasure to see you. Give my best to your family."

Elise watched him go and wondered what Henry's comments to Pam had meant. She hadn't realized they were that well acquainted, but the meeting seemed to suggest otherwise. Sliding into the booth opposite Pam, Elise contemplated the best way to get the woman talking.

"I spoke to Darrell Yancy today, and he said he'd run into you and Uncle Edmond."

Well, El, that was a lame opener.

And of course, Darrell hadn't actually said that in so many words, but his earlier reaction at her guesses had told her she was on the money.

"Is that so?" Pam eyed her with suspicion. "And what did the fine deputy have to say?"

"Just that you two thought things were going to somehow change at the vineyard in the near future," Elise reported with mock innocence. "You know, I can't imagine what that would be."

"Oh, just you wait. Change is coming, all right."

Elise blinked and gave Pam another clueless look. Maybe just a little nudge of information was in order. "Do you mean the restraining order? You know, I tried to talk them out of that, but Uncle Edmond behaved so badly last night that the rest of the family wouldn't listen to a word."

Pam's head snapped up sharply at that little nugget, a shocked look on her face. "Restraining order? What restraining order?"

Gotcha! Elise smiled inwardly and glanced at her watch. "Uh, the one that's going into effect this afternoon or early tomorrow morning at the latest. It will bar Uncle Edmond from vineyard property. I thought you knew, being that you two are so close and all."

Elise watched Pam's face go red and mottled with anger. She also thought Mrs. P. might have been wrong about Pam; there was a whole lot more than bipolar going on here, for sure.

"That dirty, rotten, no good son-of-a—"

"Pam?" Elise interrupted. "What's the matter?"

"If Eddy Beckett thinks he's going to screw *me* over, he's got another thing comin'," the other woman yelled. Heads turned all over the restaurant.

"I don't understand," Elise leaned forward with false concern. "What has Uncle Edmond done?"

Pam scrambled out of the booth, babbling

madly. "I will not watch my business go under because of that *loser,* I'll tell you that right now."

"Where *is* Uncle Edmond, Pam?" Elise asked as the owner turned to stalk away.

Pam spun around and glared at her. Elise held her breath, thinking the woman might have a complete meltdown right then and there. But after a moment she shook her head. "I haven't seen him since this morning, but if he comes back here, I just may choke the life out of him with my bare hands."

Once Pam was out of range, Elise let out the breath she hadn't been aware she'd been holding. *Yep, crazy lives right there behind Pam's eyes,* she thought.

Another glance at her watch told her she had plenty of time to order some lunch. When she was finished she could even run a few errands and be right on schedule to drop by her uncle's place before heading home for the day.

Her phone later rang while she was in line at the post office, but it was Stuart and she let it go to voicemail. She didn't have the energy for another push-pull conversation at the moment.

Her next stop was dropping off some soil samples at the Extension Service, where her friend C.C. Duncan worked in the office. They'd been meaning to make plans for a girl's night out anyway, so she spent thirty minutes chatting and piddling around there before heading out to her uncle's.

Edmond lived in a small house on the outskirts of Delphine, and it was just shy of four o'clock when Elise pulled into his driveway.

She didn't see his truck and decided it couldn't hurt to take a look around. As she crossed the small wooden porch, she glanced through the living room window. Though she thought she heard something inside, she saw no movement.

When her knock went unanswered, Elise rationalized her next action as something anyone would naturally do. She tried the door and found it unlocked. She convinced herself she should at least go in for a minute, make sure everything was okay. *Seriously, like the old commercial said, what if he's fallen and can't get up?*

She giggled at her own joke. At least that's what she'd say if she got caught snooping around!

Slowly she eased the door open. "Hello? Uncle Edmond? Anybody home?"

When she got no answer, she entered the house. Her first thought was a flashback to a line from an old black and white movie: *What a dump.* Empty pizza boxes and beer bottles littered the living room, along with dirty clothes that looked as if they'd been dropped where they'd been removed. Old newspapers and unopened mail covered the dining table, and the smell of stale smoke seemed to permeate the walls.

Good Lord, she thought. *Could this be any more disgusting?*

The idea that her uncle would prefer to live like this rather than to move out to the vineyard as her mother had suggested was dumbfounding. The air in the small space was as humid as outdoors but without the benefit of the occasional breeze. How the Texas air could be so humid and the soil so dry, she'd never understand.

Picking up a ballpoint pen, Elise poked around in the paperwork on the table. There were lots of unpaid bills, and a few hand-written receipts for what looked to be sports bets. That couldn't be good, but her mother had said he owed money.

And then she ran across something even more unexpected and disturbing: paystubs.

And not just any paystubs — these were from Kohler Winery. What the heck was going on? She wasn't even aware that her uncle *had* a job, let alone one at a rival vineyard. If she hadn't seen the proof with her own eyes, she would never have believed it. This was the ultimate betrayal.

But why work for Henry Kohler? Hadn't her mother said she'd offered him a job several times, but Edmond had turned her down? Was Henry the buyer her uncle had lined up in his ridiculous scheme to get out from under his debt? Though every vineyard owner in the area was looking for ways to increase their earnings, she couldn't see Henry Kohler involved in something so underhanded. Besides, she was pretty certain Kohler Winery didn't have that kind of cash just sitting around.

Elise sighed. This entire thing was making less and less sense. Though it probably wasn't a stellar idea, she shoved a few of the gambling markers and a couple paystubs into her purse. Heaven knew Edmond would never miss them in this mess, but they were something the others would need to see.

Not wanting to venture any farther into her uncle's rat's nest for fear of being caught, Elise retreated to her car. She didn't realize how guilty she felt about poking around her uncle's house without his knowledge until her cell phone rang, startling her. She jumped and let out a nervous laugh.

"Hey, El," Ross greeted her. "Just wanted to let you know that I got a hold of Jackson, and he'll be at the vineyard by eight thirty tomorrow morning."

"Oh, goody!"

Ross snickered. "I can hear the nasty thought behind that sarcastic false joy of yours. And yes, it means another early morning for my sister, the night owl."

"Sadly, I do seem to be the only one in the family who didn't get the early gene," Elise said with a shake of her head. "If I didn't know better, I'd think I was adopted. But that's okay. I'll drag myself out there at the crack of dawn — again."

"Yeah, well try not to be late. We get tired of waiting on you."

"Bite me," she replied good-naturedly and then grew serious. "Ross . . . there is something I need to talk to you and Mom about, something important you should see. But I think it would be better to do it privately tomorrow morning — *without* Jackson present."

"That's certainly sounds cryptic. What is it?"

"I don't want to discuss it over the phone."

"What's going on, Elise? Where are you?"

She almost didn't tell him but in the end decided to fess up. "I'm at Uncle Edmond's house," she said and then had to pull the phone away from her ear when Ross began to yell.

"What the hell are you doing out there? Have you lost your damn mind?"

"I know, it was stupid, but I just wanted to hear his side of the story, you know? Don't blow a gasket; he's not even here, so it's not a big deal."

She heard his deep sigh on the other end. "Get out of there before he comes back and catches you hanging around. It's after four. Go home, El, and let it go. You have to accept the fact that Uncle Edmond is a lost cause. You can't save everyone."

After she hung up, Elise drove back to her apartment with a heavy heart. She knew Ross was probably right, but she couldn't shake the feeling that something bad was coming. And when bad things happened, you counted on family to see you through.

Unfortunately, her uncle was about to lose what was left of his.

As she drove out to the vineyard the following morning in the still-oppressive heat, Elise tried to make some kind of sense of the thoughts running through her mind. Sadly, she wasn't having much luck. Stuart had called last night and brought up the job offer yet again. Their conversation had felt drawn out and tense, and she hadn't even mentioned her uncle's latest antics.

Being the only one who didn't live on the vineyard, she was again the last to arrive. Even Jackson was already there when she parked in front of the main house, so she didn't have time to talk to Ross or her mother. Her visit to Pam's restaurant and the news about finding the markers and the paystubs would have to wait until later.

Grabbing a diet soda from the fridge, Elise sat down at the table as Jackson began to explain the process for filing the restraining order.

"Once this order is signed and in place, Edmond won't be allowed on Beckett property," he told them. "If he shows up out here, you give us a call. We'll come out and take him away. It's as simple as that."

"Nothing is that simple, Jax," Ross said with a frown. "And I still say this isn't enough. I can guarantee this won't stop his harassment."

"It might not stop the harassment, Ross, but if he disregards this order, he faces a jail cell. That will be his choice."

"Jackson is right, Ross," Laura said. "And we all agreed that this would be the first step. We'll see how it plays out and go from there."

Before they could finish their discussion, there was a pounding at the back door. Laura got up and opened it to a frantic Carlos, accompanied by another vineyard employee. Both men nervously stepped into the kitchen.

"Sorry to bother you, Señora Beckett," Carlos began. "But we need the deputy right away."

"What's the matter, Carlos? Why do you need Jackson?"

"He must come quickly. There is a body."

"A body?" Elise jumped up, stunned by his statement. "Holy crap!"

Madison gasped. "Seriously? As in, a dead body?"

At the vineyard worker's nod, Jackson stepped forward. "Calm down, Carlos," he said, putting a hand on the man's shoulder. "Where did you find this body?"

"Down by the river. Please, you must come. We pulled him out of the water," Carlos said, his eyes wide and words a bit disjointed. "I watch those crime shows, I know we shouldn't have touched anything, but we didn't think it was right to just leave him there, in the water."

"Him? It's a male?"

"*Sí*. It's Señor Edmond."

FOUR

The chaos that ensued following Carlos's statement was epic. The room erupted into a cacophony of voices, all trying to speak at once, which resulted in no one actually being heard.

Jackson braced himself, shook his head, and finally ended the melee with an ear-piercing whistle. "Holy smokes, y'all! Would everyone please just shut the hell up? I can't hear myself think, let alone what Carlos is trying to tell me."

"Carlos, are you sure it was Edmond?" Laura asked in the lull. Hope that the farmhand might have been mistaken was written all over her face, and she looked crestfallen when he nodded.

"*Sí*, Señora Beckett, I'm afraid so. He was face down in the water along the bank when we found him. But when we pulled him out and turned him over . . . well . . . it's him."

"Tell me what happened from the beginning, Carlos." It was obvious the guy was freaked out, and Jackson gave his shoulder a gentle squeeze as he tried to coax more details from him.

The older man swallowed hard and briefly glanced in Elise's direction. "There are several rows of vines down along the river at the south end of the vineyard that Miss Elise asked us to remove."

Jackson looked over at her for confirmation, and she nodded. "That section was planted years ago with a pretty frail variety. Those vines aren't as disease-resistant as I'd like. Add in the drought we've been having, and they're going to cost us more money in the long run than they're worth. I asked Carlos to remove them to make room for the next wave of my hybrids that are almost ready for transplant."

Satisfied with her explanation, Jackson turned back to Carlos. "So, you and your crew went out to removes some vines. How did you find the body?"

"We were unloading our tools from the truck and Bernardo spotted him. We all went running down the bank to pull him out, but it was obvious he was already dead. I had Bernardo and Casey stay with him, and Antonio and I came to get help."

This was so not the way Jackson had

expected or wanted the situation with Edmond to end up. Rubbing a hand over his chin, he shot a quick look at Ross before addressing everyone in the room. "I'm going to have the men take me down to the scene, and I'd like a family member to come along. The rest of y'all should probably wait right here."

"Fine by me." Abigail plopped down in a chair. "I didn't much care for the man in the first place. I certainly have no desire to see his dead body."

"Mom!" Laura's mouth dropped open. "For the love of God."

"Well, it's not like it was a secret, Laura. I'm sorry he's met with misfortune, but I'm not about to be a hypocrite, either."

"Think what you like but please keep it to yourself. And have a little more consideration for the dead."

At Abigail's grunt of disapproval, Laura turned to Jackson. "Having said that, I'd rather not go, either. Ross can go with you, if that's okay."

"Why Ross?" Elise wanted to know.

"Why not me?" Ross asked. "I am the business manager for the farm."

Jackson watched Elise roll her eyes at that and thought, *Here we go.*

"Big deal," she returned. "I make sure the

grapes grow and produce so you have something to manage. What difference does that make?"

Deciding he'd better nip this argument in the bud before it got too far along, Jackson stepped in between them and put up a hand in both directions. "Okay, seriously? You want to argue over sibling crap *now*? Since you seem to need it, let me give you a reminder: your uncle is dead. He may not have been the most well liked man on the face of the planet, but I would think that you two would have a bit more consideration, like your mother just said."

When the two continued to stare at each other, he went on. "Elise, you're more than welcome to come along, but I can guarantee it's not going to be pleasant. Ross is probably just better suited —"

He took a step back before he could stop himself when she rounded on him with her hands on her hips. "If you say he's better suited because he's a man, I just may have to thump you." She took a breath and then blew it out slowly. "Look, this has nothing to do with sibling rivalry, trust me. And I realize how unpleasant it will probably be. I mean, how could it not be horrible, right? Uncle Edmond was family. And no, I'm not looking forward to it, but I think there should be at least a couple of family members present, that's all I'm saying."

"Well, *I* don't want to go down there," Madison spoke up. "I'm with Gram. I have no wish to see *any* dead body — for any reason."

Jackson looked to Laura for confirmation, and she nodded. "Ross and Elise can go with you, if that's what they want to do. The rest of us will stay here and wait, just as you asked."

With that settled, Jackson took his keys out of his pocket and gestured toward the back door. "All right, fine. Let's go."

The five of them piled into Jackson's cruiser and it didn't take long to get to the spot where Edmond had apparently met his maker. As they pulled up, Jackson saw that the two vineyard employees chosen to stay behind with the body stood off to one side looking very uncomfortable. Finding a dead body had to rate as one of the crappiest ways to start your morning.

Putting the car in park, he turned off the engine. "I don't suppose y'all would agree to stay in the vehicle while I check this out?"

"Not gonna happen." Ross shook his head and put up both hands in surrender when Jackson gave him a hard look. "But I promise we won't get in your way."

He climbed out, opening the back door for Elise. Together with Carlos and Antonio, Elise and Ross went to stand with the other employees while Jackson approached Edmond's supine body.

The morning air felt sticky and close, holding the earthy scent of river bottom and sandy loam. The warm sunshine made the dew that had accumulated overnight sparkle like a million tiny jewels. Elise reflected that it was the start of another lovely day, with the exception of a man lying dead on the riverbank thirty feet away.

"Poor Uncle Edmond," Elise said, her words sounding stark even to her own ears. "What on earth was he doing down here this morning?"

"Who says this is where he died or that it happened this morning?"

Elise frowned at Ross.

Seeing her confused expression, he went on, keeping his voice low so the others couldn't hear. "Well, think about it, El. When was he last seen? We know he was here causing trouble two nights ago, but he could have died anytime between then and now. He wasn't at home when you stopped there yesterday, right?"

She quickly put a finger to her lips in an

effort to silence him. Until they found out exactly what had happened here, she'd just as soon not broadcast that she'd been poking around at her uncle's house only yesterday afternoon — especially with a sheriff's deputy within earshot.

Ross snuck a glance at Jackson, who was taking photos of Edmond and the surrounding area. "Look, all I'm saying is that we don't know when this happened yet. It's entirely possible that he went into the water upstream, and this is just where he ended up."

Ross had brought up some good points. But as Elise studied the river and thought about his comments, she had to reject his theory.

Shaking her head, she pointed out at the water. "Look out there, Ross. The current is really slow along this stretch of river. I mean, it's barely moving here. And it's wide as well for at least half a mile in both directions."

"So? What are you getting at?"

Elise rolled her eyes. "Well, if he did go into the water upstream, depending on when and where, I'm wondering how he ended up in the shallows right here." She watched Jackson snap several more photos of the body. "Plus, you know Uncle Edmond was on the swim team back in his high school days. He may have been older, but he was still a strong swimmer; with that sluggish current, he would have easily been able to get himself to shore."

Ross obviously wasn't convinced. "Not necessarily. If he wasn't conscious when he went into the water, it wouldn't have mattered how well he could swim. He wouldn't have had a chance to save himself. But we don't know what happened yet, El. He could have fallen and hit his head. He knocks himself out and goes into the river. Game over."

"Maybe," she replied, as Jackson searched Edmond's front pockets and came up empty. Until they figured out just what had happened to her uncle, she knew this whole thing was going to prey on her thoughts. In her mind the mystery was compounded by the odd paystubs and numerous betting slips she'd found at his house. She hadn't mentioned that aspect yet, but the whole thing was beginning to take on a decidedly sinister feel.

"Ross, would you and Carlos come over here and help me turn him?" Jackson asked as he laid out a tarp next to Edmond's body.

Ross made a face but went to help. For this job, Elise was more than happy to wait on the sidelines and let her brother assist. *Seeing* her uncle this way was one thing, but no way did she want to have to touch his cold, dead body.

Edmond had been a good-sized man. At just over six feet tall, he'd been slender but solid as granite, like her father, and it took the strength of all three men to roll him over onto the tarp.

What they found was not pretty by any stretch of imagination.

From where she stood, Elise could see that the back of her uncle's head was a bloody mess. She loved police dramas and had seen this kind of thing on television, but it was a whole other story from just thirty feet away. Putting a hand to her mouth, she swallowed hard and prayed the toast and diet soda she'd had for breakfast wouldn't make a stunning reappearance.

"He must have hit his head on something," Elise heard Ross say, repeating what they had just been talking about.

"Yeah, but what?" Jackson checked Edmond's back pockets and found them empty. He stood and did a quick search of the area.

"There's a good deal of blood over here," he said, pointing at the ground along the bank. "But I don't see anything that would do that kind of damage to the back of his head. And if he did just accidentally fall here, it's a good twenty feet to the riverbank. How did he get into the water?"

"Like I was just saying to El, maybe it didn't happen here."

Elise watched as Jackson continued to scan the ground like a bird dog on the scent. He took several more photos and then hunched down next to the large patch of blood he'd found. She could almost hear what he was thinking, because she was thinking the same thing. What he said next came as no surprise.

"Whatever occurred, it took place right here. This is way too much blood to have happened when the crew pulled him out of the water. And I've gotta say, this is looking less and less like an accident to me."

Ross shook his head. "Now hold on, Jax. Don't get ahead of the facts here. You don't know anything for sure yet."

"You're right, buddy," Jackson said as he stood. Pulling his cell phone out of his shirt pocket, he punched in a number and put the phone to his ear. "But he hasn't got a scrap of ID on him — not one single thing in his pockets. Where's his wallet, Ross?"

"Robbery? Way out here?" Ross wondered aloud. "That seems a little far-fetched, don't you think? What could Uncle Edmond have had on him that was worth killing him over?"

"I don't know. But no matter how implausible it all *seems,* in my opinion this is a suspicious death. Since we don't have a coroner in Bastrop County, he'll have to be sent into Austin. Hopefully, the Travis County ME will be able to tell me more once an autopsy is completed."

In the two hours that followed that statement, Elise saw Jackson cover a lot of ground. He called in with his report, arranged for transportation of Edmond's body, and interviewed everyone who was present when his body was found. Elise's mind was working overtime during the entire process.

As her uncle's body was loaded up and driven away, she could only hope the medical examiner in Austin would conclude that this had simply been a tragic accident and nothing more. But her instincts and everything she'd seen so far were telling her that Jackson was right, and that would not be the case. Too many things just weren't adding up, no matter how Ross tried to spin it or explain them away.

Carlos asked if the crew could finish the

work they'd started before finding Edmond's body, but Elise thought the other workers weren't quite as interested in completing the task as he was.

In any case, Jackson nixed the idea immediately. "I'm sorry, but that's going to have to wait, Carlos. This may or may not be a crime scene, but Edmond's death is certainly suspicious. I'm cordoning off the area until we hear one way or the other from the medical examiner. This scene is now off-limits and we'll be doing a more thorough examination of the site as soon as possible."

As Ross helped Jackson put up the bright yellow tape around the entire area, the crew packed up their tools and drove away.

When Elise climbed back into the cruiser with Jackson and Ross, she gave one last look to the spot that would forever be burned into her memory as the place they'd found her uncle's dead body. She had a horrible feeling that though Edmond's ordeal might be over, theirs was just beginning — and would get far worse before it was finished.

The three of them rode back to the ranch house surrounded by the incongruity of bright sunshine and uncomfortable silence. Elise, for one, was really glad that the drive was short. They dropped Ross at his cottage and continued down to the main ranch house.

"How long do you think it will take for the ME to finish?" she asked Jackson as he pulled the cruiser into a space at the front of the house.

"That depends on how backed up they are, but I'm hoping to hear something by the end of the week or the first of next week at the latest."

"I can see by your face that you aren't expecting good news. You really don't think this was accidental, do you?"

"At this point I have more questions than answers." He turned to her, a calculating look on his face. "But I'm not going to jump to any conclusions yet, and I don't think you should either. Speculating before all the facts are in is pointless. It's better to just wait and see what the ME finds and what else turns up at the scene, and then go from there."

Although Elise agreed that this was sound advice, it was easier said than done.

After Jackson spoke to her mother and left, the rest of her afternoon seemed to drag by, and it was impossible to put Edmond's death completely out of her mind.

Stuart had called her cell phone several times during the course of the day, and she let it go to voicemail each time. She was pretty sure he was wondering about the weekend and the party they were supposed to attend in Dallas on Friday. To leave town even for the weekend in light of what had happened seemed inappropriate and somehow disrespectful. Stuart would be disappointed, but she knew he'd understand once she explained.

She tried to do some work to occupy her mind, but it was a losing battle. She ended up knocking off early. By the time she got home she felt like she'd been through the wringer. All she wanted was a nice cool shower to wash off the stickiness of the day, and a bit of quiet.

That was not to be.

She hadn't been home ten measly minutes when her home phone rang. She thought about letting the machine pick it up, but in the end she answered.

"Well, finally! Elise, where have you been?" Stuart asked, concern coloring his voice. "I've been calling your cell all day long. I was really starting to worry. Are you all right?"

"I'm sorry, Stuart. I've had a really rotten day. I know I should have called you earlier, but with so much happening, I just got caught up. We had a death in the family."

"What? Oh my God! Who?"

Elise sighed, not feeling up to a rehash of the entire event but knowing there was no way around it. "Uncle Edmond, my dad's only brother, was found dead on the property by some of the workers this morning."

"Oh, darling, I'm so sorry." Stuart cleared his throat on the other end of the line. "Uh, not to speak ill of the dead, but wasn't he the slightly unpleasant man I met during my first visit at the beginning of the year?"

Elise rubbed the spot just above her left eye that had begun to pound and wondered if this heinous day would ever end. "Yes. That was Uncle Edmond, may he rest in peace."

"Do you need me to come down and be with you, for support? I would have to rearrange a few things, but it's doable. I can be in Delphine by tomorrow afternoon."

"No!" she blurted before she could stop herself. The last thing she wanted or needed now was Stuart hovering over her like a mother hen. Plus the fact that she hadn't even mentioned his job proposal to the family yet. If he said something about it in their presence, the result could be disastrous.

Especially now.

The guilt she felt over what she was sure was an inappropriate reaction to her boyfriend's attempt at kindness and support had her softening her response. "I mean, that's really thoughtful of you, Stuart. But there are so many details the family will need to attend to in the next week or so, and I'll be neck deep in those arrangements. Plus, I wouldn't want you to take time away from your work to baby-sit me. I'll be fine, really."

"All right," he said after a moment of uncomfortable silence. "But if you change your mind, you just have to ask, and I'll come."

"Thank you, sweetie. I'll keep that in mind."

She spent the next forty-five minutes filling Stuart in on how it had all gone down. He had been very understanding, agreeing that she shouldn't leave her family in this time of loss for something as silly as a dinner party, which made her feel worse in light of her reaction to his offer of support. By the time she hung up, her head was throbbing like a bass drum.

Turning, she caught sight of Chunk studying her from the Papasan chair.

"Don't start with me, mister. You don't even like Stuart, and you know it. Having him here right now is not in either of our best interests. Besides, this whole situation is going to get very ugly before it's finished, I just know it."

FIVE

Though the week may have started off with a bang, the remainder of it flew by without further incident, and given the circumstances, seemed to end on a whimper.

Like the rest of the family, Elise tried to put her uncle's disturbing sudden death out of her mind. They had yet to hear anything from the Travis County Medical Examiner, and she was trying to stay optimistic. As Jackson had put it, to worry about the outcome was pointless. But nothing could be done and no arrangements could be made pending the ME's ruling. Until then, Uncle Edmond couldn't be laid to rest and they were all in a state of limbo, but it was funny how the oddest little thing brought it to mind when you were the least prepared.

Like the paystubs and gambling markers that she'd pilfered from Edmond's house and kept stumbling across every time she opened her purse. Sooner rather than later, she'd have to mention them to the rest of the family. At the very least she should have discussed them with Ross by now, but she'd been waiting for the right moment.

So she'd tried not to think about the situation for most of the week, preferring to concentrate on her hybrids. The latest batch was coming along well, and she hoped to have starts ready for transplant by the first of the month. The young vines would replace the rows Carlos and his crew would remove as soon as Jackson cleared the area where Edmond's body was found.

In time, her hybrids would produce a stellar grape, giving River Bend a leg up in the market. Drought- and disease-resistant, their predecessors were already in the ground at the south end of the vineyard and would hopefully yield a unique grape for an exceptional wine within the next couple of years.

Until that time, she was holding the specifics of her process very close to the vest. Even Stuart had jokingly called her paranoid when she refused to give him details.

Maybe she *was* being paranoid, but she wasn't about to have all her hard work and innovation stolen before seeing it come to fruition. It wasn't that she was worried Stuart would steal from her, but all it would take is one slip at the wrong time to the wrong person and she could potentially lose everything she'd worked toward.

As Friday rolled around, Elise was ready for some major R&R. With all that had happened, combined with having to wait on the ME's office, it had been quite the stressful week. She and C.C. had plans that night with several other women for a girl's night out. Elise intended on leaving work early and was just about to pack it in when Ross swung into the greenhouse.

"You're still here?" he asked. "I was sure you'd be gone by now."

"I was just about ready to head home and change clothes. I take it you're knocking off early today too?"

"Yep. I'm beat. I needed a break to get my circulation moving again. I've been sitting in one place looking at rows of figures all friggin' day." He rubbed his eyes and then stretched. "What are your plans for the weekend? Anything fun? I have nothing waiting for me but more work when I get home. Some of us do have to earn a living, you know."

"Awww, poor baby," she said with a sympathetic pout. "I'm meeting the girls for dinner at Toucan's on Main at six thirty."

"Mmm, Toucan's. I'm jealous."

Ross practically salivated with the words, which made her giggle. "I know, I can hardly wait, myself. Just thinking about it actually makes my mouth water. And I hear Rueben has added some new sculptures."

Toucan's was Elise's favorite Mexican restaurant and within walking distance of her apartment. They served incredible food, and the owner was a neon artist who displayed his amazing sculptures throughout the restaurant.

"Man, I wish I could afford one of his pieces. But Caroline would kill me, and I don't know where we'd put it," Ross said with a laugh.

"Hey, you should have Sancia come over and sit with the boys. Bring Caroline and come have dinner with grown-ups for a change. We're heading down the block to the Dew Drop after dinner for drinks."

Friday nights at the Dew Drop Inn were usually a hoot and always packed. It was technically a private club, with Bastrop being a semi-dry county. But for a dollar a year you could buy a membership, and it was all good.

"When was the last time you guys had a night out?" she asked with a stern look.

Ross blew out a breath. "I can honestly

say I don't remember the last time Caroline and I went out *without* the boys, and that's a sad statement." He shook his head and appeared a little woeful. "But don't tempt me. With the balloon payment coming due and a few other considerations, I've got tons to get done. I'm going to have a tough time working tonight knowing y'all will be eating spectacular food and partying it up while I'm going cross-eyed with numbers."

Elise laughed at that and then decided that maybe this was the time to tell Ross what she had hidden in her purse. "Ross, there's something I've been meaning to discuss with you about my visit to Uncle Edmond's the day before he was found. I made a disturbing discovery that I —"

"Daddy!" The name was shouted from the doorway in unison cherub voices, interrupting Elise before she could get any further. Turning, she watched Ross's two boys race toward them with Caroline strolling in behind.

"Hey, guys." His wife greeted them with a smile. "We were on our way back from the bus and thought we'd take a detour through the greenhouse."

Elise gave an inward sigh. *There goes my opportunity to spill the beans,* she thought. Not that she didn't trust Caroline, but she really wanted to talk through what she'd found with Ross before going to the rest of the family. That Edmond had been working for Henry Kohler, a direct competitor of River Bend, was a big deal. There was no telling how many ways her uncle may have compromised their security, and she needed some uninterrupted, private time with her brother to talk about her findings.

"Now, what were you saying about a discovery, sis?" Ross asked after a few minutes of chit-chat.

"You know what? It can wait until later. Besides, I need to get home and change clothes." She grabbed Caleb, Ross's youngest son, and had him giggling as she made loud, slobbery, smacking noises against his neck. "But first, I need to gobble me up some boy!"

Toucan's was crowded when Elise and the group arrived. They ended up waiting for thirty minutes for a table but knew it would be worth the time spent.

"El, I was so sorry to hear about your uncle," Brenda Peterson said once the waitress had seated them and taken their drink orders. "I heard he drowned and was found right there on the property. Is that true?"

"Actually, we're not sure what happened just yet." Elise sighed and resigned herself to repeating the story one more time, a story which was rapidly becoming tiresome. "It did look that way when he was found, but we won't know the exact cause of death until the medical examiner is finished with the autopsy."

Miranda Rollins cocked an eyebrow. "I thought they only did an autopsy when the circumstances were questionable — and *not* accidental."

"I'm not sure about that, but there were some inconsistencies," Elise admitted, trying to skirt the issue.

"What kind of inconsistencies?" Tina Babcock asked. It was an innocent enough question, but it had every woman at the table perking up and tuning in.

"It looked as if he may have hit his head on something before going into the water."

"Looked like he hit his head on something? Or someone bashed him on the head *with* something?" Miranda asked with a smirk.

"Geez, Miranda." C.C. whipped around and gave the voluptuous blonde an evil eye. "What the hell kind of question is that? Elise loses a family member and you're looking for ghoulish juice to spread around town?"

"I'm just saying." Miranda sat back and folded her arms over her ample chest. "Besides, that kind of *ghoulish juice* is already out there and being spread around without my help."

C.C. glowered at the woman. "Yeah? Well, how about we don't hitch ourselves to the gossip bandwagon just yet."

Elise put up a hand in the direction of both women. "Ladies, ladies — and I do use the term loosely — let's not come to blows right here in the restaurant, okay?"

The waitress picked that moment to come back to the table with their drink orders, and nobody said a word while she handed them out.

Elise jumped back in the moment the girl walked away. "Okay, I know there are all sorts of rumors flying around town about Uncle Edmond's death, but I think C.C. is right. I don't want to add to the conjecture. In any case, I prefer to wait until the ME makes a ruling."

C.C. made a squeamish face. "And *I* think that's really all the talk about death I want to hear for one evening. Can't we just have a nice dinner and gossip about fun stuff? Like what kind of gaudy mess Deana

Wilkinson will dream up to torture her bridesmaids with on her wedding day?"

Elise laughed along with the rest of the women but was secretly relieved when the conversation moved on. There would be a whole lot more talk if the ME ruled her uncle's death anything other than accidental. With the mayor's daughter getting married at Lodge Merlot next weekend, gaudy mess or not, the negative publicity of a homicide would be devastating. She didn't even want to *think* about what that would mean for her family or River Bend, but she knew it wouldn't be good.

The rest of dinner passed with great food and pleasant conversation, the subject of Edmond's demise forgotten, at least for the moment. The girls walked down the street and through the door at the Dew Drop Inn at twenty after eight. They were seated with drinks in their hands and tequila poppers on the table ten minutes after that.

The band was already playing their first set of the night and C.C. had to shout over the music to be heard. "Here's to a night out with good friends." She banged her shot glass on the table and downed her popper with the toast. Grimacing, she licked her lips and declared, "We so need to do this more often, girls."

"Amen, sista!" Miranda called out, as in turn they each banged their glasses on the table, downing the first shots of the evening.

"Ack!" Elise made a face and chased her popper with a gulp of her beer, as if it would miraculously rid her of the lingering taste of tequila. Poppers were *not* her choice in drinks.

Tina laughed and shouted, "Geez, El, you're such a wimp."

"Why? Because I prefer a good Merlot to shooters and beer? Hello! I've grown up on a vineyard. It's in my blood."

"You can have your fancy Merlot," Miranda said over the music with a shake of her golden curls. "I'll take shooters, beer, and the sight of so many fine-looking cowboys in snug-fitting jeans any day of the week."

"Mmm, girl, you know I'm with you on that!" C.C. chimed in just as the band ended the current song. "It's a dang shame that we're the only two unattached women at the table, but someone's got to pick up the slack."

Miranda gave an exaggerated sigh. "Yep, we'll just have to carry on."

Just then C.C. sat up a little straighter and stared through the crowd toward the door. "Yes, Ma'am! Speaking of fine-looking

88

cowboys in snug jeans . . ."

They all turned and followed her gaze, watching Jackson and Jeff Turney, Tina's fiancé, make their way down the bar.

"Okay, that's not fair," Tina complained. "How can I drool over other men with Jeff here to watch?"

"Can't," Brenda stated with a wry grin. "That's what you get for being in a relationship."

Elise's pulse jumped at the sight of Jackson in civilian clothes. He did indeed fill out a pair of jeans with exceptional style, she noted.

"I'm telling you, I could eat Jackson Landry up with a spoon," Miranda drawled.

C.C. hooked a thumb over her shoulder. "Get in line, sweetheart."

"Yes, it's a damn shame that he's taken, girls." Elise wrinkled her nose. "Although, how Maelene McKinney got her hooks into him in the first place, I will never understand."

"You mean *was* taken, don't you?" Brenda asked with a twinkle in her emerald-green eyes.

"What?"

C.C. gave her a sad look. "Uh, El, he and Maelene called it quits over a month ago. Where've you been?"

"How do you know that?" Elise demanded to know. Jackson was single again? The air in the bar suddenly seemed thin, and she found it difficult to catch her breath.

"Sweetie, he's your brother's best friend. How is it that *you* didn't know that?" C.C. slapped a hand to her forehead. "Oh, wait. You've been busy with what's-his-name. That's right."

"Very funny," Elise said, watching Jackson flirt with just about every female he came across as he and Jeff headed toward their table. "And I wish you'd quit calling Stuart that. I don't know why you don't like him; you don't even know him."

"Honey, I don't have anything against Stewie, per se, other than the fact that the *few* times I've met him, he seemed terribly stuffy and pretentious, that is. That's also the point, El. He's been here, what? Three or four times? With each visit I got the impression he felt he was slumming it in the sticks, and that he couldn't wait to get back to the big city." C.C. slung an arm around Elise's shoulder and spoke quietly into her ear as the two men arrived at the table. "I'm sure he's very nice and I'm probably judging him harshly. I just don't think he's the guy for you, that's all. But that's another conversation for another night."

Jeff circled around, pulling a chair up next to Tina, giving his fiancée a peck on the cheek. Jackson stood between Brenda and Miranda, and his eyes found Elise's from the other side of the table.

His smile grew.

Despite her best effort to remain unaffected, her pulse went wild in response even as she returned his warm look with a bland stare.

This is ridiculous, she told herself. *It's just Jackson.*

To her irritation, white teeth flashed in a grin that was just a teensy bit wicked and told her he was reading her thoughts perfectly and enjoying every bit of it.

The band started the next lively song in their set, and without taking his eyes from hers Jackson annoyed her a tad more by holding a hand out to her best friend. "Hey, C.C., you wanna dance?"

C.C. jumped up and gave a hoot. "You know it, gorgeous! I *love* this song."

Elise watched them make their way through the crowd to the dance floor. Though she was loath to admit it, she recognized jealousy as it reared its ugly head in the middle of her chest.

Which, of course, is just stupid, she thought with a frown. She and Jackson may have a strong chemistry, but she had a damn boyfriend. For crying out loud, she had no business mentally drooling over her brother's best friend. A friend she'd known for most of her life. Besides, if they hadn't been able to hook up by now, it probably wasn't meant to be in the first place. Who wants to mess with a close family friendship like that? Not her.

She tried to rid herself of the feeling by silently repeating Stuart's name, and it irritated the hell out of her that she couldn't quite picture his face. Every time she tried, all she could see was Jackson's handsome face smiling at her from across the table.

"I'm hitting the ladies' room," she announced to no one in particular. Maybe all she needed was some air.

As it turned out she'd been right and the break did wonders. By the time she'd freshened up her makeup and fluffed her hair, she was feeling much more in control.

"Hey, Elise," a soft voice said from behind.

She looked up as Harmony Gates came out of the third stall. "Hey, Harmony, how you doin'?"

"I'm good." The other woman giggled and swayed a bit as she stepped to the sink to wash her hands. "Man, it's really packed tonight, huh? Like a great big party. I'm having the best time."

"Yeah, they're making a killing, all right. Are you here with Bud?"

"Hell no! Bud and I broke up awhile back. No, I'm just here with some friends, same as you." Harmony snickered and wiggled her eyebrows. "We got us a designated driver, so the rest of us are cuttin' loose."

Maybe it was the poppers, or maybe it was her imagination, but as Elise touched up her lipstick, she got the distinct impression that Harmony was studying her in the mirror.

And it felt a little creepy.

"I saw Jackson come in," the woman said, never taking her eyes off Elise as she dried her hands. "You know, he and Maelene called it quits. You think you two might finally get together?"

Good Lord, is that what this is about?

Maybe Harmony wanted to make a move on Jackson and she was trying to clear the way. Or maybe it was the alcohol talking. She was unsteady on her feet and obviously a little tipsy. Either way, her question was too close to Elise's earlier musings, and she thought it was prudent to set the record straight immediately. The last thing the family needed now, with a murder investigation getting underway, was the rumor mill powering up at her and Jackson's expense.

"Look, Harmony, if you want a shot at Jax, you go right ahead. I have a boyfriend in Dallas."

Harmony laughed out loud. It was a harsh, unpleasant sound that grated on Elise's nerves. "No. I'm engaged to someone else now — someone smarter and better lookin' than Bud will ever hope to be. You and Jackson have always seemed perfect for each other, that's all. You should go for it now that he's a free agent. You know, Elise, Dallas is a long way off." The woman gave her a quick wink, took a last look in the mirror, and then slipped out of the ladies' room, leaving Elise a bit baffled by the conversation.

But by the time Elise returned to the table, she had not only gotten her wayward libido under control but had put the odd exchange out of her mind. Jackson and C.C. were back from the dance floor, and he'd taken up residence in her chair.

She dropped her purse on the table and tapped him on the shoulder. "You're in my seat, pal."

He looked up at her and grinned but stood to give her the chair. As he did, his arm brushed her purse — which was sitting too close to the edge of the table — and knocked it off onto the floor.

To make matters worse, she'd failed to zip it closed when she'd left the ladies' room and it landed upside down. Jackson reached down to pick it up as she dove to keep her lipstick and a few other things from rolling under the table. Her good fortune at snatching up the loose items quickly took a downward spiral as she stood up and then froze.

Jackson had her purse under one arm and was staring down at both Edmond's paystubs and gambling markers in his hand. He raised his eyes to hers, his charming smile now gone.

"Where did you get these, Elise? And what are they doing in your purse?"

Six

Elise's mind went utterly blank as she stared first at the offending papers in Jackson's hand and then up at the stern look on his face. How on earth was she going to explain this? There was no good reason why her uncle's paystubs and gambling markers should be in her purse — at least not one that didn't involve breaking and entering.

And they both knew it.

He raised a questioning eyebrow. "I'm waiting, El."

"Okay, I know how this looks," she began, "but there is a reasonable explanation."

That is, there will be as soon as I think of one, she mentally amended and went into a slight panic mode.

Before she could elaborate — or come up with that reasonable explanation — the band kicked in again, and she prayed she might put off having to provide any details until she had time to manufacture something plausible.

She should have known better. Jackson simply grabbed her by the upper arm in a vise-like grip and hauled her up against his rock-hard frame.

"Say your goodbyes, sweet pea," he murmured next to her ear, sending shivers rippling across her nerve endings. Though his tone was deceptively pleasant, she wasn't fooled. Jackson was annoyed. "We're going to your place to have us a little chat. Right now."

Elise couldn't help wishing her friends would put up a fuss and save her from the chewing out she was sure to get from Jackson when he found out what she'd done.

Unfortunately, Jeff and Tina barely looked up, Brenda gave her a happy wave as she headed toward the dance floor with Earl Wiggins, and C.C. just smiled knowingly.

Miranda didn't say much, either, but did give her the stink-eye. Elise figured she was being blamed for stealing the recently unattached Jackson out from under the woman's nose before she'd had a chance to corner him. If only Miranda knew that the glint in Jackson's eye was anything but affectionate right now.

What she was sure of was that their departure made quite the sight. Jackson — with her purse still under one arm — dragged her out of the club while she attempted to keep up with his long-legged strides.

When they got partway up the street, she tried to reason with him, but he slid a steely-eyed glance her way and muttered a terse, "Zip it."

Which she did. They walked the rest of the way to her apartment in uncomfortable silence. By the time they'd climbed the stairs and unlocked her front door, she had just about talked herself into a full-blown anxiety attack. So she went on the offensive.

"I don't know why you're being so pissy about this," she began, trying to deflect attention from her actions by attacking his demeanor. "What's the big deal, anyway?"

Jackson closed the door and leaned against it, her purse still under his arm, which under any other circumstance would have been amusing.

"What's the big deal?" He tilted his head as if considering. "Well, depending on where and when you got this stuff, it could be a very big deal."

Elise crossed her arms and watched Chunk jump down from his living room perch in the Papasan chair to stroll over and give Jackson a curious sniff. "I don't see how that would make a difference. What does when, or even where, I found them have to do with anything?"

"Well, for one thing, it makes a difference if you broke the law to get them." Jackson bent over and scooped up her tubby feline with his free hand. "I'd hate to have to haul your butt in for obstruction of justice."

"Obstruction of justice? What the —"

"You never think of the consequences do you? Those papers could be important evidence in a homicide investigation," he said as he crossed into the living room.

Stalking into the room behind him, she snatched her purse up off the coffee table where he'd deposited it and held it to her chest like a lost friend. "A *homicide*? Who said anything about a homicide?"

"The ME's office said, that's who."

"The ME ruled Uncle Edmond's death a homicide? When did *that* happen? Are they sure? And why am I just hearing about it now? Have you told Mom or anyone yet?"

As she fired off question after question, Jackson plopped down on the sofa and shook his head.

"What?" she demanded when she'd run out of steam and he'd made no effort to jump in with information.

"Are you through? Good God, woman, you jabber more than an agitated magpie. If you'd shut up for two seconds, I just might answer your questions." As he scratched Chunk's ears the cat began to purr with gusto and rub against his chest.

Traitorous little twerp, she thought with a frown.

"Well?" she asked out loud. "I'm listening."

He stared at her for a bit longer, and just when she was about to pop a vein, he finally spoke. "I got the call from Austin with a preliminary ruling at about quarter to five this afternoon. Seeing as it was so late in the day on a Friday, I thought tomorrow morning would be soon enough to come out to the vineyard to break the bad news to the family."

Elise sank down into a chair. "Oh."

"And I gotta say you don't look too surprised with the ruling."

"I'll admit, while I was hoping Uncle Edmond's death was an unfortunate accident, it seemed less likely after actually seeing where and how he was found. Too many questions, you know?"

Jackson nodded. "We also now have an approximate time of death — on Monday, early evening, between six and seven." He pulled the stubs and markers out of his shirt pocket and waved them at her. "So I'll ask you again. When and where did you get these?"

She had another bad moment as she worked to come up with something believable and failed miserably. It didn't help that Jackson sat there smiling at her as if he could read her mind.

"If you can't come up with a decent story, El, you should probably think about just telling me the truth," he said when she'd just about given up. "You know I'll find out eventually, anyway."

"Jackson Landry, I take offense at that insinuation." She sniffed and flipped her hair over one shoulder. "What makes you think I wouldn't tell you the truth?"

"Elise Brianna, how long have we known each other?"

She sighed, rolled her eyes, and thought about holding out awhile longer just on pure principle. But in the end she relented and told him about going out to her uncle's house on the day he was killed.

"Jesus, Mary, and Joseph! What in God's name were you thinking?" he demanded to know when she'd finished her explanation. "If someone saw you poking around his place on the day he was murdered — and trust me, there's *always* someone watching — that will not look good."

"Oh please! Nobody saw me. And besides, how was I supposed to know someone was going to kill the man on that particular day?"

It was Jackson's turn to roll his eyes. "That is *not* the point, Elise. Once word gets out that Edmond was murdered, there are people in this county who will be following the case with a magnifying glass. I'm going to have to be extremely careful on how I handle this investigation."

"I don't see what that has to do with —" She stopped abruptly and shot him a hard look when his earlier words sank in. "Wait. What did you mean, 'that will not look good'?"

"Are you kidding me? You think snoopin' around and taking stuff from Edmond's house on the day he's murdered will go unnoticed? Geez, El, wake up. Your family will be the first to be scrutinized, and I mean each and every one of you."

"My family?" She blinked several times and her mouth dropped open. "Why would my family be scrutinized over a robbery gone bad?"

"First of all, you can't assume this was a robbery simply because his wallet was missing. The killer could have just been trying to make it look that way. And second, I'm gonna have to look at this crime from all angles."

"You can't be serious."

"I'm serious as a heart attack, darlin'. Stop and think about it for a minute," he insisted. "Your mom has had several very public arguments with Edmond over recent months. Ross and your vineyard foreman, Neil, have both had confrontations with him *and* made threatening comments. In front of witnesses, I might add."

"Mom? Ross? Don't tell me you suspect either of them of killing Uncle Edmond."

"And then there's your little pilfering excursion to his house when he wasn't even home," he continued as if she hadn't spoken. "This kind of behavior will only serve to make my job that much harder."

"My excur—" she sputtered. "Jackson, are you insane? Have you fallen down recently and smacked your pointy little head? That's just ridiculous and you know it! How can you even think that, let alone say it out loud?"

"You really don't get it, do you?" He shoved Chunk aside and scrubbed his hands over his face before explaining. "I was first on the scene. It's my *job* to ask the tough questions — before someone else does. If there's even a whiff of impropriety with this investigation, the sheriff could replace me with someone else."

"You don't really think that could happen, do you?"

"I don't think it, I *know* it. There are folks who will say I should step down simply because of my relationship with your family. And mark my words, Darrell Yancy will be one of them. He would do a friggin' happy dance up Main Street to get his hands on this case. And just think about how much fun *that* would be for everyone involved, especially Ross."

"Oh God, it would be horrible, Jax. He doesn't know my family like you do, and he's never gotten over Caroline choosing Ross over him. Plus, he's a small-minded idiot."

Jackson smiled at that. "You won't get an argument from me on that front." Then he sobered. "But that's why it's so important that you tell me this stuff before someone else does. Or better still, don't do something stupid like this in the first place." He finished by waving the paystubs and gambling markers in front of her again.

She narrowed her eyes at him but bit back the snarky remark on the tip of her tongue. Instead, she nodded at the documents and countered with a thought of her own. "You know, those bring up a good point."

"Yeah? What's that?"

"Well, that there are others besides my family who may have had motive for wanting Uncle Edmond dead."

"Like Henry Kohler? What would be his motive?"

"For crying in a bucket, Jackson, I don't know. That's your job, isn't it?" Elise got up and threw her hands in the air. "But I find it odd that my uncle was secretly working for a rival vineyard, don't you? I mean, why would he? He'd been offered a position at River Bend on several occasions."

"True, but giving Edmond a job doesn't make Henry Kohler a murderer."

"No, but there's the security factor to think about."

"What do you mean? Don't all wineries operate pretty much the same? What would you need to keep secure?"

"Well, there's my hybridization process, for starters. And here's one more thing: I happen to know that Uncle Edmond had heavy gambling debts. You have proof of that right there in your hand. Maybe someone killed him when he couldn't pay up."

"Wow. You've been watching a lot of TV lately, haven't you?"

Elise let his comment go but glared at him

and jabbed a finger in his direction. "Another person you should talk to is Pam Dawson. She loaned him a bunch of money, and I think she may have even taken out a loan against the restaurant to do it. Plus the woman is crazy as a loon. I think she'd bash in his head in a minute if she thought he was trying to weasel out of repaying her."

"Uh-huh. And how is it you know she loaned Edmond all this money?"

"She told me," she blurted out before she thought.

"I see." Jackson paused and ran his tongue over his teeth. "And when did this incredible, information-packed conversation take place?"

Realizing the quagmire she'd babbled herself into, Elise tried unsuccessfully to backpedal. "Oh, you know, awhile ago," she replied vaguely, waving a hand in the air.

He gave her a speculative stare. "Pam was in a *talkative mood,* was she? Awhile ago? When you happened to run into her?"

"Uh, sure."

"Ha! Have you *met* Pam Dawson?"

"Oh, shut up," she grumbled.

"Lord love a goose, you are the most pathetic liar I think I have ever seen in my entire life. We both know Pam's so tight she squeaks and wouldn't just volunteer anything, let alone information like that. Why don't you tell me what really happened?"

Elise flopped back down in the chair and pouted. "Okay. But you have to promise not to yell at me, and I mean it, Jackson."

"I'm not promisin' anything. Spill it."

Elise heaved a sigh and began to fill him in on her visit to the Pit Barbeque.

"Let me get this straight. You did this on the very same day you went poking around at Edmond's?" As Jackson's voice rose, Chunk scampered back to his Papasan chair and began to bathe himself.

"I said no *yelling!*" she hollered back at him.

"And I didn't *promise!*" Jackson answered in kind, and then pinched the bridge of his nose. She could almost hear him counting to ten in his head.

"For the love of God, woman," he said when he finally looked up. "You wear me out."

"Oh, quit your bitchin'. Do you want to hear the rest or not?"

"Might as well. How much worse can it get?"

She finished up by telling him about finding Pam and Henry Kohler cozied up in a booth when she'd arrived and her crazed conversation with Pam after the vintner left.

"The whole thing was very strange. And for a minute, I thought Pam might have a meltdown right there in front of God and everyone."

Jackson sighed. "Didn't your mama teach you not to go poking at crazy people? It's dangerous and it never ends well."

"Jackson." She uttered his name in a warning tone.

"All right, I admit it does sound odd, and I'll check it out, but you have to promise me you'll butt out. I can't have you stickin' your nose into police business, El, especially when you could end up on my suspect list."

"Stop sayin' that." She picked up one of Chunk's stuffed toys and threw it at him. He caught it left handed and nailed her with a narrowed gaze. "I didn't kill Uncle Edmond, and you know it."

"Makes no difference what I think, sweetheart. I'm going to have to follow the evidence — no matter where it leads." He looked at his watch and got to his feet. "It's almost eleven. I should get going. I want to be out at the vineyard early."

"Of course you do," she muttered as she rose and followed him to the door. "I don't know what everyone thinks is so fabulous about the crack of friggin' dawn. I say if God wanted me to be up at that hour, he'd have made it light out."

Grumbling about the time, she was following him too closely and not paying particular attention. She ran right into him when he stopped and turned, and he took her by the elbows to steady her. When she looked up into those brilliant, green eyes, and then down at his full lips hovering so close, she thought her heart might literally have skipped a beat.

And she couldn't think of a single coherent thing to say.

Jackson seemed to be as discombobulated as she was. *And Lord above, doesn't he just smell good enough to eat?* Suddenly she wanted nothing more than to melt against him and feel his lips pressed to her own.

Then the stupid cat rubbed up against their legs and the feeling passed. She was left wondering what in the world she'd been thinking and how her thoughts had gotten so out of control in a matter of moments.

"I guess I'll see you at the vineyard tomorrow," he mumbled, setting her away from him. Opening the door, he stepped out onto the landing and then turned back. "Lock this behind me."

"Uh, Jax, this is Delphine," she reminded him with a smirk. "Nothing ever happens here."

"Don't suppose I need to remind you that your uncle was murdered a short fifteen miles up the road, right? Just lock the damn door, El."

Jackson sat in his truck for a good long time looking up at Elise's window and thinking. For a brief moment there, when he all but had her in his arms, his mind had gone haywire. That was the only explanation for what he'd felt.

And he wanted a taste of her in a big, bad way.

Fortunately, her cat had snapped him out of it in the nick of time. He may be a free agent now, but Elise was in a relationship with . . . crap, what was the guy's name? Stephen? Anyway, he had no business panting after her when she was unavailable.

No matter how much he'd like to.

Add in the fact that this investigation was going to get downright messy before it was all said and done. He could feel it in his bones. That said, he would be smart to put a little distance between them now.

He drove home with a jumble of information playing over in his mind. He'd need to hit the ground running with this case, be on top of every facet and not give anyone a reason to think about taking it away from him. Because no matter what Elise said, just about every member of the Beckett family had a reason to want Edmond Beckett out of the way.

What he'd told her earlier had been true; he was going to have to follow the evidence and go wherever it led him. He could only hope and pray that it didn't point him toward anyone at River Bend.

Seven

"Oh, my gosh! Uncle Edmond was murdered?" Madison sat down hard on the dining room chair. The color drained from her face and her soft, blue eyes filled with tears. "Are they sure?"

"Yes, sweetheart." Laura went to her daughter and rubbed her shoulders. "Jackson says there's no doubt."

"Good Lord! Who would do something like that? And then leave him to be found right here on River Bend land." Abigail shook her head. "I don't know what the world is coming to. Bunch of crazy people out there, if you ask me."

"Although, when it comes to Uncle Edmond, I have to say, I'm not all that surprised," Ross muttered.

"Ross Alexander! What a thing to say," Laura admonished in a shocked voice.

"I'm sorry, Mom, but I'm just saying what everyone else in this room is probably thinking. Uncle Edmond pissed off a lot of people."

"Well, you can keep those kinds of comments to yourself, please. Edmond may have been many things, but he didn't deserve this."

"You're right. He didn't, but who knows what Uncle Edmond was into recently that might have gotten him killed."

Jackson stood in the doorway of the dining room, where Laura had called the family meeting, as he'd requested. Studying their faces now, he watched how each of them in turn responded to the news. These were people who were as close to him as his own family, yet he was unable to predict just what their reactions would be, particularly Ross.

Upon hearing that Edmond's death had been ruled a homicide, most folks had been under the impression that it had simply been a random act of violence or perhaps a robbery gone wrong. Elise had thought the same thing the previous evening. Obviously, Ross had at least considered the possibility that Edmond may have known his killer. Nevertheless, the next step in the investigation was going to be touchy.

"Poor Uncle Edmond," Madison murmured as she swiped at the tears tracking down her cheeks. "And like Gram said, right here, so close to home. That's really scary. I mean, we don't even lock our doors at night."

"It's all going to be fine, sweetie. Jackson will figure this out." Laura looked up at him, and when their eyes met, hers pleaded for him to calm her family's fears. Her voice, on the other hand, didn't plead so much as demand. "Isn't that right, Jackson?"

When he and Laura had met earlier that morning, they'd discussed some of the issues the family was sure to face once the report of the murder got out. The next few weeks would not be easy. And he had no illusions that the path his inquiries would take would be welcomed by the community, least of all by the people sitting around this dining room table.

"Yes, ma'am," he finally answered. "I'm going to do my level best to clear this up as quickly as possible."

Sliding a quick glance in Elise's direction, he pulled a small notepad out of his pocket and then turned to the family, taking in the anticipation on their faces. "Which brings me to the next step. I'm going to need to know the whereabouts of each of you last Monday night between six and seven p.m."

In much the same way as the day the vineyard workers had found Edmond, the room erupted into chaos and outrage.

"What the hell are you saying, Jackson?" Ross shouted over everyone else. "That we're all suspects? You seriously think someone in this room is capable of robbing and killing a family member?"

"Ross, honey, that's not what Jackson is saying," Laura answered for Jackson before he could form a response of his own. "You need to hear him out."

It was an obvious attempt to defuse the tension, but Ross ignored her. "For the love of God, Jax, you practically grew up here at the vineyard," he said, and Jackson could almost feel the waves of fury radiating off his friend. "How can you even suggest that? Where's your loyalty, bro?"

"Ross, you need to think about this rationally." Laura made a second attempt to calm her son down. "It's important that the entire family be excluded from the process as soon as possible. Jackson is just doing his job."

"That's exactly right, Miss Laura. The family needs to be cleared first, preferably before the news breaks." Jackson met Ross's heated gaze with an icy one of his own, and he tried with limited success to beat back

115

his own temper. "I'm going to have to walk very close to the line with this investigation, and I don't want any surprises down the road, *bro.* "

Being an only child and spending so much of his youth at River Bend, Jackson thought of Ross as the brother he never had. At the moment, however, it was all he could do not to give his *brother* a damn good thumping.

"And as for loyalty? Half the folks in this county know that I consider River Bend my second home." In an attempt to stay as objective as possible, Jackson took a deep breath and made the extra effort to rein in his emotions. "That's what makes this situation so dicey. There can't be so much as a whiff of partiality in the air. Each step I take will have to be strictly by the book. I'm sorry if you have a problem with that, Ross, but you'd better get on board."

"Yeah? Or what, Deputy Landry?"

Jackson shook his head. "What the hell's the matter with you? I would think you'd want to cooperate in any way you could, would want the family cleared as quickly as possible so the spotlight could move on. Instead, here you are, throwing up road blocks right out of the gate."

"Jax, please —" Elise began, but he put

up a hand in her direction, effectively cutting her off in mid-sentence.

"You got something to say to me, Ross? Or maybe something to hide, something you don't want me to know about?"

Ross frowned at him from across the table and folded his arms over his chest. "Not a thing. I just don't care for someone who should be protecting this family — someone who should know better, I might add — insinuating that one of us could be a killer, that's all."

"Ross, that's not fair and you know it," Elise said quietly. "You need to cut Jackson some slack. This isn't going to be easy on any of us, least of all him."

Ross sighed and rubbed his eyes with the heels of his hands before looking up and pinning Jackson with a glare. "You want to know where I was Monday night? I was at home with my wife and kids while someone was out there killing my uncle. Anything else I can help you with?"

Jackson stared at Ross for a moment longer before pointedly looking to Caroline. "Caro?"

Ross's wife looked up at him with brown eyes that had grown big and round. Her mouth opened and closed several times, yet she didn't confirm or deny her husband's alibi.

Ross's caustic laugh cut through the silence. "That's awesome, Jax. Very nice. Now my word isn't even good enough for you."

"That is enough!" Laura snapped out the three words rapid-fire before skewering each one of her family members in turn with a look that conveyed her displeasure. "Listen up, all of you. This is an ugly business, there's no way around that. But from here on out, we're all going to cooperate fully with Jackson's investigation — right up to the moment he catches your uncle's killer."

She flung a hard stare back at Ross when he started to speak, and he clammed up in a hurry. "I'll be damned if this family will behave like a bunch of spoiled ingrates and give half the county something to gossip about. We are going to work together and assist Jackson with whatever he needs or asks of us. Do I make myself clear?"

When nobody spoke, she turned back to Jackson with a beleaguered sigh. "And having said that, I suppose I should lead by example. Neil Paige and I spent most of Monday out at the north end of the vineyard working on fencing with several other employees. I can give you their names if you need them." She paused and ran a hand through her short, dark cap of hair. "I came back to the house covered in grime sometime around five and spent about an hour soaking in a hot tub. We sat down to a late supper just before seven. Isn't that about right, Mom?"

Abigail pursed her lips and nodded. "Yep, I'd say that about covers it. I didn't see her come back to the house because I'd headed into town to pick up a few things for dinner at the grocery store. Must have gotten back between five and five thirty." She shrugged. "Then I cooked that late supper while watchin' the evening news. When we finished dinner, I cleaned up the kitchen and went upstairs. Miriam Graham called goin' on eight thirty, and we chatted about the upcoming Lost Pines Food & Wine Festival for a good hour, hour and a half before I turned out the lights. She'll verify that conversation and the times. I can give you her number if you need to check on it."

Jackson nodded and looked up from his scribbling. "Miss Abby, on your way to or from town, did you happen to notice anything or anyone out along the highway that didn't belong? See anything odd at all?"

"No, darlin', I'm sorry, I didn't see anything out of the ordinary that afternoon."

"That's okay. I didn't really think it would be that easy," he replied with a smile. "Who's next?"

"I'll go." Madison's bright, blue gaze skittered around the table before coming to rest on Jackson. "I worked late last Monday. The Adams/Wilkinson wedding and reception have been kicking my . . . uh . . . butt," she finished when her mother frowned in her direction.

Jackson tried not to smile. "Go on."

"Deana keeps changing her mind, and Mayor Wilkinson has yet to put her foot down. I don't know what we're going to do about this mess. If the mayor cancels the event it'll be a big, black mark for the vineyard's reputation, not to mention it will cost us a ton of money."

"I meant, go on about your account of Monday."

"Oh. Sorry." She closed her eyes briefly and took a deep, cleansing breath. "Anyway, I was in my office at the lodge until right before dinner. Gram had to call down to get me to come up to the house to eat. Remember, Gram?"

"I do, yes." Abigail nodded in Jackson's direction. "I called down about six forty-five. And she came right away too. The three of us ate meat loaf together in the kitchen."

"Well, I don't have an alibi for that night or anyone that can vouch for my whereabouts," Elise spoke up. "As you well know."

Jackson glanced up at her and rolled his eyes.

"Care to tell us where you were?" Laura asked. "And why Jackson would already know that you don't have an alibi?"

Elise sighed, and at Jackson's nod, explained how she'd gone snooping at Edmond's, and about the paystubs and gambling markers she'd found while there. "I spoke to Ross on the phone as I was leaving, and he told me to go home and forget about it, which I did. I was there the rest of the evening, though I don't have any way to prove it."

"Oh, Elise, what were you thinking?" Laura asked.

"I was actually looking for Uncle Edmond. I couldn't understand why he would want to break up the vineyard that way. I just wanted to hear his side of the story, that's all." Elise paused and shook her head. "Then I found the gambling markers and the paystubs. I couldn't believe it. Why on earth would he work for the competition when he could have worked with his own family? He betrayed us all."

Abigail got up and came around the table

to her granddaughter. Slipping an arm around Elise, she hugged her close. "Sometimes we do hurtful things to those we love without thinking, sweetheart. I think Edmond would have come to his senses eventually and realized what he was losing, but someone cut short his time, that's all."

"Unfortunately, there's no way to know what his motives were, and we can never be sure of how it would have ended." Suddenly, Elise sat up straighter and her blue eyes lit up. "Wait a minute! Stuart called me on my house phone just after I finished my own dinner and we talked for an hour or so. We hung up about seven, so I guess that does give me an alibi."

Jackson shot her a narrow glance and then shook his head.

"What?" she asked in an exasperated tone. "It covers the time you're talking about."

Jackson ignored her. "I think that's all I need for now." Flipping his notepad closed, he put it back into his pocket. "Thank you for your cooperation, Miss Laura. I will try to keep you updated, if I can."

"I appreciate that, Jackson. But if you can't, we'll all understand. I don't want you to get into any hot water because of us." She made a point to send a sharp glance at Ross before patting Jackson's shoulder.

"And if you need anything else, just give me a call, you hear?"

"Yes, ma'am."

"Jax, can I talk to you for a minute before you leave?" Elise asked and inclined her head toward the hallway.

He ignored the sly look Ross gave them and followed her out of the dining room. "What's up?" he asked as she dragged him down the hall and into the office.

Closing the door behind her, Elise leaned back on it and gave him a sympathetic look. "First off, I just want to say that I know that was as hard on you as it was on the rest of the family. I'm sorry. And I'm sorry Ross was such a butthead. You know he didn't really mean half of what he said, right?"

"He's angry right now and doesn't want to think that this kind of thing could happen to his family. I get that." Jackson rubbed his forehead, where a dull ache had begun. "Unfortunately, it has, and he's gonna have to come to grips with it on his own. Like your mom said, the sooner he cooperates, the better."

"I wish there was something I could do, but you're right, he's going to have to work it out himself." She paused, and he could almost see the wheels turning in her head.

"Spit it out, precious."

"Spit what out?"

She looked up at him all innocence, but he wasn't fooled. She was hatching something. "Spit out whatever it is that you're not saying."

"Okay, not to change the subject, but are you going to talk to Pam today?"

Closing his eyes, he counted to ten before answering. "Yes, El, I'm going out to the Pit Barbeque next, if it's any of your business — which of course, it's not. Did we not talk about this just last night?"

"Geez, don't blow a gasket. I was just asking." Elise crossed her arms and cocked a hip. "But come to think of it, you should probably take a look at Uncle Edmond's house too. I didn't have much time on Monday, and there's probably more clues buried out there in that pig sty."

"You just can't help yourself, can you?" Jackson blew out an exasperated breath and jabbed a finger at her. "You need to let me do my job in my own way and keep that pretty little nose of yours out of it. Are you listening to me?"

"Kinda hard not to when you're hollerin' in my face."

"I've got several interviews left to do and my own timeline for *my* investigation. I don't need you poking around to worry about as well."

"Okay, okay, don't be so touchy. I'm just sayin'. Anyway, I've got my own work to do. Why in the world would I want to take on yours, too?"

"I mean it, El. Stay out of my investigation."

"Now who's not listening? Didn't I just say I don't have time to do any more poking around in *your* case?"

He watched her adopt an air of nonchalance as she flipped her hair over her shoulder.

Oh, yes. She was up to something, all right. He could feel it. He just couldn't quite see what.

EIGHT

Elise was pretty sure Jackson hadn't bought her wide-eyed innocent act when she'd told him she wasn't interested in his investigation. The truth was, she wanted to know exactly what her uncle had been up to in the months before his murder.

Jackson was wrong when he'd said it was none of her business. Whatever Edmond had been planning had obviously included the vineyard. And the vineyard involved her family as well as her work. In her opinion, that made it her business.

She'd have to be careful not to get in Jackson's way and stay as far under his radar as possible. But she had a gut feeling that whatever she was looking for was buried in that rat-hole Edmond had been living in, and she was going to do her level best to find it. That meant going back and doing a better search, no matter how repugnant the thought might be.

She'd waited until the family meeting had broken up and she knew Jackson was long gone before calling C.C. and recruiting her for some amateur sleuthing. Then she headed over to pick her up the minute she could break away from the vineyard without raising any red flags. The last thing she needed was for Jackson to get wind of her plan to go back to her uncle's house.

True to form, C.C. didn't even blink when Elise suggested she put on her breaking and entering hat. However, the closer they got to Edmond's place, the guiltier Elise began to feel. It was one thing to place oneself in a hot seat with the law — maybe even in the middle of harm's way — but quite another to drag a friend there with you.

"C.C., there's still time to back out if you want," she said as she pulled her sports car into her uncle's driveway. "We really shouldn't be here at all, and Jax will pop a vein if he finds out. I'll understand if you want to wait in the car."

C.C. turned toward her with a smirk on her face and leveled a bland stare in her direction. "So, let me get this straight: if I say I'm backing out, are you going in there anyway?"

Elise shut off the motor and sat staring at the house as she gathered her thoughts. The

127

last time she'd gone snooping here she'd been alone and hadn't stayed long. She'd freaked herself out after being inside for only a few minutes. Her search hadn't been as thorough as she'd wanted it to be, but this time she was going to do a better job. Though she honestly had no idea what she was looking for, she hoped she'd know it if and when she saw it.

"Yeah. Yeah, I am," she finally answered with a firm nod. "I want a closer look and I'm going to take my time, be thorough. I just know there's something in there that will give me a clearer understanding of what Uncle Edmond was up to before he was killed. There might also be a clue as to who killed him and why. I can't *not* do this."

"Uh-huh. That's what I thought. So, if that's the case, then you're not going in there all by your lonesome. And let me just say, if there's sleuthing to be done, I'm gonna be in on it. Besides, this car is a bright red beacon, and I'd probably be more conspicuous sitting out here than going inside with you."

"You know, if we get caught doing this, we'll probably be in big trouble — maybe even be charged with obstruction or tampering with evidence or some stupid thing."

C.C. laughed out loud at that. "Please.

Let them try to pull something that pathetic. This is your uncle's house, and I don't see any crime scene tape. So I say, as long as we aren't picking the lock or smashing a window to get inside, we're not *actually* breaking and entering."

She unearthed two pairs of latex gloves from the depths of the huge bag she called a purse and dangled them in front of Elise's face. "Of course, I'd rather not get caught. Just to be on the safe side, we should probably wear these so as not to leave any prints behind."

Elise grinned. This was one of the reasons C.C. was her BFF. The woman was always willing to jump into Elise's latest adventure with both feet, regardless of the consequences. That, to her mind, was the definition of a true friend. "Wow, you really came prepared."

"You bet," C.C. replied with a wink. "I was a Girl Scout, you know. Now let's get this party started, shall we?"

They each snapped on their gloves, climbed from the car, and headed for the house.

"Uncle Edmond rarely locked his door, but just in case, I think there's a key hidden somewhere in that overgrown planter on the porch."

But as they reached the porch, they saw that the door was standing slightly ajar and they didn't need a key.

"Okay, that's kinda creepy," C.C. said and stepped behind Elise. "You go first."

"Don't be such a wuss. The last person out probably just didn't get the door closed properly and it blew open with the wind or something, that's all."

"Uh-huh. I repeat, you go first."

Elise shot a glance over her shoulder. "What happened to 'Let's get this party started'?"

C.C. jiggled her eyebrows up and down, and her dark brown eyes twinkled with mischief. "I said I was up for some sleuthing; I didn't say I wouldn't be a wuss about it if we ran across some creepiness."

"Oh, brother."

Elise gave the door a push, and the prolonged *creak* the door made as it swung open sent a chill down her back. When she made no attempt to enter, C.C. nudged her shoulder.

"What are you waiting for?"

"I'm going. Don't push me."

Moving into the dim light of the living room, she took a cursory look around and then glanced back at her friend. "See. Nothing out of the ordinary here, just an average living room."

C.C. stepped inside and immediately wrinkled her nose. "Yeah, a really filthy, disgusting, and smelly living room. My God, Edmond was a pig!"

"I know. It's pretty bad, so let's get this done and get the hell out of here as fast as we can." She pointed to the right. "You take that end of the disgusting living room, and I'll start over here in the nasty dining area."

They spent thirty minutes going through the enormous amount of crap that Edmond had accumulated and evidently felt compelled to keep. Random stacks of papers — which seemed to be piled in every damn corner — contained everything from old letters to delinquent bills to more gambling markers and paystubs.

"I think Uncle Edmond may have been spying on River Bend for someone," Elise said and held up a fairly recent copy of a book on grape varieties and hybridization. "And it looks like he was doing a little research to boot."

C.C. looked up from the heap of paperwork she was digging through and frowned. "What makes you think he was spying for someone? Maybe he was just boning up in case your mom caved and gave him his own slice of the pie."

131

Elise snorted and went back to sorting. "Besides living in a dung heap, my uncle — God rest his blackened soul — avoided work in any form. The only reason he wanted a slice of our fabulous River Bend pie was to sell it off and pay down his debts so he could start all over again."

"That's just sad, not to mention so very wrong."

"I know, right?" Elise waved a hand around in the air. "I just can't get over the fact that he'd rather live like this and be employed by a competitor than work with his own family — and in a cleaner environment."

"Amen to that," C.C. muttered. "The dust bunny I just stumbled across is the size of a small dog."

"Gross."

"El, you know it's going to take forever to get through all this junk." C.C. stood and moved on to the bookshelf. "How much time do we have here and how thorough do you want to be?"

Elise pushed the hair back out of her eyes and looked around the cluttered dining room table, then squealed and jumped back.

"Cockroaches!" she explained with a hand to her chest when C.C. whipped around with a look of concern. "Geez, I hate those things, and this one is huge. I think I'm just about done here. I'll come and help you in a minute."

"Uh — El? You might want to come take a look at this now."

The urgency in her friend's voice had Elise abandoning the bug-infested papers on the table to see what she'd found. "What have you got?"

C.C. offered her an old hardback book she'd taken from the shelf she'd been perusing.

Elise frowned as she took it, brushing the dust and grime from the cover. "*Arabian Nights?*"

"Open it."

When she did she almost squealed again — this time with delight. Her uncle had carved out a nook inside the novel just big enough for the small journal it held. The notebook couldn't have been much larger than five by seven, but Elise imagined it must have been extremely important for her uncle to go to such trouble to conceal it.

"Oh man, this is exciting." C.C. licked her lips. "A hidden clue. Like one of those mystery shows you see on television."

Gingerly taking the journal out of its hiding spot, Elise dropped the shell of the novel on the end table. Opening the small notebook, she skimmed through several pages, and her smile began to grow.

"So, what's in it?" C.C. asked. "Anything important? Any hints to what Edmond was into?"

"Yes. Do tell, Elise. What's in it?" Startled by the deep voice that boomed from the doorway, both women jumped like felons and then screamed like little girls.

"Jackson!" Elise cried when she was able to catch her breath. "For the love of mud, what's the matter with you? Are you trying to give me a heart attack?"

Unnerved when he didn't speak right away and continued to look at her with one of his inscrutable Landry stares, she went into offensive mode. "What are you doing here, besides trying to scare us witless?"

"What am I doing —" Jackson looked stunned for a brief moment. "What am *I* doing here? You're kidding, right?"

"Okay, now there's a really good reason for us to be here."

"Don't. Just don't even go there," he growled, and she knew he was spitting angry. "Because we both know whatever you say is going to be bull. You're wearing latex gloves, for God's sake!"

"And there's a reason for that as well."

"Please! I mean, really, did you even wait

for me to clear the driveway before you called C.C. and roped her into coming out here with you? And I'm not even going to touch on your 'witless' comment, because *that* seems pretty self-explanatory."

"All right, very funny."

"Jackson, to be fair —" C.C. began, but he cut her off with a hard look. She'd been watching the exchange like a spectator at a tennis match, but now he fixated on her.

"And you!" he muttered, stabbing a finger in her direction. "You should know better, but I bet it didn't take long for her to talk you into this fiasco. Hell, knowing you, you probably supplied the damn gloves."

Elise and C.C. looked at each other, and their mouths dropped open.

Before either could respond, Jackson held his hand out to Elise. "Give it up."

"Give what up?" Elise asked, slipping the journal behind her back.

"Oh, for God's sake. Don't be such a child," he replied with disgust. "Give me the notebook. Right now."

"Jack-son!" His name came out in a whiny two syllables, and she stomped her foot for emphasis. "I found it."

"From what I saw, you did no such thing. C.C. found it."

"Regardless, this isn't even a crime scene.

135

So I don't see why I should even have to give it to you."

When he simply gave her a *come on* gesture with his hand, she folded like a bad poker hand.

"I should at least get the chance to look through it before you confiscate it," she said with a pout. Crossing the room, she shoved it at him. "Fine. Take it, and I hope you choke on it."

He made a clucking sound with his tongue and shook his head as he took the journal from her. "Now, you don't mean that, do you, darlin'?"

She glared at him. "You have no idea."

For the first time since arriving, his laughter filled the room before he grew serious again. "Let that be a lesson to the two of you. You need to stay out of this. I don't want to have this conversation again." When she continued to glower at him, he stepped right into her personal bubble. "Are you listening to me, pal?"

As much as she wanted to take a step back, she forced herself not to. She wasn't about to show weakness. "Yeah, yeah, I heard you the first time."

"Evidently not. Christ, El, I can't believe you came out here to snoop around after we just talked about this."

"Okay, okay!" She cocked a hip and crossed her arms between them for effect. "I don't see what you're getting so worked up over."

"I'm getting worked up because you said 'okay' the last couple of times we've had this chat. You're starting to work my last nerve with your Pinocchio act, if you get me."

"Oh, now who's acting childish?"

Instead of answering her, his head snapped up and he stared toward the hallway. "Shhh."

"Don't you shush me, Jackson Landry. You may be in charge of this investigation, but that doesn't give you the right —"

She got no further when he reached out and firmly pressed a finger to her lips. "Would you shut up for a minute and listen?" he whispered.

She slapped his hand away, but in that instant she heard the distinct thumping sound, like someone pounding on a wall somewhere toward the back of the house.

"What the hell is that?" C.C. asked with wide eyes. "Again with the creepiness."

Elise pointed in the direction of the hallway. "Sounds like it's coming from back there."

Setting the journal down on the edge of

the dining room table, Jackson unsnapped his holster and drew his gun. "You two stay here."

"Alone?" Elise crowded up behind him with C.C. right behind her. "We most certainly will not."

"Oh, for Pete's sake." Jackson rolled his eyes. "Then stay behind me. I wouldn't want to shoot one of you by mistake."

"Ha ha. You're just so funny, Jax," Elise snarked to cover her fear.

Jackson started down the hall with the two of them following closely. He checked the small front bedroom and minuscule bathroom, which both held nothing out of the ordinary.

Then they heard the sound again. It was definitely coming from the second bedroom, and they slowly moved in that direction. As they stepped into what had been her uncle's bedroom, the pounding got much louder. The muffled noise seemed to be emanating from the closet.

Jackson put a finger to his lips and then motioned for them to stand back. As they did, he opened the closet door with one quick motion.

And a bound and bloody Pam Dawson fell out into the room.

NINE

"Oh my gosh! Pam?" Elise rushed over to help Jackson carefully extricate the older woman from the confines of the closet. "Good Lord, Jax, there's so much blood."

Jackson nodded. "It looks like she took a pretty nasty blow to the head. That's probably where all the blood came from. Head wounds are bad that way."

Turning, he handed his phone to C.C. "Take this and call 911. Get an ambulance out here ASAP."

As C.C. stepped into the hallway to make the call, Elise lifted the edge of the duct tape and removed it from Pam's mouth in one swift jerk.

"Ouch!" The woman moaned and licked her lips. "Was that really necessary? My head is already pounding. I don't need the skin ripped off my face too."

"Sorry, but with duct tape on skin, I figured it would be better to rip it off in one shot."

Jackson took out his pocket knife and cut the tape that bound the woman's wrists and ankles. "We're going to get you to the hospital as soon as the ambulance gets here."

Pam's eyelids fluttered, and then she squinted up at them as if the light caused her great pain. "Where am I?" she asked in a rusty voice.

"You're at my Uncle Edmond's house. We found you in his bedroom closet. Do you remember how you got here?"

When Pam stared up at her and blinked several times as if trying to piece it all together, Jackson took her hand. "What were you doing here?"

The older woman scoffed, and tried to sit up, but Jackson shook his head. With a hand on her shoulder, he lightly pressed her back down. "You need to keep still. At the very least, you probably have a concussion. With that head wound, you could also have a skull fracture. We'll let the EMTs earn their pay when they get here. Okay?"

"I guess that sounds good." Closing her eyes, she winced in pain and didn't give him an argument. Considering the fact that Pam Dawson was cantankerous as hell and would argue with the devil himself given an opportunity, Elise thought this was probably a first.

C.C. came back into the room and held out Jackson's phone. "The ambulance is on its way."

"What were you doing here, Pam?" Jackson asked again as he slipped his phone back into his pocket.

"I was looking for clues and something I gave to Eddy that I wanted back — something important."

"Yeah? What's that?" Jackson asked.

Elise nodded her understanding. "You were looking for the money, weren't you?"

"The money?" Jackson frowned. "What money?"

"The money she gave Uncle Edmond when she took out the loan using the Pit Barbeque as collateral. That's what happened, isn't it, Pam?" Elise asked and then mouthed "I told you so" at Jackson. "He asked you for money, and you gave it to him, didn't you?"

"Is that true, Pam?" Jackson asked, taking his notepad out of his pocket and scribbling down the information.

"Dirty cheat!" she spat and then opened her eyes. "That man could charm the bark off a tree, but he couldn't be trusted. I should've seen it coming."

"If you used the Pit as collateral, you must have borrowed a substantial amount. What did he want it for?"

"Said if he could just get out from under his IOUs — and he had a bunch of 'em — he'd quit gambling. He told me we could cash in his part of the inheritance and be living the highlife in nothin' flat."

Jackson looked up at that. "Inheritance? You mean the part of the vineyard he'd been trying to get Laura to give him?"

Elise rolled her eyes and answered before Pam could respond. "Uncle Edmond was hoping Mom would deed him half of River Bend. He said he had a buyer already lined up, but that was never going to happen."

Pam grunted. "Yeah, I figured that out when you came by the restaurant on Monday. Didn't take a rocket scientist to realize I'd been weaseled."

"I take it you didn't find anything here before you were attacked," Elise commented.

Pam barked out a laugh in response. "Honey, there's nothin' left to find. That donkey's ass took my money and did just what he said he wouldn't; he racked up more gambling debt out at that dive on Highway 20 — on top of what he already owed."

"How do you know that?" Jackson asked.

"I put two and two together when Eddy dropped outta sight. I drove out there and had me a talk with that Rodriguez fella who runs the joint. He wasn't too happy to hear that Eddy had run off, either. He wouldn't tell me how much Eddy owed him, but I could tell by his reaction that it was a boatload."

A fierce gleam came into her eyes, and she jabbed a finger at Jackson. "And I know just what you're thinkin', Landry, but I didn't have nothin' to do with Eddy's death. Can't say beatin' him senseless didn't cross my mind and that I wouldn't have whupped the ever-lovin' crap out of him if I'd found him. But the fact is I didn't, though I have no way to prove it."

Jackson made a few more notes before looking up and pinning the older woman with a stern gaze. "You understand that we're gonna need to have a much longer conversation about all of this at some point in the near future, right?"

Pam made a sour face but gave a slight nod. "Fine by me. I ain't got nothin' to hide."

"Well, until that time comes, first things first. You've been unconscious at least part of the time you've been here and you probably don't know how long you were in the closet, but can you tell me when you arrived?"

The woman let out a resigned sigh. "I got here at about half past ten. Figured I'd get in and out without much bother and be back at the restaurant before the lunch rush."

Jackson glanced at his watch. "It's almost two now. Do you remember what happened — how you ended up in the closet?"

"I'd already done a pretty good search of the front rooms. Came back here to see what Eddy had snaked away in his room. He's got . . . uh . . . *had* several hidey-holes in here." She drew in a shaky breath before going on. "I didn't even hear him. Bastard hit me hard from behind — clocked me at least a couple of times. The first strike took me down. And I didn't just see stars, I can tell you that; it was like the entire universe exploded in my head. Sonofabitch didn't even wait for me to try to get up before bashing me again, and I was gone. The next thing I know y'all are draggin' me out into the light."

Sirens could be heard in the distance now and were getting louder. They were running out of time. Pam would be taken to the hospital, and they wouldn't get any more

144

information from her until later. Elise exchanged looks with Jackson and knew he was thinking the same thing.

"Pam, you keep referring to your attacker as male, but you don't really know who attacked you, do you?" he asked. "If the perp hit you from behind, you can't actually tell me if it was a man or a woman?"

"Well, no. I guess it could have been either."

Disappointment was written all over Jackson's face, but he pressed for more. "I know this is hard and your head probably feels like it's about to split wide open, but is there anything else you can think of that would help me figure out who did this to you? The scent of perfume or aftershave? A sound — no matter how small?"

"I'm sorry, Deputy." Pam put a hand to her forehead. "Whoever it was, they were sure light on their feet because I didn't hear a thing. Like I said, I didn't even know there was someone else in the house. But if somethin' comes to me, you'll be my first phone call. Believe me, I'd like to know who did this as much or more than you do."

Elise could tell that Jackson was frustrated — she was frustrated herself. As the EMTs arrived and began to work on Pam, she knew that was the last bit of information they were going to get out of the woman for some time.

However, Pam surprised them all a few minutes later as the techs started to wheel her out on the gurney. Reaching out, she grabbed Jackson's sleeve as they passed.

"Hang on a minute," he said to the techs. "What is it, Pam?"

Pulling the oxygen mask to the side for a moment, she frowned up at him. "There is something else I remember, Deputy. Out on the road . . . there was a car parked off to one side. At the time, I thought someone had just had car trouble and left it there. Could be nothin', but . . ." She shrugged and put the mask back in place.

"Thanks, Pam. I'll check it out," Jackson replied and watched the techs take her from the room.

Elise's mind raced with the possibilities. There had been no car parked out on the road when she and C.C. had arrived. Could the car Pam noticed have belonged to her assailant? And could the person who attacked Pam perhaps be the same person who had killed Edmond?

"So was there a car parked out on the road when you two got here?" Jackson asked as if reading her thoughts. "There was nothing there when I pulled up."

Elise shook her head. "No, I didn't notice anything. Did you, C.C.?"

"Nope."

"Could be just a coincidence," Elise commented, but by the look on Jackson's face, she knew he didn't believe that.

Jackson closed his notepad and put it back into his pocket. "Could be, but I don't like coincidences."

"How do we find out who the car belonged to if it's no longer there?"

"*We* don't do anything." Jackson narrowed his eyes and shook his head. "Again, you just can't help yourself, can you? I want you two to go home, and I mean straight home. I don't want to find you doing any more snooping around, do you hear me?"

"You don't have to tell me twice," C.C. said, shaking her head almost before the words were out of his mouth. Noticing the annoyed look on Elise's face, she shrugged. "What? Sleuthing is one thing, but that was a little more drama than I was anticipating, if you know what I mean. I'm ready to go home."

Elise huffed out a breath. "Fine. Whatever. Let's go."

"Remember what I said, El," Jackson called after them as they headed down the hallway. *"Directly home."*

Elise had to fight to keep from throwing up a very naughty hand gesture. Instead, she called out a terse, "Heard you the first time, butthead."

"That's Deputy Butthead to you, pal."

C.C. laughed out loud at the exchange, eliciting another dirty look from Elise. "Do *not* humor him."

"I'm sorry, but I can't help it. He's just so dang cute."

"I worry about you, C.C.," Elise replied absently. "I really do."

All thoughts of Jackson's attributes dissolved like sugar in water a moment later as they passed through the small dining area and Elise caught sight of the notebook Jackson had left on the table.

Without a second thought, she snatched it up and continued through the living room and out the front door.

"Mmm, girl," C.C. murmured with a cluck of her tongue on the way to the car. "You're just gonna get yourself into more hot water. Jax will know where that journal went the minute he comes out of the bedroom and realizes it's not where he left it."

"Well, until he comes looking for it," she began, looking over at her friend as she climbed into the car, "I'm going to go through as much of it as I can."

"You better be quick about it. Jax is a pretty sharp guy. You won't have much time."

"I know." Elise started the car and slowly backed out of the driveway. "Not much time at all."

TEN

Jackson realized within ten minutes of the women's departure that the journal he'd left on the dining room table was gone. And as Pam had put it earlier, it didn't take a rocket scientist to recognize he'd been weaseled; that his weasel was a damn sight more attractive than Pam's had been was of no consolation.

Annoying him further was the fact that he had to wait for assistance and then process the bedroom before he could do anything about Elise's sticky fingers. Which he was certain she would have been well aware of when she lifted the notebook on the way out of the house. The woman could be infuriatingly clever at times, too clever for her own damn good.

That she kept him off balance was as intriguing as it was exasperating. One minute he wanted to throttle her with his bare hands, and the next he was having very different thoughts about where he wanted to put those hands. Thoughts he had no business thinking, especially with her in a relationship with another man. He'd felt a flash of it off and on during the years they'd known each other, but this was harder to set aside. It was something he was going to have to get under control, and quick.

It was nearly five o'clock when he finished up at Edmond's and headed into town, and by then he'd built up a pretty good head of steam. Elise would be lucky if he didn't haul her pretty behind down to the station just on pure principle.

It wasn't just the fact that she'd taken the notebook or that she kept nosing around in his investigation whenever and wherever she could that kept eating at him. It was that she and C.C. had been very lucky to arrive *after* the perp had attacked Pam and left the scene. Who knew what could have taken place had they turned up at the house any earlier? That one thought had him by the throat, and he couldn't shake it. If something would have happened to her, to either of them . . .

He took the stairs at her apartment building two at a time and pounded on her door. When she didn't answer right away, he pounded some more. Her car was parked in

151

front of the building, so he knew she was home. He decided he would just keep banging on the door until she opened it, no matter what her neighbors thought.

"Come on, El, I know you're in there. Open the damn door before I bust it in."

He finally heard the locks being disengaged and her curt, "Keep your pants on, for heaven's sake. I'm coming already."

When the door finally opened, he pushed his way past her and stalked into the living room. "Where the hell is it?"

"Well, criminy, Jax, why don't you just come on in?" she answered with irritation.

"Don't even start with me! You took evidence from a crime scene. I would be perfectly justified in my actions if I decided to haul your ass to jail."

"Oh, please. It wasn't a crime scene when we found the journal."

Jackson threw up his hands in exasperation. "That's not the point. That journal is now evidence in a *murder investigation,* dumbass! And you lifted it from the scene of a *related crime,*" he yelled and then had to back away before he ended up with his hands around that long, lovely neck of hers.

"Jax, it's just a journal," she said quietly, raising her hands in a gesture of surrender when he whipped around to glare at her.

"Okay, I get that it's evidence and could hold clues to Uncle Edmond's mindset before his murder — maybe even to who killed him — but that doesn't justify this kind of anger. What's going on with you?"

Taking several deep breaths, he scrubbed his hands over his face and struggled with the fear that still had a hold on him.

When she came over and pulled his hands away from his face, the anger he'd felt drained away only to be replaced by something else, something perilously close to longing.

Pulling her into his arms, he gave her a squeeze and kissed the top of her head. "Damn it, El. You guys scared the crap out of me."

"Scared you? Why?"

Jackson sighed and shook his head. "Do you even realize how lucky you and C.C. were today? To get there after Pam's attacker had gone? If you had gotten to Edmond's earlier, you two could have been in serious danger."

"Yes, I understand that now," she murmured with her head on his shoulder. "But Jax, we had no way of knowing that then."

Jackson growled and couldn't decide if he wanted to strangle her or hold her close. "That would be why you need to quit poking around. There's still a murderer out there somewhere, and the next time you could stumble onto something much more dangerous."

When she leaned back and looked up at him with those big, liquid-blue eyes, he was a goner — probably always had been. His mouth dried up like a deserted watering hole and his mind went hazy. He literally felt himself leaning closer.

Her face tilted up, eyes wide, and her lips parted. Those full, moist-looking lips were just inches away, and he suddenly wanted a taste of them more than he wanted his next breath.

In his befuddled state, it took him a moment to realize the knocking sound he heard wasn't just his heart pounding in his chest but someone at her front door. He watched her blink and step back as she realized it too.

"Someone's at your door," was all he could think to say.

"Uh-huh. Someone's at the door," she repeated and then ran a hand through her hair. "I'll . . . uh . . . just go see who it is. Be right back."

Someone's at your door? Geez, how lame was that? he thought as he watched her go to the door.

Her next word doused him with ice water. "Stuart!"

ELEVEN

Elise stared at the man on her landing, her mouth hanging open like a guppy suddenly chucked out of a fish bowl.

What the hell is he doing here? was her only thought, and that question nearly popped out of her mouth before she caught herself.

Even in her confused state, she knew such a question would be an inappropriate response to finding her boyfriend on her doorstep. However, it was a reaction borne out of the mortification she was now feeling over what had almost occurred between her and Jackson. At least . . . what she thought had been about to happen.

In truth, she wasn't entirely certain *what* had taken place after looking up into those deep, green eyes of his. Other than the fact that she'd come close to making a colossal fool of herself, of course. She'd nearly jumped her brother's oldest friend in the middle of her living room.

And with her boyfriend right outside her front door, no less. What in God's name was *wrong* with her?

"I know this is a surprise, darling, but I had to come down to Austin on business and thought I'd just swing over for the evening."

Stuart's voice jarred her out of the mental rerun of the near-kiss with Jackson, and she swallowed hard, hoping her face wasn't reflecting the guilty thoughts swirling around inside her head.

Evidently, he didn't notice anything amiss because he gave her one of his charming smiles and leaned in for a peck on the cheek. "So, are you going to leave me standing out here, or can I come in?"

Her awkward pause — followed by his puzzled look — was enough to snap her into action. "I'm sorry. Of course you can come in. I'm just surprised to see you, that's all."

Stepping back, she gestured toward the living room, where Jackson stood observing the exchange with a guarded look on his face.

"I don't know why you're surprised," Stuart said as he entered the apartment. "I left you several voicemails, starting about mid-morning."

"I turned my cell phone to vibrate for a meeting this morning, and with so much happening I guess I forgot to turn the sound back on. I haven't checked messages all day."

"So much happening? You mean more than just the preparation for your uncle's services?"

At a loss, she looked to Jackson for help, but he just stared back at her with a blank look.

She knew it was irrational, but for some perverse reason she couldn't help feeling the need for Jackson to somehow share in her guilt and discomfort. So she tossed the ball toward his side of the court. "Stuart, you remember Jackson Landry, don't you?"

She had a bad moment when the possibility entered her mind that Jackson might not have felt the same chemistry with her that she'd felt with him just moments ago. How humiliating would *that* be?

And why am I even thinking about Jackson with Stuart standing right there? What kind of girlfriend does that?

"Ah, yes, it's *Deputy* Landry, right?" Stuart asked while she mentally shook the disturbing thoughts away and tuned back in. He gestured to Jackson's uniform and then laughed. "As you can tell, not much

158

gets past me."

If she thought Jackson would feel the least bit uncomfortable, Elise was mildly disappointed, because he didn't show it. He simply grinned and stepped forward to shake Stuart's hand.

"How're you doin'?" was all he said, and then he looked to her as if passing the ball back to her.

Butthead!

"Jackson is in charge of the investigation into Uncle Edmond's death," she explained, trying to remember not to babble. She tended to run off at the mouth when nervous. "We were just discussing . . . uh . . . a few things that have come up."

And I was briefly contemplating a make-out session with him right here in the living room . . . isn't that neat?

"Really?" Stuart looked back and forth between them.

She almost laughed out loud before she caught herself when she realized his reply could have been meant for either of her comments — spoken or unspoken.

Geez, she so needed to get a grip! She was making way too much out of the situation. After all, she'd actually done nothing wrong, unless you counted the very sexy scene involving Deputy Landry that her imagination had conjured up.

"Wait. There's an investigation into your uncle's death?" Stuart frowned. "I don't understand. I thought it was an accidental drowning. What is there to investigate?"

"As it turns out, it's now a homicide case," Jackson answered, pulling his keys out of his pocket. "Speaking of which, I should probably be getting back to it."

"Wow, you must be very dedicated."

When Jackson looked bewildered by the comment, Stuart chuckled. "You realize that it's almost seven o'clock on a Saturday evening. Does the sheriff's office work you around the clock?"

"No, of course not. I just meant that I should probably head out."

For a few more uncomfortable moments, they all stood staring at each other until Jackson finally broke the tension. "Well, it was good seeing you again, Stuart. Uh, El, why don't you get me that journal you were holding for me. I'll go ahead and take it with me now."

If she thought he would forget about the journal after Stuart's arrival, she should have known better. He gave her a pleasant enough smile, but she could definitely read between the lines. Jackson wasn't leaving without her uncle's notebook, and he'd made the statement in front of Stuart to make damn sure of it.

"Of course, let me get it for you."

She thought about giving him a bit of grief over the whole thing, but since she'd stopped at Fairfax Office Supply and photocopied the journal after dropping C.C. off, she cut him some slack.

"Here it is," she told him when she returned from the bedroom. "Hope it wasn't too inconvenient for you to have to come by here to get it. I wouldn't want you to miss your dinner."

"No trouble at all, El. It was on my way home . . . and it was my pleasure." The smile he gave her then, along with the warm glow in his eyes, told her she hadn't been the only one to feel the sensual energy that had snapped between them earlier.

And was it her imagination, or did that smile turn just a touch wicked now?

"Speaking of dinner, I'm actually starving," Stuart said, reminding them both that he was still there and dissolving their unspoken conversation. "Is there a decent restaurant close by where we could grab something to eat? Jackson, you could join us and catch me up on what I've missed over the last week or so. That is, if you don't have plans." He put a possessive arm around

Elise's shoulder and pulled her close. "This one has been hard to reach lately and pretty tight-lipped about events."

"I'm sure Jax doesn't have time to —" Elise began.

"Sure. I'd like that, Stuart." Jackson gave her another evil grin. "Why don't we walk up to Toucan's? It's late enough that there shouldn't be much of a wait."

"Outstanding." Stuart beamed and gave her another squeeze.

"Yeah, isn't it just?" she muttered under her breath as she went to get her purse. Turning, she gave the two men a bright smile. "Shall we?"

Since the restaurant was just up the street, the walk there didn't take long. And though the evening air was still, thick, and a bit muggy, the sunset was spectacular and colorful.

"So, tell me about this investigation," Stuart said after they'd been seated and ordered their food and drinks. He lowered his voice so as not to be heard outside their table. "How on earth did you decide Edmond's death was actually murder?"

Jackson leaned in as well and spoke just as quietly. "I didn't. The Travis County medical examiner did. And I just got that

162

information yesterday afternoon, so it's not really common knowledge yet."

"I see. So he didn't drown?"

Jackson shook his head. "There was no water in his lungs, so he was dead before he went into the river."

"Then how did he die?"

Jackson looked over at Elise, and she could tell he was contemplating how much to say.

"Jax, for heaven's sake, the report's out. It's not like it's a big secret or will compromise your investigation. And word travels fast, especially around here."

"I know, and you're right. But that's not what I'm worried about. I just figured it wouldn't be easy for you to hear."

"Oh." That he would consider her feelings hadn't even crossed her mind. And while his sympathetic tone filled her heart, it made her feel petty and small at the direction her thoughts had taken. "No, it won't be easy, but facts are facts."

He nodded then and addressed Stuart's question. "Edmond died of blunt force trauma to the head. He was hit repeatedly from behind with enough strength to fracture his skull."

"Wow. That's . . . well . . . really horrible." Stuart turned to Elise. "Sweetie, I'm so

163

sorry. It was bad enough when we all thought that Edmond's death was accidental, but this . . ."

"I know. Hearing about it really is awful."

"Well, at least you were spared seeing that kind of horror. I can't even imagine how terrible the scene must have been."

Elise shot another glance to Jackson, and then turned back to Stuart. "Well, actually . . ."

"Oh, darling, you weren't there, were you?" When she didn't answer, he went on in a surprised tone. "My God, Elise, why would you put yourself through that?"

"I wanted, no, *needed* to spare Mom," she acknowledged with a sigh. "She and Uncle Edmond had been so combative lately, and I knew it would just devastate her. I also thought there should be more than one family member present. So Ross and I went with Jackson down to the scene when the workers reported it."

Stuart shook his head and gave her a sad smile. "That's my girl, always thinking of family first. But you really should have let Ross take care of it. It had to be traumatic for you, and you can't take on everything for everyone."

"Don't be so dramatic, Stuart. It's not like I'm Mother Teresa or anything. Was it pleasant? No. But we got through it, and now it's over." She hesitated and then looked over at Jackson. "Except that's not true, is it, Jax? It isn't over yet."

"No, darlin', I'm afraid it isn't."

"And it'll probably keep being awful until it's finally done and Uncle Edmond has been laid to rest."

Jackson put a warm hand over hers on the table. "It probably will, but we'll handle it. No matter what comes at us, the family will handle it, right?"

"Yes." She took a deep breath. "We will."

There was comfort for her in the fact that no matter what happened between them, Jackson was as close as family and would always be there for them.

"So, where does your investigation go from here?" Stuart asked, breaking into her train of thought.

Elise realized then that she and Jackson had left him completely out of the conversation, and she felt guilty all over again. She slowly withdrew her hand from beneath Jackson's, who cleared his throat and looked away as the waitress brought their drinks.

When the server left the table, Jackson spoke. "To answer your question, Stuart, I've just begun my inquiries, but I'm pursuing several avenues. You understand that I can't really comment on an ongoing investigation, right?"

"Oh no, of course not," Stuart answered with a nod. "But do you even have any suspects at this point?"

When Jackson only smiled at the question, Elise began to chuckle, and then to laugh. "Oh, yes, Jackson already has several folks on his suspect list, which includes me. Isn't that right, Jax?"

Jackson huffed out a breath and looked up toward the ceiling. "Give it a rest, El."

"Funny!" Stuart started to laugh along with her until he realized she wasn't kidding, and his mouth dropped open. "What? You're joking, right?"

"Unfortunately, no, I'm perfectly serious," she replied with a mischievous grin. "I was at Uncle Edmond's house that Monday — alone; and then I was at home that evening during the time he was killed — again, alone."

"But . . . but you can't really believe Elise had anything to do with this, can you?" he asked Jackson. "You know that's just ridiculous. Any fool could see that she's no more capable of such violent behavior than I am, especially toward a family member."

"Stuart."

"No, darling, I have to say that I find it

appalling that someone so close to your family would take this attitude."

"Stuart, let me ease your mind," Jackson replied, putting up a hand to Elise before she could speak. "First of all, I don't believe any such thing. I've known Elise all my life, and I'm certain she would never harm anyone, let alone a family member. Having said that, you have to understand my position. I'm in charge of this investigation, and I have to make sure everything is done by the book."

"Yes, but really —"

"I have to look at all the evidence and follow where it takes me, even if I don't like what I find."

"Surely —"

"And the first step is to eliminate each member of the family as suspects, which is the point we're at right now."

"I see." Stuart frowned and then nodded. "I appreciate that you've been placed in a difficult situation, Jackson. I also realize you'll do your best to shield the Becketts. I'm sorry if I insinuated anything different, but this is very upsetting."

"Hey, no harm, no foul," Jackson said and leaned back as their meals arrived. "It's a disturbing situation, and you're entitled to feel protective of Elise."

Elise breathed in the heavenly scent of her favorite Fajitas Grande as it was placed sizzling in front of her. "Now that we've cleared that up, can we drop the subject? I need to apply all my focus to this fabulous plate of food."

Jackson snagged a pepper off of her plate and grinned. "Amen to that!"

Reaching for a tortilla, Elise contemplated what Jackson had implied. Even though he had no choice but to treat her as a possible suspect, he'd just admitted to Stuart that he didn't believe her capable of murdering anyone.

That left no clear-cut suspects for him, unless you counted Pam Dawson, and he'd yet to interview her in depth.

Elise couldn't wait to get back home and check out the pages of the notebook she'd copied. Surely they held a clue that might lead to her Uncle Edmond's killer, and better still, officially take the heat off her and her family.

TWELVE

Though it was Sunday, Jackson went into the office mid-morning to set up a bulletin board and arrange the information he'd gathered so far. With the investigation into Edmond's murder getting underway, he knew the shit was fixin' to fly, which meant his to-do list was going to grow at a rapid pace. He needed to get organized, figure out his next steps.

He needed to get ahead of the game.

Tacking Edmond's picture to the top of the board, he methodically gathered his supplies. After opening a new packet of index cards, he pulled out several and jotted down one name on each.

He'd spent several hours going over the first half of Edmond's journal after his dinner with Elise and Stuart the previous evening. Most of the entries listed there were in some kind of code — which he'd only begun to chisel away at — but he had deciphered a couple of the initials that had been used with some frequency. He figured they were a good place to start.

One of those sets of initials — and the first name he wrote on a card — belonged to Denny Rodriguez. Denny owned El Diablo, the honky-tonk out on Highway 20 where Edmond had gambled away just about every dime he'd managed to borrow or steal. Lord knew the man had rarely actually worked for anything.

The journal had an entire section dedicated to the countless wagers Edmond had placed at the dive, his meager winnings, and — more often than not — his heavy losses. There were also several dated entries noting harassment, and a number of threats had been made regarding repayment of what he owed.

After he'd pinned Rodriguez's card onto the board beneath Edmond's photo, Jackson stood frowning at it.

With Edmond up to his eyebrows in debt and no way to get clear, it wasn't inconceivable that Denny had sent someone around to give him some physical incentive to come up with the cash. And it wouldn't be the first time in history a simple roughing up had ended in murder. Still, you'd have to be pretty stupid to kill someone who owed you that much green. After all, it would make it impossible to recoup your losses.

Jackson leaned back against the desk and rubbed his jaw as another possibility ran through his head. The murder could have been presented as a message to others in the same situation: pay your debt or suffer the consequences. In that case, Rodriguez would have to weigh what was more important — getting paid or making a statement to keep others in line. It was something to think about and to confront Rodriguez with when he questioned him.

The next name going on a card was Henry Kohler. Kohler's vineyard was one of River Bend's biggest competitors, and Henry had employed Edmond for several months before his death. Of course, that wasn't illegal or even immoral, but as Elise had pointed out, it was odd. And now that he really thought about it, why *would* Edmond work for Kohler Winery when he could work at a vineyard that had been in his family for decades?

Jackson supposed there could be an espionage angle there. The boutique wine business was extremely competitive. Coming up with a unique hook to set your vineyard apart from others — finding that edge — was imperative. Was Edmond spying for

Kohler, perhaps passing on secrets about River Bend's operation? It was possible, but what secrets would that include? It would have to be something exclusive to River Bend. Elise's hybridization process crossed his mind.

He followed Kohler's card on the board with one for Pam Dawson. She was probably a long shot, but Jackson believed her perfectly capable of killing Edmond in a fit of rage. And along with being bat-shit crazy half the time, Pam had no alibi to speak of and plenty of rage.

She also had a powerful motive: money.

Edmond had sweet-talked close to ten grand worth of motive out of her. And the fact that she'd used her restaurant as collateral to get him the money in the first place had to have added fuel to that anger. Had she found out about Edmond's deceit earlier than she'd said? Jackson could see how that could have pushed her right over the edge.

As hard as it was to do, Jackson made himself add Elise's name to a card and stuck it up on the board as well. He knew in his heart she wasn't the murderer he sought, but until he could clear her without question, she had to be considered.

She had no decent alibi, other than the

phone call Stuart confirmed they'd had, but what about motive? Elise was passionate about her work and incredibly tight-lipped where her research was concerned. Could she have somehow found out that her uncle was giving away her secrets to a competitor?

Jackson shook his head. "No way. Not even then," he said to the empty room.

Finally, with disappointment, he added one more name to a card and tacked it up next to Elise's. Though he had a tentative alibi, Ross wasn't being as forthcoming as Jackson hoped he'd be. Maybe his best friend wasn't outright lying, but Jackson had known the man from boyhood and could tell when he was hiding something.

And Elise's brother was definitely hiding something.

His alibi was weak at best, and they both knew it. One look at the shock on Caroline's face when Ross had said he'd been home during the time of the murder, plus the fact that she didn't confirm or deny it, told Jackson that it was probably a fabrication.

But why? What would Ross want to hide so badly that he'd put his wife on the spot and lie to his best friend? With no way to refute Ross's claim, he'd have to wait and see how it played out. But it was disturbing.

"What're you doing here on a Sunday,

Jackson?"

He looked up to find Darrell Yancy, arms crossed, leaning against the door frame. The deputy lifted his chin toward the bulletin board. "Suspect board?"

"Yep. Gotta start somewhere, Darrell. With the ME's report making this a homicide, I thought I'd get a jump-start before beginning interviews tomorrow."

Yancy made a *pfft* sound. "Must break your heart to have to put a couple of your precious Becketts up there."

The smirk on the other man's face did exactly what it was designed to do — push Jackson's buttons. But he wasn't about to let this donkey's ass press him into saying or doing something he'd regret later.

So he took a deep breath and reined in his irritation. "No, I don't like having to consider my friends as suspects, but I can't rule them out simply *because* they're my friends."

Yancy narrowed his eyes as he shoved away from the door frame. "Are you sayin' you think I'd ignore evidence that involved my friends?"

"I don't know how you run your investigations, Darrell, and I don't much care. I'm just telling you how I intend to run mine." Jackson tapped Edmond's photo for emphasis. "A man is dead, and it's my job to follow the evidence trail — no matter where it leads. Now, is there anything else I can help you with?"

Yancy's face turned a nasty shade of red, and he wrinkled his nose as if he'd smelled something rotten. "Whatever," he muttered and headed down the hall.

"Asswipe." Turning back, Jackson gave the board another once-over. No, he didn't like having to put Ross or Elise up on his murder board, but he had no choice until he could get them cleared. Making up a game plan in his head for most of the following day, he figured he would hit the ground running and hopefully come up with evidence to do just that.

In the meantime, he thought grimly, he'd head out to River Bend this afternoon for the Sunday family dinner and see what trouble he could stir up there.

Elise and Stuart arrived at the vineyard just after two in the afternoon and headed into the greenhouse first thing. Stuart had been interested to see how her new starts were coming along and wanted to go out to the southernmost field to see the transplants there as well.

"We can head out to the south end of the

vineyard after dinner," she told him as they entered the greenhouse. "I think you're going to be surprised at how well those vines have taken root. They're a much more hardy and disease-resistant hybrid, and they're growing at a fast pace. I'm really very pleased."

"I have no doubt. These look promising," he said, gesturing to the table where some of her newest starts flourished under grow lamps. "They seem to be developing with vigor."

Pleased at his reaction, she gave him a tour of the rest of the greenhouse. The last time he'd been to the vineyard, Stuart had been less than complimentary, though he'd nagged her about the details of her process. When she had been hesitant to give him those details, they'd argued. She hoped this time around would be different.

As if reading her mind, he stepped right back into the damned arena. "Elise, darling, are you ever going to trust me enough to share your process with me? After all, we could be working together very soon."

Elise sighed and shook her head. She didn't want another fight, but how could she make him see? "Let's not have this conversation again, okay? It's not an issue of trust, Stuart. I designed this specific process for River Bend. I just don't want any leaks, however innocent, before the patent on the process is in place."

"Yes, I understand that, but —"

"No buts. It's my decision, and I would hope that you would respect that, if not as my boyfriend, then at least as a colleague."

He immediately put up his hands in surrender and the look on his face was rueful. "Okay, okay. We'll table the discussion for now. I don't want to ruin our time together with an argument."

"Good. I don't either. So how about we go in and see what Gram has cooking for dinner instead?"

Stuart chuckled. "You certainly know how to get around me, don't you? I'm starving."

They walked out into the lovely afternoon sunshine and started up to the main house just as Jackson roared up on his huge motorcycle looking all macho and male.

"Hey, El," he said as he climbed off of the enormous machine and removed his helmet. "Stuart," he acknowledged with a nod.

She couldn't help admiring the way Jackson's faded jeans conformed to his long, long legs and hugged his fine —

And geez, she really needed to get a grip! Here she was, ogling Jackson's form with her boyfriend standing right next to her. Of course, she wasn't dead and Jackson had some fine form, but that was no excuse.

"Hello, Jackson. That's quite the motor-cycle you have there," Stuart said in greeting.

"I have to admit, it's a weakness." Jackson's grin was quick and full of pleasure. "A weakness I try to indulge in every chance I get when the weather is this spectacular. Do you ride, Stuart?"

Amusement burst out of Stuart like a shotgun blast. "Good God, no! I prefer plenty of metal surrounding me when I'm out on the highway where any yahoo could plow into me."

"Man, you don't know what you're missing."

"Jax is a true road warrior," Elise said with a tilt of her head. "And he does love the rush of speed."

"You got it, darlin'." His laughter was warm and infectious, and his gaze held hers just a bit longer than she was comfortable with. "But then, you know me so well."

"Yeah, yeah." Rolling her eyes, she hooked a thumb over her shoulder toward the house and tried to ignore the erratic jump of her pulse. "Let's go in before Gram comes out with a rolling pin. You know she doesn't like to serve a late dinner."

The three headed into the house and were met by Madison as she came down the stairs. "Hey guys. And Stuart? What a surprise. Elise didn't tell us you were coming this weekend. Nice to see you again."

Stuart smiled in response. "Nice to see you, too, Madison. To be fair, Elise didn't tell you I was coming because she didn't know. It was a surprise."

"How long are you staying?"

"I'm afraid I have to hit the road right after dinner. I have early meetings tomorrow morning."

"That's a shame, but at least you get to indulge in another one of Gram's extravaganzas before you go," Madison said, leading the way into the dinning room.

"I wouldn't miss it. Your grandmother is a genius in the kitchen."

"That I am," Abigail said as she brought a platter of stuffed pork chops and a dish of collard greens in to join the huge salad already on the table. "The food is hot. Are there enough place settings?"

Laura came in behind her carrying a basket of dinner rolls and a gravy boat, which she set in the middle of the table. "Caroline took the boys into Austin to visit with her parents for the day. Ross will be a

179

bit late, but we should have plenty of room, Mom."

"All right, then. Let's hop to it before it gets cold. Ross will just have to fend for himself."

Everyone took their seats. Laura and Abigail sat at each end of the table, leaving Elise, Stuart, and an empty place for Ross on one side, Jackson and Madison on the other. Abigail said grace, and they all dove in.

"So, Stuart, when did you get here?" Laura asked as she passed the greens.

"I had a business meeting in Austin yesterday. It got out a little early, and I thought since I was so close and didn't have to be back in Dallas until Monday morning, I'd pop over and see my girl."

Elise patted his hand. "So sweet."

"You kids these days." Abigail made a face. "I just don't get this whole long-distance relationship stuff."

"Mom."

Undeterred by Laura's warning, Abigail gestured to Elise and Stuart with her fork. "Well, really, when do they see each other? Once or twice a month?" She skewered them both with a sharp glance. "No offense, but what kind of relationship is that? How do you know if you're actually compatible or not if you spend so little time together?"

Stuart chuckled and shook his head. "No offense taken, ma'am. I actually agree with you. Hopefully, that little problem will be solved with the move and the new position."

Elise froze with her fork halfway to her mouth.

Oh no, he did not just do what I asked him not to do!

"You're moving, Stuart?" Laura asked, obviously confused by his statement. "I thought your new position with the foundation was still located in the Dallas area."

Crap!

"Uh, no. That is to say, it is." He glanced over at Elise with an apologetic look. "*I'm* not moving."

"So that must mean you are, little sister," Ross said from the doorway.

There was a gasp from Madison, and Laura set down her fork with a clatter. She placed her elbows on the table and folded her hands together, looking to Elise expectantly. "Elise Brianna, is there something you haven't told us?"

Elise cleared her throat and threw a hostile look at Stuart before meeting her mother's gaze. "Stuart has offered me a position at the new research facility, but nothing has been decided yet."

Ross slid into the seat beside her. "Sounded like it's a done deal to me."

Stuart leaned in to look around her at Ross. "No, let me be clear about that right now. What you heard was just wishful thinking on my part. I've been nagging her about a decision, but she's continued to put me off until she had a chance to talk it over with y'all." He turned to her. "Sorry, darling. It just slipped out."

She ignored him and spoke to her mother. "Mom, I would never make that kind of decision without discussing it with the family first. You know that, right?"

"And when did Stuart make this fabulous offer?" Ross asked, disregarding the way Stuart had tried to come to her rescue.

"You're not helping," she muttered under her breath.

"Not trying to," he replied out loud. "Sorry, Stuart, but I think this is a crappy idea. Especially now. Your timing couldn't be worse."

Glaring at him, Elise directed her comments to her mother. "Stuart only made the offer last weekend. I've been meaning to talk to y'all about it, but with everything that's happened this week, There hasn't been a good time."

"Did you know about this?" Ross suddenly asked, pointing at Jackson.

"What?" Jackson eyebrows snapped together, and he sat up straighter in his chair. "Why the hell would I know about this if she hasn't said anything to the rest of the family?"

"Oh, come on. Why do you think?" Ross smirked at him across the table.

"What's that supposed to mean? She's just as tight-lipped with me as she is with anyone else."

"*She's* sitting right here! Geez, it makes me so crazy when you two talk around me like that."

"Children, that's enough," Laura said in an attempt to stem the outbursts.

Elise huffed out a frustrated breath. "Look, I didn't tell anyone, okay?"

Turning to Ross, she gave him a flick on the side of his head. "I wasn't keeping it from you, and there was no hidden agenda. With Uncle Edmond's death — and then it suddenly becoming a murder investigation — I just wanted to wait until things calmed down a little before throwing something else onto the pile. That's all."

"Yeah, well, the cat's out of the bag now, huh?" Ross pointed out with a snicker. "And don't flick me."

"Act like a normal human being and I

won't," she replied, trying to keep from grinning back at him.

But the amusement pushing to get out died a quick death when she looked up and met Jackson's gaze. There she saw not only disappointment, but something else she couldn't quite get a handle on. For some reason, it made her feel as if she'd hurt his feelings.

Before Elise had a chance to think it through, he looked away. Pushing back his chair, he got to his feet and directed his remarks to Abigail. "As riveting as this conversation is, I'm afraid I have to head out."

"What? You're not going to stay for dessert?" her grandmother asked, clearly let down. "But I made peach pie."

"Mmm, you know that's my favorite, but I've got a ton of work to get done before tomorrow." He circled around to give Abigail a loud smooch on the cheek. "Next time. Promise."

The woman gave a resigned sigh and waved a hand in the air. "Well, at least let me put some in a container for you. There are compartments or saddle bags or some such thing on that monstrosity you ride, aren't there?"

"Yes, ma'am. And I would be much

184

obliged if you'd make me up a to-go bag with a ginormous piece of your fine pie."

Elise watched Jackson follow her grandmother from the dining room with a sudden sense of melancholy. He'd made the excuse of work, but she got the distinct impression that *she* was the reason for his hasty departure, though she wasn't quite sure why. Of course, that could just be her ego projecting.

"Elise, we'll discuss this new development tomorrow morning in my office," Laura stated, snapping her out of her thoughts. "Ten o'clock sharp."

"Yes, ma'am. I'll be there."

Right after I beat the living crap out of my boyfriend.

THIRTEEN

Jackson had no real reason to leave before dinner was over, but the news of Elise's job offer — and impending move it required — had hit him hard. Harder than he wanted to admit.

He told himself it was brotherly concern that had him so twisted up about it, but he knew that wasn't entirely true. Yes, he had some strong feelings for Elise Beckett, but none of them were very brotherly.

So, he'd gone home and spent the rest of the evening brooding over a couple of beers and then trying to console himself before bed with Miss Abby's scrumptious peach pie.

Neither helped much.

Fortunately, he had a murder investigation to take his mind off things, and after a night of tossing and turning, he jumped right into it on Monday morning. There was a full list of interviews to conduct, which would leave little time for obsessing over Elise's future plans.

Though Darrell Yancy had tried to weasel his way into the investigation, Jackson had blocked the other deputy's efforts, choosing Jim Stockton to assist him with the interviews instead.

Jim was sharp, quiet, and observant. He was a good judge of character and would be an asset in an interrogation, unlike hotheaded Yancy. The deputy was also twice Darrell's size, which would be helpful should they run into trouble once they got out to El Diablo later in the afternoon.

However, their first stop would be Kohler Winery. It was on the way and would probably be an easier, less hostile meeting.

There were several cars in the winery's parking area when he and Jim pulled up. It was tourist season, and with the weather they'd been having, vineyard hopping had become almost a sport, even at midmorning.

However, one of the cars in the lot piqued his interest far more than the others. He parked the cruiser next to a little red sports car, pretty sure it belonged to a certain Nosey Nancy from River Bend.

What the heck is she up to now? Obviously, he needed to have yet another stern talk with Elise about steering clear of his investigation.

They were met at Kohler's front door by Henry's grandson Paul, who seemed unsurprised to see them.

"Gramps is in the living room with Ms. Beckett. Come on in," he said and led them down the hall. "Hey, Gramps, these deputies are here to see you. I gotta get going, so I'll see you later."

"All right. Drive careful."

Henry watched his grandson leave. When he heard the front door close, he turned to Jackson with a shake of his head. "Kids these days. Always on the go."

"I hear that," Jim replied.

Jackson cast a narrowed glance in Elise's direction. "Looks like you're having all sorts of company today, Henry."

"Don't get your panties in a wad, Jackson. I just stopped by to return a couple books that I borrowed from Henry last month," Elise replied defensively.

"Books. Uh-huh." When she huffed out a breath, he shook his head and gave her a doubtful look. "I think we're gonna need to revisit a few ground rules, but that'll wait."

"What brings you out our way, Jackson?" Henry asked in an attempt to defuse the tension suddenly filling the air. "Does this have something to do with Edmond's drowning?"

"Well, yes and no, Henry." Jackson sat down in the chair across from the man and took out his notepad. "I received the medical examiner's report on Friday afternoon. Edmond didn't drown. He died of blunt force trauma, which would be the reason for our visit. His death is now a murder inquiry, but I'm betting Elise has already filled you in on that." Jackson tilted his head and shot her a look, at which she just rolled her eyes.

"Yes, she did mention that," Henry said. "Terrible news, just awful. And there's no chance he simply fell and hit his head before going into the river?"

"No," Jackson answered. "There's no way it was an accident. Anyway, I do have some questions that I need you to clear up for me, if you will."

The older man nodded vigorously. "Of course, anything I can do to help."

"Did Elise also happen to mention that we ran across Kohler Winery paystubs in Edmond's name? Can you explain that to me?"

Henry looked back and forth between them, and confusion was plain on his face. "As I told Elise, there's really nothing to

189

explain. Edmond had been working for me for several months. I thought his family was aware of that."

Elise shook her head. "No, we had no idea Uncle Edmond was working here."

"Why *was* Edmond working for you?" Jim asked. "And what did he do for you?"

"He did odd jobs," Henry answered vaguely.

"Odd jobs?" Jim prompted. "What kind of odd jobs?"

"Oh, this and that, anything extra I wanted done. He didn't have specific job duties." The vintner shrugged. "He needed a job. I tried to help out an old friend. Is that a crime, deputy?"

Jackson shook his head at the older man's defensive attitude and decided to cut to the chase. "No, it's not, Henry, but corporate espionage is."

"What? You think Edmond was spying for me?" the vintner asked in a wary tone, before scoffing at the notion. "That's just foolishness. Who would he be spying on? River Bend? And for what?"

"That's just what I'm trying to figure out. Stranger things have happened. Surely you were aware that Edmond had been on the outs with his family. He'd tried to get Mrs. Beckett to give him a large portion of River

190

Bend, and she'd refused. Maybe he was of a mind to get even."

Jackson had played poker with Kohler on several occasions, and the man couldn't bluff for shit. He watched closely now as Henry blinked then looked away.

"I don't know anything about that," he finally said.

You lying old goat.

It was clear they weren't going to get anything else from the man just yet, but it was early in the investigation. Jackson had no doubt they would be back to Kohler Winery eventually with more questions. In the meantime, he'd let the old buzzard stew over the fact that they'd been here and were looking in his direction.

"Well, if you think of anything else that might be pertinent, give me a call. Thanks for your time." As he stood, he glanced at Elise and nodded. "And I'll be seeing you very soon for that little chat."

Henry saw them to the door, and as they climbed into the cruiser the quietly observant Jim said in a mild tone, "Kohler knows a whole lot more than he's saying, and he's lying through his teeth about it."

"I'll say. In the first place, he and Edmond were never friends. They barely tolerated each other most of the time."

191

Jim snorted. "Not foolin' anyone."

"No, but that's okay. We'll be back," Jackson replied as he turned the cruiser back toward town. "Let's grab some lunch and then go see what Denny Rodriguez has to say."

"Yeah, that ought to be fun."

They decided on a quick lunch of Chinese at Peking Palace before heading out Highway 20. El Diablo was quiet when they pulled up, the parking lot close to empty. Of course, it was early yet; other than a few regulars, most customers probably wouldn't show up until late afternoon or early evening.

As they stepped from the bright sunlight into the dimness of the bar, Jackson detected the faintest scent of cannabis in the air. He and Jim exchanged glances and headed toward the back booth where Denny Rodriguez sat eating lunch.

They hadn't gotten but ten feet into the room before an enormous Hispanic male with a shaved head and what looked to be a very bad attitude stepped into their path.

"You're gonna want to move out of our way, son." Looking around the big, bald bouncer, Jackson raised his eyebrows at Rodriguez. "You know, Denny, we can do

192

this here in your office, or we can take it into town to mine. Your choice. You have about ten seconds to make up your mind, or I'll make it up for you."

Baldie looked over his shoulder and got the signal from his employer to back off. He joined his buddy at the bar, but not before giving both deputies a look of disdain as he went.

Jackson slid into the booth opposite Rodriguez, and Jim pulled up a chair at the end of the table.

"So, what can I do for Bastrop County's finest?" Denny Rodriguez leaned back in the booth like he didn't have a care in the world and wiped his lips with a napkin.

"I have a few questions for you regarding Edmond Beckett."

Rodriguez's shoulders moved slightly. "Eddy? What about him? He was a good customer. Damn shame."

"When was the last time you saw him, Denny?" Jim asked.

"Maybe two weeks ago. Why?"

Jackson folded his arms on the table and leaned in. "I have it on good authority that he owed you quite a bit of money." He slid his gaze to the other deputy. "You know, gambling is a terrible addiction, isn't it, Deputy Stockton?"

"It is — a terrible addiction, indeed."

A crafty smile stole across Rodriguez's face. "Now, Deputy, maybe I *loaned* the guy some money, but we both know the kind of gambling you're talkin' about is illegal in our fine county."

"True, but I'm more worried about murder than gambling."

"Murder? What murder?" A sober look crossed Rodriguez's face and he sat up straight. "I heard Eddy drowned."

"You heard wrong. Someone cracked open his skull."

Rodriguez shook his head. "I don't know nothin' about no murder, man."

"Right. But the journal I found at Edmond's place said he owed you big — like close to ten grand big — and that you'd made threats. Did you maybe send a couple of your boys around to give him a nudge? Maybe that nudge turned into something more?"

"Noooo." Rodriguez drew the word out for emphasis. "Huh-uh. No way. Rafe and a couple of the guys went out to *talk* to him, that's all. Look, maybe sometimes Eddy was late with a payment, but he usually came through. Besides, I don't know where you got ten large; he only owed me four plus change. And the last time he was in here, he paid his bill."

Jackson sat back and studied the man for a moment. "He paid you in full?"

"Yeah, man. That's what I'm telling you. I had no need to put the hurt on Eddy. Like I said, he was a good customer. That night he told me his ship was about to dock and it was carrying a belly-full of *dineros.*"

"He was expecting a payoff? From who?"

"I don't know." The man shook his head and there was concern in his dark gaze. "He shut down when I asked, told me to forget he'd said anything. Got real jumpy, actually."

"But he didn't owe you anything after that night?" Jim asked.

The cunning smile was back. "Now, I didn't say that, did I? He paid his *tab,* all right . . . and then spent the rest of the night jackin' it back up. If he was about to hit a payday and wanted to spend some of it at my establishment in advance . . . well, I don't judge, man."

Rodriguez chuckled then and pointed a finger in Jackson's direction. "That *loco* bitch he was hangin' with like to went off the rails when she heard that, I can tell you. Maybe you should talk to her."

Jackson and Jim exchanged another glance. "And when did Pam find this out?"

The bar owner made a pained face. "She was in here the night after he was — checkin' up on him."

"Was she alone?" Jim asked.

"Dude, have you *seen* her?" Rodriguez gave an exaggerated shudder. "What dude's gonna get with that but Eddy? Say, are we about done? I don't need my customers comin' in here and catching me all cozied up to cops. Bad for my image. I got a rep to uphold, you know?"

"Yeah, yeah," Jackson nodded. "One more question, Denny. Where were you last Monday night?"

Rodriguez stretched and leaned in. "Where I always am on Monday nights, man — sitting right here. You can ask anyone."

Jackson mirrored Rodriguez's body language from his side of the table and got right into the man's face. "We're gonna go now, Denny. But if you're lying to me about any of this, we'll be back — and it won't be near as much fun then as it has been today. You get me?"

Rodriguez swallowed hard. "Sure, man. I get you. I'm telling you like it was — I got no reason to lie."

Jackson slipped on his sunglasses as he and

Jim headed back out into the bright sunshine.

"You buying all that?" Jim asked when they climbed into the cruiser.

"Yeah, unfortunately I am. At least, for the most part."

"Me too. Okay, so it would be a simple thing for Rodriguez to send a couple of his goons out to do Edmond. It would leave him with a perfect alibi. But if Edmond had already paid his previous bill, even if he had just jacked his tab back up, there'd be no need."

"Right. Here's another thing that's bothering me — Edmond wheedles close to ten grand out of Pam, supposedly to pay off Denny, but he only owes four and change. Where's the rest of the money? And where was the additional payoff coming from that Edmond told Denny about?"

FOURTEEN

Elise's weekend had finished up on quite the sour note, thanks to Stuart's blunder during the Sunday family dinner. His gaffe had also served as a catalyst, propelling her into her work week by way of an uncomfortable meeting with her mother first thing Monday morning.

Laura Beckett had made it clear she was not pleased that her oldest daughter had kept something so important from the family. That she'd kept it to herself during a time of family crisis, while admirable, didn't win her any points.

As Elise worked to redeem herself during that meeting, she'd been consoled by the fact that she'd sent Stuart back to Dallas with her voice ringing in his ears. Still, it was frustrating that even as he'd driven away on Sunday afternoon, he hadn't seemed to understand the uproar he'd caused or why she'd been so upset by it.

Because Stuart's parents had been killed in a car crash during his early twenties and he'd grown up very independent, he'd never had close relatives hold him accountable for his actions. For this reason, Elise tried to cut him some slack at times like this when he worked her very last nerve. Despite his incredibly high IQ, he wasn't always the sharpest knife in the drawer when it came to social skills.

Still, the meeting with her mother had put Elise off her stride, and her morning had continued to deteriorate when Jackson had caught her snooping out at Kohler Winery.

He'd nearly popped a vein when he and the other deputy had arrived to interview Henry and found her there. By his attitude and the look on his face when they'd left, she figured he'd seen right through her flimsy book explanation. She had no doubt there would be another thorough chewing out in her near future.

She'd been pretty successful in dodging him as Monday rolled into Tuesday, even though she was dying to find out what they'd learned from Denny Rodriguez. She knew he and Jim Stockton had gone out to El Diablo to question the bar owner, and she'd contemplated tracking Jackson down to pump him for information. She figured it would almost be worth the lecture she was sure to receive.

Unfortunately, wheedling information out of Jackson had been bumped down on her to-do list when the Travis County medical examiner finally released her uncle's body. Edmond had been transported back to Clemmons Funeral Home late Tuesday afternoon and cremated on Wednesday for interment at the end of the week. The funeral was scheduled to take place at the Delphine Methodist church Friday afternoon, followed by a short graveside service at Oak Hill Cemetery out near Camp Swift.

By the time Friday morning dawned, the vineyard was abuzz with all sorts of activity as last-minute arrangements for the funeral were completed.

Adding another layer of stress to the family's plate were the final preparations for the Adams-Wilkinson wedding and reception, which would take place the following day at Lodge Merlot. Madison had been on the phone putting out fires left and right all morning long after numerous panicked calls from the bride, as well as a few from Mayor Wilkinson, the bride's mother.

Elise sighed as she loaded the back of Ross's SUV with the last of the flowers sent by family friends for the memorial services.

It seemed as if everything was happening at once without much time to catch a breath. But then, such was the circle of life. One day you were mourning the loss of someone close to you, and the next you were celebrating a marriage and a new beginning.

"Is that it?" Ross asked as he came down the porch steps.

"I think so. Are Mom and Maddy about ready? We should get going if Mom wants to have time to go over anything with Greta at the mortuary before the service."

"I think Mom is, but the last I saw of Maddy she still had her cell phone glued to her ear." He shook his head. "I'm telling you, I don't know how she does it without going postal. And I definitely would have sent the mayor and her precious daughter packing weeks ago."

"I know what you mean." Elise had to laugh at the crabby look on his face. "We should count ourselves lucky that our baby sister loves what she does; neither one of us has the patience to deal with it. More than likely I would have burned the lodge to the ground by now."

"Man, isn't *that* the truth?"

Just as he acknowledged her statement, Madison and Laura came out of the house and headed toward the vehicle. Laura looked preoccupied, and Madison — who was still on the phone — was sporting a terrible frown.

"More wedding troubles?" Elise asked as her sister hung up and stalked over to the SUV.

"I can't *wait* until tomorrow is over. It never ceases to amaze and baffle me how a normal, rational individual can become so unrecognizable when they're planning a wedding."

Ross smiled. "The mayor again?"

With a roll of her eyes, Madison growled. "Charlotte Wilkinson is just as calm and steady as she can be as mayor. I've never even heard her raise her voice. Yet in the last couple of weeks she's become a train wreck over the smallest details. Now she wants to move the cake and buffet tables out onto the veranda next to the bride and groom."

Elise giggled. "Uh . . . and you said . . . ?"

"Well, for the love of God! What could I say? I had to put my foot down and give her a reality check. All that food out in the Texas sun for hours? Seriously? She's completely lost her mind."

Laura ran a calming hand over her daughter's shoulder. "And from what I heard, you handled the situation with your usual tact and diplomacy. Now turn off your phone and put it out of your mind for a while. You've done all you can do. This afternoon is for your uncle, may he finally rest in peace."

They all climbed into their respective vehicles, with Laura riding with Ross, Caroline, and the boys, and Madison riding with Elise. Once they arrived at the mortuary, Laura went in to talk with Greta, the director.

"Mom looks tired," Madison said as they unloaded the flower arrangements from the SUV. "She's taking Uncle Edmond's death a lot harder than she lets on."

"I know." Ross frowned. "She's blaming herself for not trying harder to find a solution or some sort of compromise with him. But the truth is his demands had become totally unreasonable; nothing she did would have been good enough for him."

"I wish someone could have talked some sense into him," Elise said with a sigh.

Ross gave a snort as he closed the SUV's hatch. "I tried, but it didn't get me very far. Like I said, he was completely unreasonable."

Something in his frigid tone had her putting down the basket and facing him. "You talked to Uncle Edmond?"

"Damn straight. Somebody had to. His behavior toward Mom had become abusive, and she continued to ignore the situation."

"Why didn't you tell us?" Madison asked.

"I didn't tell anyone. Mom thought he'd get over it — that he'd eventually focus on something else — but his tantrums just kept escalating. Somebody had to do something."

An uneasy feeling spread through Elise. "When did you talk to him?"

He shrugged. "What difference does it make now? He wouldn't listen; told me to butt out and mind my own business. It was a very short, unpleasant conversation. End of story."

"Ross, don't be an idiot. The man was murdered. *When* you met with Uncle Edmond makes a huge difference! Jackson's already looking closely at all of us. If you didn't tell him about this *unpleasant* conversation and he finds out on his own, it will look like you were hiding something."

"And that's precisely why I didn't tell anyone, El! Nobody saw or heard the confrontation, so as long as you two keep it to yourselves, I'm not too worried about Jackson. It has no bearing anyway. I certainly didn't kill him."

"Geez, Ross, that's not what she meant," Madison said. "Nobody thinks you had anything to do with Uncle Edmond's death, but Elise is right. It would probably be prudent to talk to Jax about it before he —"

"For crying out loud, would you both just give it a rest? It wasn't a big deal, so don't make it into one."

As if the tense conversation had conjured him up, Jackson arrived at that moment, pulling his cruiser in next to the SUV. Ross gave them both a keep-your-mouth-shut look before closing the hatch and heading toward the building with an armload of flowers.

"Hey, Jax. Thanks for coming," he muttered as he passed.

Jackson watched Ross walk away with a frown on his face, and then he turned to Elise. "What's up with the attitude?"

"Don't mind him. Grumpy McGrumperson is having a bad day." Elise picked up a basket arrangement and, slipping an arm through his, pulled him toward the building. "Come on, you can sit by me during the service."

"You sure you want to do that? We haven't had our anticipated conversation yet." He shook his finger at her. "Don't think I don't know that you've been dodging me."

She aimed the full wattage of her smile at him. "Why Deputy Landry, I'm sure I don't know what you mean."

A little over an hour later, Elise stood next to Jackson at the cemetery. To say that she was surprised at the turnout for Edmond's funeral would have been an understatement. Although she understood that most were in attendance out of respect for the family, it was still impressive.

Henry Kohler stood directly across from the family with his arm around a tearful Pam Dawson, which Elise found interesting. He'd told her that he barely knew Pam, but this wasn't the first time she'd seen them together in a way that suggested otherwise.

Shockingly, Denny Rodriguez also made an appearance, though he hung back and seemed to be waiting for something. No doubt both he and Pam were looking to see who they could hit up for the money Edmond had owed at the time of his death. If they thought they could squeeze the vineyard for compensation, they would both be disappointed.

As fascinating as suspect-watching was, with the mugginess of the day and the threat of thunderstorms, Elise was relieved that the graveside service was brief and to the point.

"Give me a ride back to the house?" she asked Jackson as they walked away toward the vehicles.

"Why? You drove. Or did you forget that?"

"I know. I'll have Maddy drive my car back. We need to talk. Or did you forget that?"

Jackson gave her a narrow glance. "What are you up to?"

"I thought I'd take my lumps like a big girl and let you chastise me for snooping on Monday, but if you're going to be like that, then just forget it."

She started to turn away and pretended to dig in her purse for her keys. Jackson didn't let her get far before taking her arm and steering her toward the cruiser.

Lord, he is so easy, she thought as she hid her smile. "So, I take it you want me to ride with you?"

"Don't push it, El. What's that phrase? Oh yeah, be careful what you wish for."

She didn't wait for him to change his mind. Flagging down Madison, she handed over her keys and high-tailed it back to the cruiser.

"Interesting turnout, don't you think?" she asked as they turned onto the dirt road leading out of the cemetery.

"Mmm-hmm."

"I saw you talking to Denny Rodriguez."

"Yep."

"I couldn't believe he'd show up like that. It's not like he and Uncle Edmond were friends or anything."

"Nope."

"He and Pam both were probably looking to see if they could worm some of the money Uncle Edmond owed out of the family."

"That's a possibility."

"For crying out loud, Jackson," she said in frustration at his noncommittal answers. "Are you going to tell me what you said to him? Or how the interview with him on Monday went?"

He slid a brief, knowing look her way. "I figured this was the reason you wanted to ride home with me. *Taking your lumps* has nothing to do with it. You just want to pump me for information."

"That's not true." At his doubtful look, she amended her answer. "Well, not completely true. I also wanted to pass on what Henry told me before you and Jim showed up on Monday. And, yes, I am dying to hear what Denny said when you and Jim went out to El Diablo."

Jackson heaved a beleaguered sigh. "Elise, you have got to step back from this investigation. All your meddling and interference will only hinder my inquiries."

"Oh, posh. I've been very discreet."

Jackson burst out laughing. "Yeah, that's you, all right. Like that little fiasco out at Edmond's house. Very discreet, my ass."

"Okay, so that wasn't as prudent as I'd have hoped, but you would never have found his journal without me and my indiscretion."

"Please. C.C. found that journal, not you."

She ignored his dig and continued to plead her case. "And I might remind you that had we not been there, Pam Dawson may have expired in that closet by the time someone found her."

"Oh, for the love of —" Jackson burst into laughter. "I highly doubt that."

She turned to face him. "Come on, Jax. Give. Denny's initials were in the notebook. So were Pam's and Henry's. And Henry point-blank lied to me several times before you and Jim got there. Any one of them could have killed Uncle Edmond. Or maybe it was a conspiracy!"

"I don't think Denny had — wait, how do you know who was listed in the journal? It took me half the night to decipher some of those codes, and you didn't have it long enough to study."

Crap. She knew better than to look at him but couldn't help herself. She saw it in his face the moment he put together what she'd done.

"Oh . . . my . . . God! You little sneak. You had it copied when you left Edmond's, didn't you? You knew I'd come for it and copied it before I could get there!"

"Don't be so dramatic. This isn't a covert operation we're talking about, and it's a stupid notebook, not microfilm or a secret computer chip."

Jackson pulled off the highway into the H-E-B grocery store parking lot and turned off the engine. He shifted to face her. "Look me in the eye and tell me that's not exactly what you did."

"Jax —"

"You can't do it, can you?"

Throwing up her hands, she confessed. "Okay, you got me. I had it photocopied on my way home. So what? It's not a crime."

"Geez, El." He shook his head. "Between your inability to butt out and Ross's reluctance to tell me the truth . . . don't you get that it makes my job that much harder?"

After her earlier conversation with her brother, Elise didn't want to go down that road with Jackson for fear of spilling her guts. So with a guilty twinge, she changed the subject.

"Do you want to know what I found out from Henry or not?" When he just sighed and pinched the bridge of his nose with his fingers, she dove in. "For one thing, he told me he hadn't seen or spoken to Uncle Edmond for several days leading up to his death. But I ran into Boyd Cox in town — he works in the vat room out at Kohler's — and he said they were both out there the day before having a very heated argument."

"An argument about what?"

"Boyd didn't know, but he said he clearly heard Uncle Edmond say that he 'wasn't going to do it anymore' and that he 'wanted out.' And that wasn't the only thing Henry lied about."

"Yeah, we weren't buying that crap he was selling about how he was just trying to help out an old friend, either. He and Edmond were never friends."

"So what did Denny have to say?"

"El."

"Jax."

He scrubbed his hands over his face, and then relented. "Denny has an alibi for the night Edmond was killed. He was at El Diablo and has a room full of people who will attest to it."

"That doesn't mean anything. He could've

211

had a couple of his goons do it while he sat in the bar and held court. Good way to give himself a solid-looking alibi."

"True, but from what he told us, he didn't have a reason for killing your uncle."

Elise frowned. "But what about the money he owed Denny?"

Jackson finally broke down and replayed the conversation for her.

"Uncle Edmond paid him off in full and then ran up another tab?" she asked when he'd finished. "No wonder Pam was angry. Especially if she forked over close to ten grand and he only owed Denny half of that."

"Yeah. And Edmond was also bragging about a big payoff he'd be getting, but when Denny questioned him about it, he got really jumpy and clammed up. Told Denny to forget he'd said anything."

"Do you believe him?"

"Yes, unfortunately, I do. And I'm gonna have another conversation with Pam Dawson. Seems she conveniently left out the fact that she dropped by El Diablo the night after Edmond was there and that's when Denny told her everything."

"Speaking of Pam, did you notice her and Henry today? The other day, he tried to tell me that he hardly knew her, but he'd obviously forgotten that I found them all huddled up together at the Pit the day I went to see her. And then there he is today, drying her crocodile tears and murmuring words of comfort in her ear." When Jackson raised an eyebrow at her, she shrugged. "Okay, so maybe that's a bit over the top, but not by much. I'm telling you: conspiracy."

"There's nothing at this point to support that theory, and so far I've got more questions than answers." He stared out the windshield for a moment before starting the car. "Like, where's the rest of the money that Pam gave Edmond? That's been really bugging me. And the biggest question of all, who was Edmond getting a payoff from and for what?"

FIFTEEN

Saturday turned out to be a perfect day for a wedding and just the ticket to brighten the somber mood at the vineyard after Edmond's funeral services the day before. The gray skies of Friday night's thunderstorms had given way to the softest pastel blue Elise had ever seen, and the sun warmed the Hill Country air without the terrible humidity they'd endured for weeks.

Women roamed the Great Lawn of Lodge Merlot in dresses of every hue, some with matching summer hats adorning their heads. Men dressed in warm-weather attire strolled with them or stood talking in groups.

Elise loved weddings and the way they made her heart grow light and put a smile on her face. This one would hopefully scrub away — at least in the short term — the dark cloud that had begun with Edmond's murder. Not that Jackson's investigation would magically disappear, but it wasn't something she even wanted to think about today. Today was for hearts and flowers, joy and celebration.

Madison had outdone herself this time.

The vows would take place on the back lawn under an arbor bursting with wisteria blooms. Rows of white wicker chairs lined the flagstone walkway the bride would take to greet her groom under fragrant blossoms.

The reception would follow on the Great Lawn at the far side of the lodge with a stunning view of the vineyard as a backdrop.

Elise had to admit she was crazy for the way her sister had set up the area. Pristine white linen covered the round tables that would seat five each. At the center of each was a miniature ice bucket filled with trailing ivy, aromatic narcissus in full bloom, and perky Texas bluebonnets.

The bride and groom would sit at a similarly adorned table on the side veranda, overlooking the spread of guest tables that were situated under huge canopies to shield them from the worst heat of the afternoon sun. The bandstand and flagstone dance area were off to one side within view, but out of the main pattern of foot traffic.

The wedding cake — an incredible four-tiered display of decadence — held court inside Lodge Merlot. Colorful sugar paste flowers matching the bride's bouquet swirled around the top tier and then poured cheerfully down the sides. The artful cascade ended by wrapping halfway around the bottom tier. It was truly spectacular.

The mayor had spared no expense for her only daughter's wedding, and Maddy had delivered in masterful style. The effect was elaborate without being over the top, with a light, summery ambiance. The pride Elise felt for her sister swelled in her chest as she watched the proceedings from the lodge's wraparound porch.

Fortunately, the ceremony itself was mercifully short. Upon its conclusion, the guests strolled around the building to the reception area while the bride and groom, along with family members from both sides, had their photo session under the colorful arbor.

Though Deana Wilkinson wasn't the prettiest woman in Bastrop County, today Elise thought she was radiant. The new bride's face was drenched in joy, and love shone in her eyes each and every time she looked up at the man standing next to her. And Peter Adams, her groom, was all smiles and looked about ready to pop.

I would love to have that someday, Elise

thought as she walked around the lodge to the reception area. To have so much love for one person — someone you could count on to know exactly what you needed and when you needed it — would be wonderful.

However, it was a bit troubling that instead of thinking of Stuart, her thoughts seemed to naturally gravitate toward Jackson before she could redirect them. She'd felt herself drawing back, pulling away from Stuart for weeks now. If she were honest, she would have to admit that C.C. may have been right when she'd said he wasn't the man for her. And she wasn't doing either of them any favors by dragging out the inevitable.

But was Jackson the one her heart had been waiting for, or just a convenient target for her libido?

On the heels of that troubling idea, Elise scanned the sea of faces and zeroed in on him, picking him out of the crowd like he was magnetized. As if sensing her thoughts, Jackson looked up at that very moment and met her gaze. He said something briefly to the couple he was talking with and turned, striding toward her with a carefree smile on his face.

Her heart did a quick two-step in her chest.

"Hey, darlin'," he said when he got closer.

"Hey, yourself."

He made a show of giving her the once-over, his smile growing. "You look pretty today, fresh as a Texas wildflower."

Her traitorous heart did another fast stutter.

"Thanks," she managed and couldn't help the way her lips curved in response. "You clean up awfully well yourself."

He held out his hand to her. "Come on. Walk with me?"

She hesitated. "I should really wait for Stuart. He had to take a business call."

Jackson nodded. "I saw him heading down toward the Wine Barrel talking on his cell. I think you have time for a quick walk with an old friend."

An old friend I can't get out of my mind lately, she thought. "All right," she heard herself say, knowing it wasn't the smartest move, but one she was helpless to resist.

Taking his hand, she let him lead her around the side of the lodge, across the gravel road, and down into the rows of grapes away from the festivities.

"Where are we going, Jax?"

Halfway down the row and out of sight from prying eyes, he stopped and turned to her. "I was wondering if you'd made up your mind yet about moving to Dallas."

"Geez, not you, too," she said and tried to pull away from him, though he held fast to her hand. "I'm getting really tired of everyone telling me what they think I should or shouldn't do."

"Hey, I'm not judging, El. And I'm not trying to tell you what to do. I get it; this job is a great opportunity for you. I just want to make sure you've considered all the angles."

She jerked her hand out of his grasp and glared at him. "And of course, I'm such an idiot that I surely wouldn't have considered *everything.*"

He stuffed his hands into his pockets, and his eyebrows dropped as he stared back at her. "That's not what I meant, so don't put words in my mouth."

"Yeah? Well, then what did you mean, Jackson? Because that's what it sounded like. Let me tell you something, *pal,* it's my damn choice — my life!"

She stopped abruptly when she realized she was yelling at him, and for the life of her, she couldn't say why. It wasn't Jackson's fault he was voicing aloud concerns she'd been wrestling with internally for weeks. This was something she normally would have talked out with her family the moment Stuart had made the proposal, but she'd kept it to herself. Why? Though her uncle's murder had played a part, she'd used it as an excuse not to tell anyone. When she thought it through, that was probably the most telling aspect of all.

And in that instant, she knew her decision had been made long ago, whether she'd recognized it or not.

With a heavy sigh, she gave him a rueful look. "Look, Jax, I'm sorry. I've been a little stressed out with everything lately. I didn't mean to take it out on you."

He looked down at his feet and kicked around in the dirt with the toe of his cowboy boot. "I'm not trying to tell you how to run your life, El." When he looked up, something else flared in his eyes, something that made her heart pound a bit faster. "Your family doesn't want you to go. They'd miss you, even though you'd only be five hours away."

"I'm aware."

"Don't go."

"Jax —"

He pulled his hand out of his pocket and held it out to her. "It may be unfair, and I know our timing has pretty much always sucked, but I don't want you to go either."

She looked down at the hand he offered and then met his gaze. Though everything inside her yearned to take his hand, she shook her head and took a step back. "I'm sorry, but I can't do this now. We should go back. Stuart's probably looking for me."

She turned to go, but he didn't let her get far.

"Huh-uh. I don't think so." He grabbed her by the wrist and spun her back around and into his arms. "Not this time."

Then his lips were on hers in a smoldering kiss that she had no will to stop. God help her, she'd known that it would be this way with him. Desire burst into full bloom in an instant, and she found herself drawn to the heat. Slipping her arms around his neck, she sank into the kiss with reckless abandon. *This is it,* she thought. This is what she'd been craving.

Jackson.

Time spun out and moments passed as her world seemed to narrow down to only him. She could taste the cold beer he'd been drinking and smell the combination of soap and sunshine on his skin.

And then the sound of a child's giggle broke up the moment.

She and Jackson sprang apart in guilty fashion just as three children ran by them on either side.

"Kissy-face, kissy-face," the littlest of the

three, a cherub with golden curls and big blue eyes, yelled at them as she raced after the older two.

On their heels came a woman calling out, "Sasha! Angelica! Grayson! Come back here this instant."

The woman rolled her eyes and shook her head as she got closer. "Sorry for the interruption. Sometimes I wonder why I had children in the first place," she said with an apologetic grin before continuing after them.

Elise stole a glance at Jackson, who continued to watch the woman's receding back with a half-smile playing about his lips. When he turned back, the smile slowly faded. "I'm sorry, El. I shouldn't have pushed."

"Jax, I —"

She was interrupted at that moment by a woman's scream and raised voices coming from the direction of the road. Without another word, they both ran back up the row of vines, and when they emerged, saw Harmony Gates and her ex, Bud Thornton. Bud had a hold of Harmony's wrists and she seemed to be struggling to get free.

"Let go!" Harmony screamed. "You're hurting me."

"Baby doll, would you stop and just listen

to me for a minute?" Bud yelled back.

Elise and Jackson got there just seconds behind Ross and Darrell Yancy. Darrell stepped between the two and shoved Bud back several paces.

"What the heck's going on here?" Darrell asked. "Are you trying to screw up my cousin's wedding reception?"

Bud shook his head. "No, of course not."

"I want to take out a restraining order," Harmony cried dramatically, tears and mascara running down her face. "He's been stalking me, and I'm afraid for my life."

"What?" Shock flooded Bud's face as he stared over Darrell's shoulder at her. "Harm, you know that's not true. Why would you say that?"

"Bud, why don't we take a walk and you can tell me what's going on?" Darrell said as he led the big man away.

"Why would she say that? I just wanted to talk to her. That's all," Bud told Darrell as they headed down the road toward the Wine Barrel.

"Harmony, are you okay?" Ross asked, offering her his handkerchief.

She took it from him, blotting her eyes before sniffing and nodding. "I am now. Thanks."

"Would you like to go up to the house and

freshen up?" Elise offered.

"That would be good." She looked over at Ross with a shy smile. "I must look a mess."

He smiled back at her. "You look fine, but why don't you go with Elise? Might make you feel better."

When Harmony looked away, Ross gave Elise a look that very clearly said *help,* so she took pity on him. "Come on, Harmony. Ross is right. It will make you feel better."

They walked up the road to the residence in silence. When they got there, Elise showed Harmony to the powder room then gave her some space. Ten minutes later, the woman came out looking almost as if nothing out of the ordinary had taken place.

"Hey, what happened back there? If you don't mind me asking."

Harmony waved the question away. "Oh, nothing really. I probably just overreacted. Bud's been nagging me something awful since we broke up. He just won't let go. I've tried to tell him that I'm in love with someone else and what we had is over, but he doesn't want to hear it."

"I'm sorry. Breaking up can be hard if the feeling isn't mutual."

Harmony nodded. "Exactly. People grow apart or take different paths every day, but sometimes it's hard to accept."

"That's true."

"And sometimes timing that hasn't been right suddenly is and you have to act. Kind of like you and Jackson."

"Me and Jackson?" Elise gave the woman a puzzled look. "What are you talking about, Harmony. I told you the other night at the Dew Drop that I'm seeing someone from Dallas. Stuart is actually here this weekend."

Harmony nodded, but her smile was sly. "Yeah, that's what you said, but I've seen the way you look at Jackson *and* the way he looks back. Like I said, Elise — timing."

Elise stared at the woman for a moment. Her attraction to Jackson was something she didn't want to discuss with anyone, let alone Harmony Gates. But it had her wondering who else had noticed. Was their spark that obvious?

"What are you going to do now?" she asked in an attempt to change the subject. "Are you going to go through with the restraining order?"

"No. I don't know why I even said that. I don't want to hurt Bud. He always treated me like a princess, and I really do wish him the best. I just can't keep going through this with him. I'll probably have to sit him down and explain it again. And hope that it finally gets through to him."

As they walked back to the reception, Elise thought about what Harmony had said. Sometimes people did take different paths and grew apart when they found they wanted different things out of life.

Like you and Stuart, a little voice in the back of her mind whispered. It was something she was going to have to face. And soon.

The Great Lawn was alive with activity when they returned to the reception. Harmony saw a group of her friends and headed off in that direction. Elise scanned the crowd for Stuart but didn't see him anywhere. Nor did she see Jackson, which was probably for the best. She needed some time to herself and decided to slip out to the greenhouse for a few minutes for a much-needed break.

On the way there she ran into Ross, who was obviously coming back from his house farther up the drive.

"Hey, sis. Where're you goin'? The party's that way," he said pointing back toward Lodge Merlot.

"Very funny. I needed a break, so I thought I'd take ten minutes of quiet time and do a quick check of my hybrids. What about you? Why aren't you down at the reception dancing with your wife?"

"I'm on my way to do just that right now. The boys got into a scuffle that ended with Caleb scraping his knees in the gravel. I took them back to the house so Sancia could clean them up and watch them for the rest of the afternoon."

"Aw, some adult time without worrying about what the kiddos are up to." She laughed and began to walk backwards toward the greenhouse as he walked backwards toward the reception. "Enjoy your brief window of opportunity."

"I intend to. And don't you take too long with your vines."

Elise turned and made her way to the greenhouse with a smile on her face. Unfortunately, her joyful mood came to an abrupt end when she opened the greenhouse door and found her boyfriend standing at her desk, digging through her personal files.

Sixteen

"Stuart?" Elise stood just inside the door, stunned that he would violate her privacy in this blatant manner. "What do you think you're doing?"

"Elise," he stammered. "I didn't hear you come in."

"Yes, that's obvious." He looked as guilty as one could after getting caught going through someone else's personal files without permission.

"I was just . . ."

"Yes? Just what?"

She watched him struggle to come up with a plausible answer. When he couldn't quite find the words, she shook her head, disappointment bitter on her tongue. "How could you do this? I trusted you and this is how you honor that trust?"

He put out his hand in a plea. "Elise, darling, let me explain."

"Seriously? I don't think a verbal explanation is necessary, do you? Here you are, rifling through my desk, through my personal papers and notes. When I've been very clear about boundaries."

"Sweetie, I know how this looks, but I was just so darn curious that I couldn't help myself. I thought if we were going to be living and working together that I should get a handle on your process."

"You mean you wanted to get your hands on my *hybridization notes,* don't you?" She narrowed her eyes and wondered how many times they were going to have this conversation.

He dropped the offending papers on the desk like they were on fire and took a step toward her. "Elise, be reasonable."

"Be reasonable? Oh, that's rich. Did you really think invading my personal space would be acceptable?" When he didn't comment, only continued to stare at her, she shook her head. "My guess would be no since you snuck in here during the reception when you thought you wouldn't be caught."

"Okay, now that's not entirely fair. I have asked to see the notes on your hybridization method. Several times."

"That's right, and I've told you no. Several times. So, what? You thought you'd just come in here and steal them?"

"That's a terrible accusation. I was doing nothing of the kind. I was just looking."

"You know, Stuart, I was going to tell you tomorrow that I'd decided not to accept your job offer, but in light of current circumstances, I think now is the perfect time."

He came to her then and took her arm. "I've offended you, I see that now. But this isn't the time for rash decisions over hurt feelings. You have to know that I meant no harm by it."

"Oh, I do know." Tilting her head, she gave him a sad smile. "That's part of the problem, Stuart. You don't think about how your actions affect others."

"Elise, I've offered you the opportunity of a lifetime. Please think about what you'd be giving up."

"I've been thinking about the job offer — as well as our relationship in general — for several weeks now."

Though he tried to hold onto her, she pulled away from him. "I've come to the conclusion that I don't want to move to Dallas. Yes, it's a terrific offer, but I'm happy working for the vineyard — working with my family. And they need me right now."

"All right, we can talk about that." He lifted his hands in a plea. "Maybe we could work out some kind of agreement where it's possible for you to do both."

"It's not just about the job, Stuart. We both know that." She heaved a sigh, knowing that she had to be honest, not only with him but herself as well. "I think the time has come to make a clean break — to move on with our lives — separately."

He took a step back and stared at her with his mouth hanging open. "You're breaking up with me? Over this?"

"Stuart, you're not listening. It's not just about this, though it does emphasize the bigger issue. Our relationship hasn't been working for some time. I know you've felt it, too. Don't deny it. And that you would sneak in here like this shows how little you really know or understand me."

"But to throw away the last six months without notice? Can't we at least discuss it?"

"I'm sorry, Stuart. I wish you all the best, I really do, but I don't think there's anything left to discuss. I know you'd planned on staying until tomorrow, but I think it might be best if you left now."

Stuart's features hardened with anger. "I can see that you've tried and convicted me without giving me a chance to state my case."

"Stuart —"

"No, your mind is made up. You've made that perfectly clear. I'll respect your wishes and go. But you're wrong about one thing, Elise. I do know you. And you will come to regret this decision."

She'd never been afraid of Stuart but now felt an odd chill skitter down her spine. "Is that a threat?"

"A threat?" He gave a disappointed sigh. "Really, Elise? I've gone from snooping to theft and now to threats — all in the space of five minutes? Maybe you're right. Perhaps we do need a break."

The menacing feeling disappeared as quickly as it came, and Elise was sure he would have said more, but Jackson cleared his throat from the doorway, drawing their attention. "I'm sorry. Am I interrupting?"

Stuart sent a glare in his direction. "Not at all, Deputy Landry. It seems we're finished." He spared her a brief glance and then stalked past Jackson and out the door without another word.

Elise let out a long breath and stooped to pick up a handful of papers that had fallen to the floor. When she stood up, Jackson took them from her and lifted her chin with a finger. "You okay, pal?"

She narrowed her eyes at him. "Do not be

nice to me right now. I just hurt his feelings, accused him of awful things. I'm a terrible person."

He made a *pfft* sound and waved the papers he held at her. "Sounds like he got just what he deserved."

"Still, I was a little over the top with — wait." Crossing her arms, she cocked her hip. "Jackson Landry, were you eavesdropping on a private conversation?"

"Uh, El . . . this is a greenhouse, remember. The walls aren't made of stone. Kinda hard not to hear an argument when it's being carried out at a supersonic decibel inside a plexiglass building. With the windows open, I might add."

"I guess," she said with a shrug.

"So, you'd already decided not to move to Dallas and take the job?" He crossed his arms and mirrored her stance. "Were you just messin' with me earlier?"

"Maybe."

"I take it back . . . you really *are* a terrible person."

That made her laugh, which she knew had been his intension. So she threw her arms around his shoulders and hugged his neck. "Thank you for showing up when you did. And for always being there when I need you," she whispered in his ear.

Pulling back, he hesitated and then gave her a wink. "My pleasure, darlin'. Always. Now, let's go have some cake. If you're really nice to me, I might even spin you around the dance floor a couple of times."

True to his word, Stuart's car was gone when she and Jackson passed the main house on the way back to the reception — which she found a relief.

Once she'd made the choice not to accept Stuart's job offer, the stress that had been plaguing her for weeks seemed to evaporate. She was able to spend the rest of the afternoon and evening in the pleasant company of family and friends without decision anxiety weighing her down.

It wasn't until she climbed the stairs to her apartment much later that she cast another thought in Stuart's direction. She found an envelope taped to the front door containing an apologetic card and her spare apartment key.

I really am a terrible person, she thought again as she walked into her bedroom and dropped the card and key on the dresser.

She turned to find her fat cat sprawled in the middle of the bed. Kicking off her heels, she sat down next to him. "Well, you'll be happy to know that I gave Stuart his walking papers today, though I think I was a bit hard on him. So I guess it's just you and me."

Chunk stood up and stretched as only cats can do and then meowed, promptly giving her shoulder a head butt.

"Yeah, yeah. Suck-up." She scratched his head and ran her hand down his big body. "Come on, tubby. I'll give you a treat and then it's into bed for the both of us."

She awoke early Sunday morning with bright sunlight streaming through her bedroom window and the beginnings of a dull headache.

Though she'd fallen asleep quickly, she hadn't slept well. Tossing and turning, she'd gone from one bad dream to the next all night long. Obviously that last glass of champagne at the reception had been one too many, hence the nightmares and the headache.

Adding to her concern, she'd initially thought her right foot may have become paralyzed sometime during the night. That was, until she popped her eyes open and realized Chunk had draped himself comfortably across her feet. He had to have been there most of the night, as she couldn't feel anything in that lower extremity.

"Hey. You big, fat tub of lard. Get off me."

Nothing. The cat showed no reaction, not even an eyelid flickered. Unlike most cats, when Chunk slept, he slept like the dead — and he snored. She couldn't help but smile just watching and listening to him. He was such a putz, but he was her putz.

Just when she began to extricate her feet from beneath his girth there came a pounding at her front door.

Who the hell is at my door on a Sunday morning?

Turning her head, she craned her neck to see the alarm clock on the nightstand. Ten thirty-five. Okay, so it wasn't the crack of dawn, but still, it was freakin' Sunday.

"Okay, okay. Hold your water," she grumbled when the pounding began again. "I'm comin'."

Kicking the covers aside and a yowling cat to the floor, Elise rolled out of bed and tripped over one of the heels she'd been wearing the night before. "Geez, Chunk, quit your bitchin'. This isn't the way I wanted to start my day either."

Grabbing her robe from the back of the door, she struggled to slip it on without tripping over the damn cat as he wound in and around her feet. "And why is there only one shoe here? What have you done with the other one, you little twerp?"

Meanwhile, the pounding at her front door wasn't doing her headache any favors. Scrubbing her hands over her face, she stumbled down the hall and through the living room. Yanking open the front door, a few really nasty words died on the tip of her tongue.

"Morning, sunshine." Jackson stood on her doorstep looking quite tasty in a pair of washed-out jeans and a loose-fitting polo.

He held a cup of coffee in one hand, a bottle of soda and a bag from the bakery up the street in the other. Whatever was in the bag smelled heavenly, but his good mood was a tad annoying when she'd only just pried open her eyes.

"Jax, do you know what time it is?"

"I do. It's almost noon." His white smile flashed. "I brought snacks to tide you over, so get your ass dressed."

"It's not almost noon. It's not even eleven yet."

"Close enough for government work," he told her as he brushed by and headed for the kitchen.

"I don't even know what that means." Closing the door, she followed him into the tiny space. "And snacks to tide me over for what? Why are you here in the first place?"

"You obviously need a shot of caffeine to

fire up your brain and jog your memory." He handed her the soda she craved and shook his head as he opened the bakery bag. "You told your mom and Miss Abby that we would pick up supplies and be out at the house by noon for a late brunch, remember?"

"Oh my God! I totally forgot we'd decided on brunch in place of Sunday family dinner. I should never drink that much champagne in one sitting." She opened the soda and glugged down a quarter of the bottle.

Snatching a warm bagel out of his hand, she turned and headed for the bedroom. "I gotta get in the shower or we're gonna be late. Keep Chunk company, would you? And find out what he's done with my shoes."

Forty-five minutes later, she was dressed and spackled up. She'd braided her hair and was feeling much more like herself. Now all she was missing was her other damn sandal.

"Chunk!" she yelled as she came out of the bedroom brandishing a lone shoe. "What have you done with the other one?"

Jackson lifted his elbow and laughed out loud as he watched the cat try to burrow underneath to escape Elise's scolding. "Chunk says he has no idea what you're yammering about."

"Geez, he just will not leave my shoes alone. Some kind of weird fetish. Ah-ha! There it is," she said, spying the matching sandal under the rocking chair.

Turning, she glared at the cat and a snickering Jackson before slipping the sandals on her feet. "Come on. Let's get going before I stuff him in the hall closet to make sure nothing else goes missing while I'm gone."

By the time they'd stopped at H-E-B for the promised supplies and headed toward the vineyard, it was going on noon. Consequently, it was almost twelve thirty when they drove through the gates at River Bend.

"Well, for crying in a bucket, it's about time!" Abigail spouted as she watched Jackson set the grocery bags on the kitchen island. "Where've you two been? Out lolly-gagging, no doubt, when I've been waiting for these ingredients to finish my cabernet breakfast casserole."

As she turned back to drain the bacon she'd been frying, Elise slipped an arm around her grandmother and gave her a loud smack on the cheek. "Sorry, Gram. It's my fault. I had a titch too much champagne last night and I'm moving slower than normal this morning, so we got a late start. Where is everybody?"

"You mother is in her office and Maddy went down to check on the lodge cleanup. The crew she hired got started early this morning."

Abigail slapped Jackson's hand when he reached for a piece of bacon, then she turned to dig through the grocery bags. "The boys ran through here earlier, but I haven't seen Ross or Caroline yet. Now, you two get out of my kitchen so I can get this shindig put together."

"Yes, ma'am. Come on, Jax, let's go see what's holding up Ross and Caro." She giggled as he snagged a piece of bacon behind her grandmother's back and spun toward the back door.

"I saw that," Abigail called after them as they slipped out of the kitchen.

Crossing the side yard, Jackson held the gate for her and they followed the well-worn path through the field and around behind the cottage where Ross and his family resided.

As they neared the back deck, raised voices greeted them from the open windows. Ross and Caroline were obviously arguing about something, but their voices were just muffled enough that the contents of the quarrel were unclear.

She and Jackson exchanged glances. Before they could decide on whether to interrupt or not, Ethan and Caleb ran out of the wooded area along the river. Ethan was white with shock and Caleb was sobbing.

Alarmed, Elise started toward them and caught Caleb mid-flight as he launched himself at her. Ethan ran straight to Jackson and held on tight.

"Caleb, what's the matter, sweetie? Have you hurt yourself?" she asked, searching the child's body for injury.

He shook his head and wiped his nose with his shirt. "Not me, the lady in the woods," he cried.

"What lady? What are you talking about?" Elise asked, feeling panic rise in her throat.

When both boys began to chatter at once, Jackson knelt down and took Ethan by the shoulders. "Slow down, big guy, I can't understand you. Take a breath and tell me what happened."

Ethan took a huge gulp of air before blurting, "We were in the woods down by the river and found a lady. I think she's dead!"

SEVENTEEN

"What's going on out here?" Ross asked as he came through the sliding glass door out onto the deck.

Caroline followed close behind. When she saw her youngest child in tears, she hurried down the steps to take him from Elise. "Caleb, baby, what's the matter?"

"He's okay," Elise said. "I think they both just had a good scare."

"What kind of scare?" Ross asked.

Elise shot a look to Jackson before shaking her head. "That's not been determined exactly. It seems they stumbled onto something down by the river."

"By the river?" Caroline leaned back and looked down into Caleb's tear-stained face. "You boys know you're not to be anywhere near the river without an adult."

"Mom." The word was drawn out and full of chagrin as Ethan came to their defense when his brother began to blubber again.

"We weren't *at the river.* We were in the woods."

Jackson stood up and aimed a meaningful look at Ross. "He says they found a woman in the woods and he thinks she's hurt. I'm going to need him to show me where."

The dread on his friend's face when he nodded told Jackson he understood the gravity of the situation, and that they probably weren't talking about someone who was just *hurt.*

Ross turned to his wife. "Sweetheart, why don't you take Caleb in the house and I'll go with them."

"I'll bring Ethan back as soon as he shows them the location," Elise said when her sister-in-law started to protest.

Caroline reluctantly nodded and carried Caleb into the house, while the three of them followed eight-year-old Ethan along the trail that led back into the woods.

When they entered the copse of trees, Ethan stopped short and pointed. They didn't need him to go any farther; in the dim light Jackson could see bits of the woman's clothing through the brambles.

Even from a good fifty feet away, he knew by instinct that they were looking at a dead body.

"Ethan, you come with me now," Elise

said, taking him by the hand. "We'll let your dad and Jax take it from here." She met Jackson's gaze. "I'll take him back to the house. Call me on my cell if you need anything."

He nodded and waited for them to cross the tree line before turning back to Ross and the unpleasant task at hand. "Come on, Ross, let's get this over with."

As they carefully made their way along the thin trail — and then through the shallow undergrowth to the body — Ross gasped when he caught sight of the woman's face. "Sweet Jesus, it's Harmony."

"Yeah."

Harmony Gates lay nestled in a small grassy area with her hands folded at her mid-section and her legs crossed at the ankles. Though her shoes were gone, the rest of her clothing was neat and tidy, everything in its place. If not for her eyes — wide open and staring blindly at the oak canopy above — one would think she might have stretched out in the shade for a short nap.

He'd check for further injury, but with the amount of bruising around her slim neck and the petechial hemorrhaging around her eyes, Jackson was pretty sure strangulation was the cause of death. However, he'd have to wait for the Travis County ME to make it official.

"Okay, I'm going to need you to take three or four giant steps back the way we came. This is a crime scene now and I don't want to disturb it any more than we have to."

When Ross continued to stare down at the unfortunate woman without answering him or moving away, Jackson put a hand on his friend's shoulder. "Ross? You okay, buddy?"

"We just saw her yesterday, Jax. We talked to her; El took her up to the house after that argument she had with Bud. Remember?"

"I know."

"I mean, Uncle Edmond made enemies left and right, so having somebody murder him wasn't all that shocking. But Harmony?" Ross looked over at him then with eyes full of disbelief. "How does something like this happen? And so close that my boys could find her. God, Jax, she was harmless. Who would have done this?"

Jackson shook his head. "I don't know. But I'm damn sure gonna find out, I promise you that. Now move on back. I'm going to do a preliminary check of her body and the surrounding area, and then call it in."

■ ■ ■ ■

Just under four stressful hours later, Harmony's body was finally carried out of the woods to be transported into town. Ross had hung in there long enough for the crew to arrive before Jackson had sent him back to the house to wait.

After overseeing a search of the immediate area — and finding precious little to go on — Jackson was more than a little frustrated. Though the brush had been broken down from the trail to where Harmony had been left, the ground cover was too thick to get lucky with footprints.

He needed to head into the office to file his report as soon as possible, but while the crew finished up at the scene, he hiked back to Ross's house.

Jackson found Ross and Elise sitting out on the deck. At first glance, they looked like a couple of folks simply enjoying drinks in the late afternoon sun.

Until you looked closer.

Ross still had a shell-shocked look about him, and Jackson knew the scotch he held in his hand probably wasn't his first. Though Elise held a glass of wine and smiled as he approached, he could tell by her body language that she was keyed up and more than a little upset.

He really couldn't blame either of them. Two deaths on the property in as many weeks could be considered tragic. But that they were both homicides? What were the odds? It was pretty disturbing.

And in Jackson's opinion, more than coincidental.

"Did you find anything, Jax?" Ross asked.

"Not much." He sat down on the end of Elise's lounge, took her glass, and sipped. "I'm fairly sure strangulation will be the cause of death, though we didn't find the murder weapon. Other than the bruising around her neck, she didn't have any other visible injuries that I could see. The ME will tell us for sure."

"What's happening here, Jax?" Elise asked quietly. She dashed at angry tears that threatened. "What the hell did Harmony Gates do to anyone? It makes me so mad. And I feel so helpless, which only serves to make me more furious."

"Who would have done this?" Ross asked. "Do you think it was the same person who killed Uncle Edmond?"

"Possibly."

"But what link could there be?"

"I won't know what connection there may

be until I find it. But at this point, I'm not ruling anything out." Jackson rolled his shoulders, where tension seemed to have taken up residence. "All I know for sure is that I have two murders now within a two-week period, and the only common ground that I can see so far is River Bend." He held up a hand before Ross could ramp up again. "Look, you're right. Harmony's death may well be random or a case of wrong place, wrong time. But I have to check every avenue, Ross. And I gotta be honest; my gut's telling me this is somehow all connected."

Ross's perplexed expression didn't change. "But how? I don't think Harmony and Uncle Edmond even knew each other. They certainly didn't travel in the same social circles. Hell, there was thirty years or more in age difference alone."

Jackson shook his head and stood up. "I don't know. I don't have all the answers — yet. But trust me when I say I'm going to get to the bottom of this."

He looked down at Elise. "I have to go back into town, file my report. You want a ride home?"

"No, you go ahead. I think I'll stay here tonight. It's been a terrible day, to say the least, and Mom is a mess, though she's trying not to show it. I'll get a ride home from someone tomorrow."

"Okay. Call if you need me."

As Jackson drove back to the office, fragmented bits of information churned in his head. He couldn't explain it — and he knew it seemed like a stretch — but a small voice at the back of his mind insisted that Harmony's and Edmond's deaths were somehow connected.

Perhaps they were both part of some bigger picture. He just needed to figure out what that picture looked like. Whatever it was, River Bend was smack-dab in the middle of it. He needed to go back to the beginning, sift through everything he'd already learned.

Later, as he sat down to write his report, he thought a good place to start the process was Edmond's journal. He had a gut feeling that the key to the entire mess was concealed there somewhere. He hadn't had the time to slog through every entry, nor had he deciphered all the initials and codes the man had used.

By the time he put the finishing touches on his report, he realized it was almost ten at night, and his vision was beginning to blur. Revisiting the evidence and Edmond's journal would have to wait until the morning.

Going home and getting a good night's sleep sounded like a good plan. Unfortunately, when Jackson finally got to bed, he tossed and turned, had the strangest dreams, and woke just before the alarm feeling like someone had beaten him with a stick. So he decided to get up and get moving. There was a ton of work to do, and he had the uncomfortable feeling things were spinning out of his control.

That feeling only increased an hour later on the way into the office when he decided to swing by the small house that Harmony Gates had been renting. As he pulled up in front of the house, he noted that her car wasn't in the narrow driveway, but then, he hadn't expected to find it here.

Since she was still wearing the dress she'd worn to the wedding when she was found, she'd been killed before making it home. He'd need to conduct interviews to establish a timeline, and he'd start with the friends she'd been seen with at the reception.

In the meantime, he'd take a look around her place, see what clues he could dig up. Climbing out of the vehicle, he walked up to the small porch.

And his trepidation increased when he saw

that the front door was slightly ajar.

"Hello?" he called, giving the door a push. "Anyone here?"

When there was no answer, he stepped inside. The place was trashed. Figuring Harmony probably hadn't trashed her own place before heading to the wedding, he deduced someone else had been here recently. And the *way* it had been tossed told him that whoever did this was either looking for something or trying to cover their tracks.

Whichever the case, he'd call in the crew to process the house. As much as he itched to look around right away, he backed out instead and closed the door.

Pulling out his cell, he called the office and got Jim Stockton on the line. "Hey, Jim, it's Jackson. I'm out at Harmony Gates's house and it's been tossed."

"No shit? That's an interesting development," Jim said.

"Yeah, isn't it just? I'm going to hang some tape before heading in. Send a crew out to process the place, would you?"

"You got it. By the way, her folks were here bright and early. Darrell handled it, but man, they were wrecked."

"I guess finding out that your daughter

has been killed would have that effect on you."

"Yeah, but get this: she was supposed to go out to their place after the wedding reception on Saturday night. Then she called around seven o'clock that evening to say that something had come up she needed to take care of and that she'd call later."

"Did they say what?"

"No. Her mom got the impression that she was meeting someone, but she didn't know who. Evidently that was the last they heard from her."

"Okay. At least it gives us a starting point. I'll talk to Darrell and get the full rundown when I get in."

Hanging up, Jackson went back to the car for crime scene tape and hung it across the door before heading into the office.

Darrell had already left for the courthouse when he arrived, so he went to his office to sort out his thoughts and work on a game plan. He spent an hour sketching out what he knew on paper from the time they'd found Harmony and Bud arguing around four thirty to the last time he'd seen her at the reception just shy of six. He added anything that he thought could possibly be tied to Edmond Beckett.

Jackson had stayed out at the vineyard

until almost ten o'clock himself before heading home Saturday night. And he had a vague recollection of Harmony walking toward the parking lot with a group of her friends as the reception was winding down. That had been around six forty-five. The call to her parents had to have happened not long after.

Where did you go after that? he wondered as he stared at a picture of Harmony's eerily still body.

Just as he was adding the photo to the board, there was a knock at the door. Jackson was not surprised to see Darrell Yancy standing there, but he wasn't prepared for what had brought Darrell to his office in the first place.

"You got a minute, Jackson? I've got something I think you'll want to hear."

"Yes, I need you to fill me in on your meeting with Harmony's folks."

"Actually, it's not about that."

"Shit's kinda hit the proverbial fan with this case, Darrell. Can whatever it is wait until later?"

"I don't think you want to wait on this. It directly affects your case — maybe both of them."

Jackson studied the man. Where Darrell Yancy could be a total dick most of the time, he wouldn't waste time on a murder investigation with something that wasn't pertinent. "Okay. What to you have?"

"It's not what — it's who. A witness has come forward with information you're not going to like much."

"What witness?"

Darrell jerked his head toward the hall. "I've got him in Interview One. Come on."

Jackson followed Darrell down the hall and entered the room behind him.

And found Carlos Madera seated at the small table.

"Hey, Carlos. What's going on?"

Darrell smirked, and Jackson felt the first touch of unease slide into his system.

"Carlos witnessed something interesting that I know you'll want to follow up on," Darrell said. "Go ahead, Carlos. Tell Jackson what you saw — and better still, when you saw it."

Jackson looked back and forth between the two men before sitting down at the table with Carlos.

"I'm sorry, Señor Jackson, but I had to come forward."

"Come forward with what, Carlos? What did you see?"

"I saw Señor Ross and his uncle arguing."

Jackson sat forward. "When did you see

this, and where?"

"Like I told you before, me and my crew were going to remove the sick vines for Elise, so I went down the afternoon before to prepare."

"So, this was Monday afternoon? The Monday before Edmond was found?"

Madera nodded. "It was probably somewhere between four and five o'clock that afternoon. I was marking the plants in the two rows we were going to dig up when I heard voices. They were very angry."

"Where were the voices coming from?"

Carlos swallowed and glanced at Darrell Yancy.

"Go ahead, Carlos," said the deputy. "Tell him the rest."

"They were coming from up along the riverbank. It was Señor Edmond and Señor Ross. They didn't see me, and I couldn't hear all of it, but I did hear Señor Ross say 'you won't get away with it — I'll make sure of that.' Then Señor Ross pushed his uncle and they struggled some."

Jackson leaned in and looked into the other man's eyes. "Carlos, did you see Ross hit Edmond? Did he assault him in any way?"

Madera shook his head. "No! They shoved each other back and forth a couple times.

Then Señor Ross walked away."

"And Edmond was still there? Unharmed?"

"*Sí.* He said something, and Señor Ross turned back for a minute, but then he walked away. Señor Edmond left a few minutes later."

"Okay. Thank you for coming in, Carlos. I'm going to send an officer in to take your statement. Hang tight, okay?"

Jackson stepped out into the hall, followed closely by Darrell.

"What Carlos saw happened awfully close to Beckett's TOD," Darrell said, his intention clear. "What are you going to do?"

Jackson knew he had no choice. Ross had conveniently failed to mention the altercation Carlos had just described.

"Well, Darrell, what do you think I'm gonna do? I'm going to go pick up Ross Beckett and bring him in for questioning."

EIGHTEEN

To say that the mood at River Bend on Monday morning was somber or tense would have been an incredible understatement. Elise thought it was a bit like negotiating a minefield — of eggshells — filled with napalm.

It felt as if everyone on the property was in denial. Like if they didn't talk about the recent murders, then they could pretend they hadn't taken place. For a family that insisted on talking about literally everything, it was disturbing.

Laura, Abigail, and Madison had retreated to their individual comfort zones — her mother to her office, her grandmother to the Wine Barrel, and Madison to her office at Lodge Merlot. After gently trying to open a dialogue about the situation with her mom and being rebuffed, Elise too had escaped to the greenhouse to repair the damage Stuart had done rifling through her files.

Ross seemed to be the only one willing to talk about Harmony's death, though he continued to insist that her murder couldn't possibly be related to Edmond's.

That was something else Elise had been dwelling on for the last twenty-four hours: Jackson seemed to think the two murders were connected. If that was the case, then he was going to have his work cut out for him. She certainly couldn't see a link other than being found on River Bend property.

On the flip side, if the murders were unrelated, then it seemed to indicate that someone could be targeting the vineyard in some way. And that raised her hackles some. If someone had River Bend in their sights, then her loved ones and anyone connected to the vineyard — no matter how loosely — could be considered fair game. Either scenario was a frightening prospect.

With everything that had occurred recently, maybe it was time to sift through her uncle's journal more thoroughly. Elise had been distracted by circumstances, but it was possible the pages he'd written held something that could connect the seemingly unrelated deaths.

Jolted from her thoughts, she heard the sound of an engine getting louder as it came up the long drive. When the car passed by the greenhouse, Elise went to the door and pushed it open in time to see Jackson's police cruiser before it went around the bend toward Ross's house.

What was he doing here in the middle of the day? Going back down to do another search of the area where Harmony had been found? As she crossed the path to the driveway, Elise could see through the trees that Jackson had pulled in at Ross's place.

She decided to take a walk up to her brother's house to see what was happening. Perhaps there had been some kind of development and Jackson was bringing the news. But if that was the case, why didn't he stop at the residence? She had an uneasy feeling there was another reason for his visit — one she probably wasn't going to like.

As she rounded the curve, she watched Jackson and Darrell Yancy get out of the car and walk up to the porch, and her concern increased.

Darrell Yancy. What the hell was he doing here? Surely Jackson hadn't been replaced as lead investigator. But if he was still in charge of the case, then what was he thinking bringing Darrell right to Ross's door? With the bad blood between the two men over Ross's wife, this *certainly* wouldn't go over well.

From halfway up the road she saw Ross answer the door and all three men head into the house.

Picking up her pace, she didn't bother to knock when she got to the porch. She let herself in and followed the sound of her brother's heated voice into the living room where a face-off looked to be already brewing.

"What the hell, Jax? Are you kidding me with this?" Ross was frowning and looking daggers at Darrell, who was standing to Jackson's left. "You bring *him* into my house and expect to haul me in because of something *he* says happened?"

"No, Ross. I'm asking you to come back to the office with me for questioning, that's all," Jackson said. "This has nothing to do with Deputy Yancy. It's my investigation — I'm the one asking."

That answers the question about whether Jackson was still in charge of the investigation, she thought with relief.

After Caroline spoke quietly to Sancia — who herded the boys out of the room like her apron was on fire — she turned and put a calming hand on Ross's forearm. "Ross, honey, why don't you hear him out before you go blowing a cork." Looking over at

Jackson, she asked, "Now what's this all about?"

Jackson ran a hand through his hair. Whatever this was, it wasn't easy for him, and Elise could almost feel the stress pouring off of him.

"A witness came forward this morning with information involving a meeting between Ross and Edmond." He directed the rest of his statement to Ross. "I want to hear what happened — and why you didn't tell me that you met with your uncle on the day he died after I point-blank asked you."

"Oh, for the love of God! Is that what this is all about? It was nothing." Ross swung around and pointed an accusing finger in Elise's direction. "I told you to keep your mouth shut. What did you do — run to him the minute I was out of sight?"

Everyone turned to her, and Elise felt heat rise in her face as she looked around the room. "What? No! I didn't say anything, but way to deflect attention from your own stupidity by throwing me under the bus, jerkwad."

"Wait — you knew about this and didn't tell me?" Jackson asked. Crossing his arms, he gave her a hard stare. "How long have you known?"

She winced but came out swinging. "Look,

don't get your panties in a bunch, okay? I only found out on Friday before the funeral."

Jackson's mouth dropped open, and he raked his hands over his face in a frustrated gesture. "Seriously, Elise? You've known about this since Friday? Since *before* our conversation that afternoon?"

"Geez, take a breath! It's not like I've been holding onto it for months. It was two *days* ago, Jackson. And Ross may be dumb as a rock at times, but he *is* still my brother, after all. I'm required by blood to do no harm, though in moments like this I'd dearly love to throttle him."

"Hey, I'm standing right here!" Ross shouted.

She whirled around and pointed back at him. "And didn't I say then that you should tell Jackson before someone else beat you to it? But, no, typical Ross. *It's no big deal, so don't make it one,*" she finished, mimicking him and what he'd told her and Madison on Friday.

Ross threw his hands in the air. "Because it wasn't a big deal!"

Jackson shrugged. "Then why not just tell me when I asked? Instead, that day at dinner you made out like I was betraying the family by asking everyone for their whereabouts. You even put your own wife in the hot seat, as I recall."

"Nice," Darrell said under his breath, shaking his head.

Ignoring the comment, Caroline spoke up. "That's not fair, Jackson."

"Maybe not, Caro, but he point-blank lied to me, told me he'd been home with you and the kids all night. Which, I might add, you didn't deny. Now I find out he actually met with Edmond — and within thirty or forty minutes of the murder."

"This is ridiculous! Uncle Edmond was fine when I left him," Ross shouted in anger.

Elise stepped between them and spoke to Jackson. "You said someone came forward this morning. Who was it?"

"Carlos Madera saw the encounter and came in a couple hours ago to report what he'd seen."

"What?" Ross asked in a stunned voice. "Carlos told you about it? I don't believe it."

With a sigh, Caroline slipped an arm around her husband's waist. "Regardless of where you got the information, Ross wasn't gone long. I can vouch for that. Really, Jackson, don't you think I would know if he'd had anything to do with Edmond's death? He was angry when he got back to the house because Edmond was being hard-headed, but that's all."

"Angry enough to kill?" Darrell asked and slid a look her way. "Caro, sweetheart, I hate to tell you, but from what I understand, he made threatening remarks in front of witnesses just a day or so before Edmond was found."

"What the hell are you talking about, Darrell?" Elise asked. "What threats? And in front of what witnesses?"

"*Someday somebody's gonna take him out and no one will cry about it.* Sound familiar, Beckett?" Darrell smirked at the shocked look on Ross's face.

Elise realized Darrell was paraphrasing what her brother had said about their uncle the Sunday before he was killed. But how had he known? The only people in the foyer that afternoon to hear Ross's words were family members, with the exception of their foreman, Neil Paige.

And Carlos Madera. She couldn't imagine the man repeating something so damning. Then again, she would never have thought he'd tell the police what he'd seen without talking to Ross first.

If Darrell's remarks were designed to create doubt of Ross's innocence in her sister-in-law's mind, by the look in Caroline's

264

eyes, Elise thought he'd made a critical error in judgment.

This time Caroline didn't ignore Darrell's remarks, but rounded on the deputy with some righteous anger of her own. "No, Darrell, he wasn't angry enough to kill. And I don't appreciate you trying to put words in my mouth. I think I know my husband just a little bit better than you do, and I can say with certainty that he's not capable of that kind of violence — especially not directed at a family member."

The deputy's reaction to Caroline's outburst was priceless. His face turned a lovely shade of scarlet so quickly Elise thought his head might explode like a cartoon thermometer. He took a step back and looked almost as if he'd been sucker-punched. She knew the man had continued to have feelings for Caroline — even after all these years — but until that moment, she hadn't realized how deeply those feelings still ran.

Jackson put up a hand and tried to get a handle on the situation. "Okay, let's all just simmer down for a minute. Right now, what I need is for Ross to come in to the station and give an official statement as to date, time, and what happened during this meeting with Edmond."

"Fine. Whatever," Ross grumbled. "But

this is a colossal waste of time. Our conversation —"

"Don't you mean argument?" Darrell interrupted awkwardly.

"Yancy, you're not helping," Jackson said without so much as a glance in the man's direction.

Ross, on the other hand, glared at the deputy but continued speaking to Jackson. "Our *conversation,* though heated, was just a rehash of the same old crap with a couple of new twists. And he was very much alive when I walked away. Any *witness* who says otherwise is a damn liar."

"Be that as it may, I'll need an official statement. And Caro, you should ask Sancia to sit with the kids for a few hours because you need to come too."

Caroline nodded and left the room to speak with Sancia Madera.

If Elise thought to make a clean getaway after Ross had ratted her out, she was mistaken. Jackson snagged her by the arm as she tried to slip out.

"Exactly where do you think you're going?"

"Me?" she squeaked.

"Yes, you. I think it would be a good idea if you rode back to the office with us as well."

"Are you joking? Why? What did *I* do? I wasn't even on the property that night."

"It's more what you didn't do that concerns me," he said as he hauled her toward the door. "And as I recall, your whereabouts that night are still unsubstantiated."

"Jackson! Stuart told you we were on the phone."

"Yeah, well, at the very least you can corroborate Ross's statement by telling me all about this conversation you failed to mention on Friday."

Ten minutes later, they all piled into the cruiser, and the ride into town was uncomfortable at best. Ross grumbled most of the way about being treated like a criminal, while Elise and Caroline sat in the back seat on either side of him, making the trip in stony silence.

Things didn't improve much when they arrived at the station. They were escorted into separate rooms to wait. Jackson obviously didn't trust them not to compare stories, which was humiliating enough, but that she felt she'd disappointed him made her feel terrible.

Over the next couple of hours, they each had their turn at being grilled. Of course, Ross's interview lasted much longer than hers or Caroline's, as neither of them knew much more than what Ross had already told them — that a meeting had taken place. However, the longer they waited for him in the lobby, the more concerned they both became that things were not going well.

"Why do you think it's taking so long?" she asked Caroline. "Did he tell you what he and Uncle Edmond argued about?"

Caroline shook her head. "He wouldn't say. When he got home, he was actually more disgusted than angry. But he didn't give me any details."

Elise looked down the hall toward the interview rooms. *Oh, to be a fly on that particular wall right about now.*

NINETEEN

In Interview Two, Jackson sat down opposite Ross at the table and leaned back in the uncomfortable plastic chair. "Okay, so walk me through it from start to finish."

"Dude, I've already told you what happened, and you have it on tape. That isn't enough?"

"Humor us," Jim Stockton said.

Rubbing his eyes with his fingertips, Ross blew out a breath and relented. "Okay, fine. I got a call from Uncle Edmond about five thirty saying he needed to talk to me right away, and could I meet him down by the river."

Jim nodded and scribbled in his notebook. "That was Monday, the afternoon before his death. And you said he seemed anxious?"

"Yes, he was jumpy. He said he'd made a big mistake and needed to talk to me. I was reluctant to go, because I'd just about written him off after he argued with Mom at the house, but something in his voice . . . I don't know. He seemed almost desperate."

"So you met him down by the river. What happened next?" Jackson asked.

"He told me that when Mom hadn't given in to him early on he'd been angry, and because of it, had made a deal he was regretting. He said he'd betrayed the family — told me how *sorry* he was, blah, blah, blah."

"Betrayed the family how?"

"He didn't say, Jax. To be honest, I thought it was just another one of his ploys. But he wouldn't explain himself, even when I got a little physical."

Jackson sat up and leaned forward. "What exactly do you mean when you say 'physical', Ross?"

"I told you before, I shoved him — he shoved back, and that was the extent of it. I said I wouldn't let him screw with the family and all that we'd built. He told me he didn't intend to go through with the deal, but that we should 'watch ourselves'. He was concerned because the plan — whatever it was — was already in motion, and he didn't know what the reaction was going to be when he backed out."

"So he was worried about the family?" Jim

looked up from his notebook.

"I guess. When I thought about it later, that's the way it seemed."

Jim looked up from his notepad. "And that was it? That was the point you walked away?"

"Yeah. Well, I started to, but then he called my name. When I turned around, he looked kind of sad and apologized again. He said he knew he'd been a pain, and he was sorry for the trouble. The last thing he said was, 'be careful, Ross, and take care of the family.' Then he turned and walked down to the river and I went back to the house. That's it. He was alive and well the last time I saw him."

"Okay. I think that's all we need," Jackson said as he reached over and turned off the recorder.

Rolling his eyes, Ross asked, "Are you sure? Maybe I should go through it one more time for good measure."

Jackson gave him a narrowed look. "Be careful what you wish for, bro. Because going through it again is definitely an option."

Ross made a face. "Very funny."

Before Jackson could reply, the door opened and Darrell Yancy stepped in. "We've had an interesting development, Jackson. I just took a phone call with an anonymous tip."

"What kind of tip?"

"The kind where the caller told me where we could find Edmond Beckett's missing wallet."

Jackson stood. Adrenaline began to pump as he wondered if this could be the lead he'd been hoping for. "And where is that?"

"In Carlos Madera's truck — the glove compartment to be exact." Darrell turned to give Ross a look of disgust. "Pretty convenient, if you ask me."

"What?" Ross looked astonished. "Well, hey, don't look at me. I've been here for the last couple of hours."

The seating arrangement in the cruiser on the way back to River Bend was much the same as it had been on the way into the station. Jackson drove and Darrell rode shotgun, with Elise, Ross, and Caroline scrunched into the back seat. However, the mood was much more thoughtful in light of the latest wrinkle in the case.

Elise's mind spun with the numerous possibilities that the mysterious tip presented. Whether Carlos had meant to or not, he had cast the suspicion of murder in Ross's direction with his earlier statements.

Now the finger was being pointed back at

him — but by who?

Carlos and Sancia Madera had been with River Bend for several years, with him working the land and her taking care of the houses. Sancia also watched Ross's boys on a regular basis.

Ross and Caroline continued to insist that Carlos would never be mixed up in something so heinous. Elise hated to think it might be true, but she'd seen enough to know that anything was possible. The only thing consistent about human behavior was its inconsistency, and even someone you thought you knew well could surprise you when you least expected it.

It was something she'd found out the hard way with Stuart's recent behavior.

Still, she was having a difficult time believing it herself and was highly distrustful of the timing of this so-called anonymous tip. Maybe Carlos had been put up to making the statement and was now being sabotaged by the same person who'd encouraged him to come forward — perhaps the real killer. But again, that would mean Carlos was connected in some way to whatever scheme her uncle had been planning.

She thought about what had been said following Ross's interview. Edmond had been caught up in something shady involving

River Bend. And he was worried enough about it to warn Ross on the very day he'd been murdered.

With these new clues in mind, she needed to scour his journal more thoroughly as soon as possible. Maybe he'd written something about it there, hidden in his weird coding.

Harmony's murder also weighed heavily on her mind. What part could it have played in this whole mess? Like Jackson, she was starting to get the feeling there *was* a connection somewhere, and they just weren't seeing it.

Her thoughts were interrupted when Ross sat forward as they turned onto River Bend property. "Don't bother running us home, dude. We're going with you."

"I don't think that's such a good idea," Jackson said from the front seat. "This is police business, Ross."

"And this is our land, Jax. We're going with you whether you like it or not. I want to make sure Carlos is treated fairly, no matter what you find."

"Ross, honey, Jackson may have a job to do, but you know he would never do anything to compromise Carlos's rights," Caroline said in a quiet voice.

"It's not him I'm worried about," Ross

replied with a nasty glance in Darrell's direction. "Besides, that anonymous call is bullshit. Carlos would never be a party to something as horrible as murder."

In truth, Elise had expected Darrell to be the one to put up a fuss. But surprisingly, the other deputy hadn't said a word and had been quiet the entire trip.

She figured he was still smarting from the reprimand he'd received from Caroline earlier. With him continuing to carry a bit of a torch for Ross's wife, it couldn't have been easy to be reamed by her in front of everyone that way.

"Fine." Jackson finally relented. As they pulled up in front of the cottage, he shut off the engine and turned to address the three of them. "I guess I don't have to tell y'all that you need to stay in the background here. Carlos was feeling pretty bad about telling us what he'd seen between you and Edmond, or so it seemed."

Ross huffed. "Don't worry about us. We won't interfere with your precious investigation, Jackson. As for him coming forward, I don't hold that against him. I'm sure he was just doing what he thought was right."

Elise noticed Carlos's truck in the driveway. Jackson would have to get his permission to search it without a warrant. For

Carlos's sake, she really hoped there was nothing to find.

They all got out of the cruiser, but she, Ross, and Caroline hung back on the sidewalk, letting Jackson and Darrell go up to the door. After a few moments, it opened and Carlos appeared.

"Señor Jackson, what are you doing here?" he asked. When he looked around Jackson's shoulder and saw Ross, worry blossomed on his face. "Does this have to do with what I told you earlier? Am I going to be fired?"

Jackson shook his head. "No, Carlos. We're here for something else entirely. I'd like your permission to search your truck."

"My truck?" Carlos looked puzzled for a moment. "Why would you want to do that?"

"Because we got a call stating that we'd find Edmond Beckett's wallet in your glove compartment," Darrell said. "Any idea why someone would say that?"

"No. Who would say that?" he began to shake his head. "It's not true. Why would I have Señor Edmond's wallet?"

"That's a good question," Darrell agreed. "Since it wasn't found on his body, you understand that it would look very bad for you if we found it in your truck."

Elise didn't like Darrell's tone and was just about to say so when Jackson put up a hand in the other deputy's direction. Darrell stepped back.

Jackson spoke calmly. "Look, Carlos, I need your consent to check it out. Now, I can get a warrant, but I'd prefer to do this in a friendly way, if possible, and put an end to the speculation."

Carlos stuck his hands in his pockets and nodded. Fear was evident on his face, regardless of his denial, and Elise's heart went out to the man.

"*Sí,* go ahead," he said after a moment. "But you won't find what you're looking for."

Jackson nodded, and he and Darrell went back to the cruiser for latex gloves. Carlos slowly walked toward the group.

"Señor Ross, I'm sorry about going to the police. I never meant to cause you any trouble."

"I know you didn't, Carlos. I should have told Jackson about the meeting right away. Then you wouldn't have been put in that position in the first place. But don't worry about that now, okay?"

"I wouldn't have done it at all, but I didn't have a choice."

Elise stepped forward and spoke in a low voice. "What do you mean you didn't have a choice, Carlos?"

"I had to protect —"

"Well, well, well. What do we have here?" Darrell's voice carried across the yard, interrupting the conversation. He held up his hand; perched between his fingertips was a wallet.

Carlos's mouth dropped open, and he shoved both Elise and Ross aside as he ran toward the deputy yelling, *"No, no, no!"*

Jackson caught the man before he could make a grab for the wallet and held onto him while Darrell opened it, confirming that it was indeed Edmond's.

"That can't be!" Carlos screamed. "It wasn't me. I didn't kill Señor Edmond. I didn't, I tell you!"

With a sinking feeling, Elise watched Darrell slip her uncle's wallet into an evidence bag. Had they all been wrong about Carlos, or was he being set up to take the blame for someone else?

"We'll get to the bottom of this, I promise you," Jackson told the man. "But right now you're going to have to come with us. Carlos Madera, I'm arresting you on suspicion of murder."

The man continued to protest his innocence as Jackson read him his rights and put him in the back seat of the cruiser.

Ross took out his cell phone as he walked

toward the car. "Carlos, don't say another word. Do you hear me? I'm calling Lyle Ingram. He's the vineyard's lawyer and a damn good one. So, don't worry. He'll take care of everything, okay?"

"I didn't do this, Señor Ross. Please make them see. I didn't kill your uncle, I promise."

While Ross called Lyle, Elise pulled Jackson aside. "Jax, you can't seriously believe that Carlos killed Uncle Edmond."

Jackson rubbed the back of his neck and gave her a grim look. "Unfortunately, it doesn't matter what I think, El. I have to follow the evidence whether I like where it's going or not."

"I know, but that's what I'm talking about. Don't you find this just a little bit too convenient? I mean, come *on.* Do you really think Carlos would be dumb enough to keep that wallet in his glove compartment if he'd just murdered the man?"

"It is troubling, but the fact is, people do dumb things all the time."

"Yes, but you found that wallet via an *anonymous call.* The caller couldn't have known it was there unless they put it there themselves to set Carlos up."

"That's a definite possibility. Or maybe the caller was an accomplice who'd been with Carlos when he put it in his own glove compartment." Jackson put up a hand when she opened her mouth to argue. "Regardless, I do find it awfully coincidental, and you know how I feel about coincidence. But if that wallet comes back with Carlos's fingerprints on it, it won't look good for him. And I'll tell you right now, at that point, how we found it won't matter much to the DA."

Elise's frustration grew as she watched him climb into the vehicle and drive away. Jackson's hands might be tied, but hers certainly weren't. She was going to figure out what had Carlos so terrified and, hopefully, the identity of the anonymous caller. And she knew just where to start.

Glancing up, she realized that Ross and Caroline had already started walking down the long driveway back toward the residence. Following them, she opened her purse, dug for her phone, and quickly punched in a number.

"C.C.? It's Elise. How soon can you meet me at my apartment?"

"We're not going to do anything to get us in hot water with Jackson this time, right?" C.C. asked when Elise opened her front door forty-five minutes later. She traipsed past her and headed for the living room. "Because I do *not* want that gorgeous hunk of man pissed off at me again."

"Please. Don't be such a whiny baby," Elise replied as she shut the door and followed. "And no, we're not doing that kind of sleuthing. We're just going to do some . . . research, that's all. Jax doesn't even need to know about it unless we find something."

"Research. Uh-huh." C.C. gave her a skeptical squint. "I'm intrigued. What kind of research?"

Elise grabbed her briefcase, pulling out a sheaf of papers and dropping them on the coffee table. "We're going to do some decoding."

"Holy crap! Girl, are these what I think they are?" When Elise just smirked, C.C. burst out laughing. "Oh, you sly thing, you. I'm impressed. You made photocopies of your uncle's journal?"

"Well, one must always be prepared, right?"

"Does Deputy Sweet Cheeks know about this?"

Elise laughed out loud at her friend's description of Jackson. "Yes, and he was none too pleased about it, let me tell you. He gave me a good ration of crap on the subject."

"He was so steamed at finding us at Edmond's house that day I'm surprised he hasn't come over to confiscate these."

"He probably would have if he'd had the time. I knew he'd hot-foot it over here the minute he found the journal missing when we left the house. And knowing him as I do, I figured he'd demand that I give it up. So I took out a little insurance by making photocopies on the way home."

C.C. made a sweeping curtsy. "I bow to you, O Cunning One."

"As well you should," Elise said with a chuckle. "It just made sense. Besides, I don't think he's had much time to peruse the journal. Like I said, he's been pretty busy lately. You heard about Harmony?"

C.C. nodded. "Word travels fast in this little burg. So sad. Does Jax have any leads?"

"There hasn't been much to go on, but there've been a few other developments just this morning regarding Uncle Edmond's death."

She explained about being hauled into the station with Ross and Caroline, Ross's recount of his meeting with Edmond, the anonymous tip, and Carlos's arrest.

"Wow! How did I miss all the fun?" C.C. asked with a stunned look. "Does Jackson really think *Carlos* killed your uncle?"

"I don't think so, but he has to go by what evidence he finds. I can't imagine Carlos killing anyone, and I don't trust this mysterious call implicating him. Unfortunately, I'm starting to think Carlos may have been involved somehow in whatever Uncle Edmond was mixed up in."

"Ooh, betrayal, murder, and intrigue — oh my! Geez, you could write a book, and it would sell like hot cakes!"

"Yeah. It is kind of deliciously sordid, isn't it?"

"Who would have thought something like this would happen here in little Delphine, Texas? Amazing."

"Yeah, and really convoluted."

Knowing her friend couldn't resist a good puzzle, she picked up some of the journal copies and waved them in C.C.'s face. "I think Carlos is being set up by the real killer, though, and the link we need may be hidden in Uncle Edmond's coding. You up for it?"

C.C. stared at the pages for a moment, and Elise could almost hear the wheels turning in her friend's head.

"Absolutely!" she finally said with a grin. "Let's do it."

They cleared the coffee table and sat down on the floor on either side, spreading out the pages in front of them.

"Okay, I've pretty much figured out the first half dozen pages, or so," Elise said. "Most of the initials in the beginning were easy to match up, though a few are still a mystery. The four or five pages after that were also a cinch. Those entries catalog his wagers out at El Diablo with Denny Rodriguez — wins, losses, what he owed — that kind of thing. But after that it gets really weird."

"What do you mean 'weird'?"

"Well, look here." She gestured to the pages in question. "On first glance, it's formatted to look like paragraphs, see? But instead of letters it's all numbers. I'm guessing the numbers at the top of each page represent dates and maybe times. But the rest of it — it's like he was doing this bizarre savant writing with random numbers."

"Let me see," C.C. said, taking the pages for a closer look.

She studied the odd script for a few minutes. Just when Elise was starting to get impatient, her friend began to smile. Then the smile turned to a chuckle.

"Okay, do you want to let me in on the joke?" Elise asked. "What's so funny?"

C.C. looked up from the pages she held and laughed out loud.

"C.C.! What?"

"Cake and pie, baby!"

Elise gaped at her friend. "You've figured it out? Seriously? That fast?"

C.C. nodded. "Easy peasy, girlfriend. This is definitely a number cipher. The military has used these kinds of codes for decades."

Elise felt an adrenaline surge and couldn't contain her excitement. "So you can read it?"

"Well, that's the tricky part. You have to know the template, but basically, it looks like one of the simpler ones. In other words, he used a specific number for each letter of the alphabet. One for A, two for B, and so on. Lots of newspapers print ones where each letter stands for another letter, so this is kind of like that."

"Oh my God! You, my friend, are a genius."

"Yes . . . I know," C.C. said and patted her short bob.

"Well, what does it say?"

Her friend blew out a breath. "Unfortunately, that's going to take some time."

Elise grinned. "Then we'd better get busy."

TWENTY

It took several hours — plus a myriad of snacks and too many diet sodas to count — but Elise and C.C. slowly made headway into deciphering Edmond's journal notes.

"Seriously, girl, it's so past my bedtime," C.C. complained, flopping back onto the carpet and rubbing her eyes. "We've been at this for hours, and I have to work in the morning. Are we going to pack it in anytime soon? Because I gotta tell you, I think my eyeballs are starting to melt."

"I know, mine too," Elise agreed. "I just want to get through this next section."

"El! I'm tired!"

"Okay, okay, but listen to this," she said and read from the section she'd just decoded. "Now, you know how furious Uncle Edmond was when Daddy left the vineyard to Mom, but when she wouldn't cave to his demands to give him the south quadrant, it sounds like he went really berserk. That's when he agreed to steal my notes on the hybridization process for Henry Kohler — which, I might add, Henry lied about when we were there the other day."

"Yeah, but you already figured that, right?"

"Uh-huh. But he also talks about Carlos. Edmond wrote here that Henry was holding something over Carlos's head to make him help." Elise read a bit more. "Oh my! He has some really nasty things to say about Henry."

"Does it say what Henry had on Carlos to make him help with the theft?"

"No, but that must have been what Carlos was about to tell us earlier."

C.C. sat up. "Wait — earlier? What are you talking about?"

"I told you. It was this afternoon when we went out to the vineyard so Jackson could search Carlos's truck." Elise glanced up from her notes, watching the cat jump down from his perch in the Papasan chair and saunter over to rub against C.C.'s arm. "Carlos kept apologizing to Ross about coming forward. Just before Darrell found the wallet, Carlos said that he wouldn't have squealed on Ross, but that he'd *had no choice.*"

"What did he mean by that?"

Elise nodded and jabbed her finger in

C.C.'s direction. "That's what I asked him, and he started to tell me, too, but then that damn Darrell hollered that he'd found the wallet, and Carlos didn't finish. All he got out was *I had to protect* before he knocked me and Ross out of the way and ran off. I got the impression he felt he needed to protect someone."

"You think it was Sancia?"

Elise shook her head. "I don't know."

"Wow. Not only murder, mayhem, and intrigue, but possibly blackmail as well? This just gets crazier by the minute."

Elise did a bit more decoding. "He says the three of them met frequently down by the river in the evenings but alludes to the possibility of others being involved in the scheme."

"Does he say who or give initials?"

"No, but he writes here, *I wonder who's really pulling the strings for this deal because it's definitely not HK.*"

"Sounds like he didn't actually know who else was involved."

Elise put down her pages and stretched. She was starting to get a kink in her neck from hunching over, and like her friend, was going to need to sleep soon. "One of the other people could have been Denny Rodriguez. His initials are in here all over the place."

"Denny?" C.C. wrinkled her nose and made a comical gagging sound. "That guy is the creepiest, if you ask me. Makes my skin crawl. But okay, what would be his motive for joining Henry's espionage party? I mean, other than the fact that it's sneaky and illegal. I can't see the guy giving a damn about your hybridization process — no offense."

"None taken." Elise shook her head then shrugged. "Yeah, it's a pretty thin theory. I don't think he gives much thought to anything other than drugs and his gambling business."

"Hey, how about Pam Dawson? Do you think she might have had anything to do with this?"

Elise yawned and leaned back against the sofa. "I don't know. Our Pammie is crazy as a loon, that's for sure. She would fit right into this mess, but she's not mentioned much in the journal so far."

"That doesn't necessarily mean anything. She's been running the Pit for how long now; she's certainly smart enough to be calling some of the shots."

"True."

"And, not to speak ill of the dead, but

your uncle was dumb enough not to have a clue about it."

"Unfortunately, also true."

"Plus, you said yourself that you caught Pam and Henry together at her restaurant, and then later at your uncle's funeral, they were together again. Could be more going on there than just a little comfort, you know?"

"Good point." Elise thought about it for a moment then frowned. "Still, she was pretty rabid about wanting to know where the money she'd lent Uncle Edmond had gone. Although, like you said, she's wily — could have been just an act."

C.C. rubbed her eyes again. "All I know for sure is that I'm done for tonight." Pulling her sandals out from beneath the coffee table under Chunk's watchful eye, C.C. slipped them on and gathered her belongings. "I'd love to stay and help you figure this out, but I gotta get home."

"Yeah, I need to go to bed too. Thanks for your help, my friend. I wouldn't have gotten this far without you."

She walked C.C. to the door and watched her friend head down the stairs.

"*Ciao,* darlin'," C.C. said over her shoulder. "Call me tomorrow."

"Will do."

Elise closed the door then turned and leaned against it. Glancing toward the living room, she thought about what they'd learned tonight — and how much more there was to uncover. Knowing she was probably too tired to make much headway, she figured the smart thing would be to give up and turn in — come back to it when she was fresh. Still, she desperately wanted to dig out more of the secrets the journal pages had to offer.

After a short debate with herself, she decided to work another thirty minutes and then go to bed. She would take the entire mess with her to the vineyard and work on it in the morning as well. Before long, she'd have the entire thing deciphered — and hopefully the killer revealed.

Adding to what she could learn from the journal, having a sit-down with Sancia Madera sometime in the next day or so was also a priority. Although with Carlos taken into custody, she'd have to be careful in her approach with the woman. Sancia would probably be a wreck and reluctant to talk, but Elise had a feeling she knew a whole lot more than any of them suspected.

Looking down at Chunk — who looked up at her and yawned — she nodded. "I know, buddy, but it'll only be another thirty minutes or so. I promise."

Sitting down on the carpet, she scooted up to the coffee table and got to work.

Running. She was in the south quadrant of the vineyard and racing between rows where grapes hung thick on her new hybrid vines. Out of breath, Elise caught a glimpse of Uncle Edmond at the far end of her row and struggled to catch up. But no matter how fast she ran, she couldn't seem to close the distance.

"Uncle Edmond! Wait up. I need to talk to you about your notebook!"

He turned and smiled, then disappeared around the end of the row.

That's when she heard the music. Celtic music to be exact. Wait — that was her cell phone ring tone. But where was her phone?

Distracted and patting her pockets in search of it, she tripped and began to fall in slow motion . . .

And woke up with a start — smacking the side of her forehead on the coffee table as she tried to sit up too quickly.

"Ouch!" she cried and collapsed back down on the carpet.

Rubbing the tender spot above her right eye, she took stock of her whereabouts. She was in her living room, on her back with her head halfway underneath the table. Surrounded by journal papers, she'd obviously fallen asleep there last night while working.

So much for thirty minutes and then to bed.

Turning her head, she came nose to nose with the fat cat. "What are you looking at, you big lump? Did you sleep under here, too?"

When he just continued to stare at her with an inscrutable look, she decided she'd better get up and answer her phone, which was still ringing.

Rolling over and being very careful not to bang her head again, she crawled over to her purse and pulled out her phone. "Hello?"

"Elise, where the hell are you, and why aren't you here yet?" The annoyance in her brother's voice grated on her nerves. She wasn't completely awake yet and didn't appreciate his tone in the least.

"I'm at home, Ross. Therefore, it would stand to reason that I'm not there yet because I'm *here*!"

"Very funny, smart-ass. Seriously, do you know what time it is?"

"Since I fell asleep on the living room floor last night and your call just woke me, that would be a no. But I'm sure you're about to tell me."

She heard his beleaguered sigh on the other end of the line.

"It's half past eleven, El. We were supposed to meet here at nine to discuss Carlos's situation, or did you forget?" There was a brief pause before he asked, "And why did you sleep on your living room floor?"

"I was doing some research into — Never mind. Look, I'm sorry I'm late. Give me an hour, and I'll see you then."

She didn't wait for his response, hanging up before he could haggle over time. Ross was the punctual one in the family. Elise thought his obsession with time often bordered on OCD, but Ross was Ross. Of course, she couldn't really point fingers. She had issues of her own, like being almost incapable of punctuality in any form.

Scraping the journal pages together, she dropped them into her briefcase and headed into the bathroom to shower. She'd better get it together and get out to the vineyard before her dear brother had a complete meltdown.

Fifty-five minutes later, she was feeling quite pleased with herself as she guided her sports car through the gates at River Bend. Since she was running so late, she didn't bother to stop at the residence as she normally would. Instead, she drove directly to her brother's home, bypassing the greenhouse as well.

"It's about damn time," Ross said when he met her at the door. "I was about to talk to Sancia without you."

She gave him a dirty look as she crossed the threshold. "Dude, chill out. Is there any news? Any new developments?"

"No. Haven't heard a peep yet. Lyle Ingram met Carlos at the station yesterday and was going to be there when he was interviewed first thing this morning."

"Then what's the rush? Relax. Sancia's husband has just been arrested in connection with a murder; the last thing she needs right now is you bouncing off the walls like a damn pinball."

"You're a tad surly today considering you slept until almost noon. Were you out of diet soda? We've got some in the fridge if it will improve your mood."

"Ha, ha. You're killing me here." She wasn't about to tell him that he was spot on. In her rush to get to the vineyard, she'd missed her morning quota of caffeine and she was feeling it. It was all she could do not to whimper.

"For your information, Caro just went to get Sancia. They have a pretty close relationship, and she thought it would be a good idea to provide some support while we talk to her."

"Have you said anything to Mom or Maddy?"

"No. They know just the basics about what happened with Carlos, but I didn't tell either of them that we were going to talk with Sancia. Thought we'd see what we could find out first."

Elise smiled and patted his cheek. "Such a good boy."

"Bite me," he said with a chuckle.

"You know, for a family that prides itself on honesty and full disclosure," she began as she followed him into the living room. "A few of us have been decidedly sneaky and tight-lipped lately."

He stopped in the middle of the room and turned to her. "If that's a crack about me not telling anyone about my meeting with Uncle Edmond, I could point out that you've held onto a few things yourself. The whole Stuart debacle — the job offer and possible move to Dallas?"

"Hey, I said a few of us, didn't I? Don't be so defensive."

She thought about the journal pages in her briefcase, and guilt sprang to life in her head. Though Jackson and C.C. knew about the journal, it was still another thing she hadn't told anyone in the family about yet. Maybe she should tell Ross now, get it out in the open.

"Ross, there's something I've been meaning to —"

She didn't get any further as Caroline entered the room with a miserable-looking Sancia. All thoughts of the journal went out of her mind as she took in Sancia's splotchy face and puffy eyes. It was obvious she'd been crying, and Elise's heart hurt for the woman. But who could blame her? Elise felt another pang of guilt about the conversation they were about to have. It wouldn't be easy, that was for sure.

"Come on over here and have a seat on the sofa, Sancia," Caroline said with a gentle tone. "Can I get you anything? Something to drink?"

Sancia Madera dabbed at her eyes as fresh tears began to fall. "Maybe some water, if it's not too much trouble."

Caroline smiled at the woman. "It's no trouble at all. I'll be right back."

Sancia watched Caroline leave the room and wept softly.

"Sancia, I'm so sorry for what's happened," Elise said. "We're goingto get to the bottom of it, and Carlos will be home before you know it."

A sob escaped the woman as she shook her head. "Everyone has been so kind." She looked up at Ross as the tears streamed down her face. "After Carlos had to tell Señor Jackson about the argument you had with your uncle, we were both sure you would send us away."

Ross sat down next to her and took her hand. "Darlin', we would never fire Carlos for doing something he thought was right. I don't blame either of you for that. I should have been honest with Jackson early on, so I'm the one who should be sorry for putting Carlos in that position."

Elise sat on the other side of the woman. "There is something that's been bothering me, Sancia, and I'm hoping you can clear it up for me."

"*Sí.* If I can. What is it?"

"Well, Carlos told us yesterday that he didn't want to go to Jackson with what he saw, but he didn't have a choice. Just now, you said, 'after Carlos had to tell'. Why did he feel he had no choice? Did someone force Carlos to come forward?"

The older woman's face crumbled, and she began to silently weep again.

"Sancia, if you know something, you have to tell them," Caroline said from the doorway. "They only want to help, but they can't if they don't have all the facts."

Caroline crossed the room, set the glass of water she carried on the coffee table, and knelt in front of the housekeeper. Taking her hands, she gave her a gentle smile. "Please let them help you."

After a few moments, Sancia nodded and wiped her eyes. "*Sí,* I will tell them what I know."

"Good girl," Ross said.

The housekeeper took the glass from the table and sipped before speaking. "Neither of our families have much money, but Carlos's family comes from a very poor town in Mexico. His brother, Arturo, came across the border two years ago hidden in the back of a delivery truck. He's here illegally."

Elise sat forward. *This must be the root of the blackmail scheme we found out about from the journal,* she thought. "Where is Arturo now, Sancia?"

"Carlos got him a job at the Kohler Winery. He works for Señor Henry."

"Does Henry know that Arturo is here without papers?" Ross asked.

"*Sí.* He pays Arturo under the table, so there won't be any records."

Elise nodded. "Was Henry Kohler the one

who made Carlos come forward yesterday?"

"*Sí.* He makes Carlos do things he does not want to do all the time! When my husband refuses, Señor Henry reminds him that Arturo is here illegally and threatens to call Immigration."

"That's despicable," Caroline said, anger firing in her eye. "What kind of person does that?"

Sancia turned to Elise. "Señor Henry wanted Carlos to steal the notes on your new vines."

"My hybridization process?"

"*Sí,* but it was the one thing Carlos would not do, even to save his brother. When Carlos said no, Señor Henry was very angry and was going to call Immigration right then. But Señor Edmond made him stop — I don't know how — but we were so grateful for his help. He was very kind to Carlos."

"Uncle Edmond? Kind?" Ross said in amazement.

They were interrupted by a knock at the door. Caroline got up to answer it, and when she came back she was followed by Jackson.

Ross stood. "Jax? What are you doing here? Is there news? Did you find fingerprints on the wallet?"

Jackson shook his head and twirled his hat

in his hands. "No. The wallet had been wiped clean."

"See! I told you," Elise said. "Someone is setting Carlos up."

Sancia looked up at Jackson, a hopeful look on her face. "Will my Carlos be coming home soon?"

Jackson paused, and by the look in his eyes, Elise had a terrible feeling that things were about to take a turn for the worst. "I'm sorry, Sancia, but Carlos won't be coming home just yet."

"Jax, what's going on? What's happened?" Elise asked.

"In the interview this morning, Carlos told us that he and Henry had met with Edmond about twenty minutes after his argument with Ross. And he's admitted to assaulting Edmond with a rock."

TWENTY-ONE

"Nooo!" Sancia cried and slumped over, sobs wracking her small frame.

At once, the room erupted in shouts and denials, everyone yelling at once over Sancia's wailing.

"I don't believe it for a minute," Caroline said. "Carlos wouldn't harm a flea, much less kill anyone."

"You're out of your mind, Jax!" Ross shouted. "Where in God's name was his lawyer during this interview? Ingram was supposed to make sure Carlos was protected."

Jackson finally let out an ear-piercing whistle to get everyone's attention. "Just hold on a minute, y'all. I didn't say he killed Edmond; matter of fact, he swears he didn't."

"Then what are you talking about?" Ross asked in anger.

"Well, if you'll sit your ass down and shut

302

up for one minute, I'll explain."

Ross sat back down, but he didn't look happy.

"Jax, Sancia just told us a few things that could have a huge bearing on the case," Elise said. "Henry Kohler was blackmailing Carlos because his brother is in the country illegally. He was threatening deportation."

Jackson nodded. "I know. Carlos told us all about that. I had Jim pick up Henry for questioning this morning after we spoke with Carlos."

Elise handed Sancia a fresh tissue and patted the woman's back in an effort to calm her fears. "See, Sancia? Jackson's going to figure this out. Carlos will be coming home very soon."

"What did Kohler have to say when you brought him in?" Ross asked. "Did he deny the allegations?"

"At first, yes, but when he realized we knew that he'd met with Edmond just before his death, he was visibly shaken and fessed up pretty quick."

"No doubt in an effort to cover his own sorry butt," Caroline commented in disgust. "I'll just bet that pathetic excuse for a human being tried to shift all the blame onto poor Carlos."

"Actually, his version of what happened

closely matched what Carlos told us. However, he adamantly denied the blackmailing allegation. Said he wasn't blackmailing anyone — that Carlos must have *misunderstood.*"

"Lying bastard," Ross said.

"Anyway, he swears that Carlos only hit Edmond once with the rock, and then they both hightailed it out of there."

"Then why are you still holding Carlos?" Elise asked. "Hitting Uncle Edmond once with a rock wouldn't have done the kind of damage we saw that morning when he was found."

"Even though they both *say* Carlos only hit Edmond once, it doesn't make it so." Addressing Sancia, he gave her a sympathetic look. "I'm sorry, Sancia, but I can't just take their word on this. I have to be able to rule the rock out as the murder weapon. Until then, Carlos will remain in custody."

Sancia nodded and blew her nose. "I understand, Señor Jackson, but my husband is a good man," she insisted. "There must have been a reason for him to do this terrible thing."

"Did Kohler say what went down in their meeting and why Carlos hit Uncle Edmond in the first place?" Ross asked. "By Sancia's account, Carlos didn't have a beef with him."

"No, Señor Edmond was very good to Carlos," Sancia added.

"Evidently, when they met that evening, Edmond was royally pissed off. Seems he and Henry had struck a deal earlier to go into business together, but Edmond had found out somehow that Henry was doing some double-dealing on the side."

"Wait — what business?" Ross asked.

"Edmond was buying into Kohler's operation, making it a partnership."

Ross scoffed and gave a short burst of laughter. "Then the joke's on Kohler, because Uncle Edmond didn't have squat in the way of funds."

"The missing money!" Elise said with surprise. "That's where the money went that he got from Pam."

Jackson nodded. "From what Henry said, Edmond gave him almost six thousand dollars as a down payment, which would have been just about what he would've had left after paying off Denny Rodriguez."

Elise drew her brows together and pursed her lips. "But where was he going to get the rest of the money he needed? Six grand wouldn't be nearly enough to buy into a deal like that."

When Ross spoke up, it was obvious that he was having an aha moment: "He was bringing property to the arrangement."

"What?" Elise asked.

"Well, think about it, El," he continued. "It makes perfect sense now, him badgering Mom to give him part of River Bend. He wasn't going to sell it like he told her. With the money he gave Henry as the down payment, River Bend *property* would be his buy-in."

Elise's mouth dropped open. "That's also why he was specific about wanting the south quadrant. Those fields are where we put the first crop of my hybrids, which is probably what Henry was counting on. That would have been very enticing to him."

"Except Mom wouldn't give in to Uncle Edmond's demands," Ross said with a shake of his head. "So that would have put the kibosh on his grandiose plans."

Elise thought about the journal notes she'd deciphered with C.C. the evening before. "Sure, but I'm guessing that was where the theft of my notes came into play." She glanced over at Jackson with a sly look. "Am I right?"

"Yes. Edmond agreed to get them in lieu of the property. Henry was also pressuring *Carlos* to steal anything he could on your hybridization process."

"But my husband refused to do it," Sancia insisted. "And when Señor Henry was going to call Immigration to turn in Carlos's brother, Arturo, Señor Edmond stopped him."

"Jax, you said Uncle Edmond found out Henry was 'double-dealing'. What did you mean by that?" Elise asked, remembering what her uncle had written about the possibility of others involved in the scheme. "And how did Uncle Edmond find out?"

Jackson sat down in the wing-back chair and crossed a booted foot over his knee. "It seems Kohler's operation was in financial trouble. I don't know how your uncle found out — we may never know — but Henry was trolling for investors. I think Edmond thought Henry was trying to cut him out of the loop, just waiting until he got his hands on your hybridization process to do it."

"And that's what the final meeting was about that night?" Ross asked. "But that still doesn't answer the question of why Carlos assaulted Uncle Edmond."

"Like I said, Edmond was furious and feeling double-crossed. In the meeting, he told Henry he was backing out of the deal and that he was going to come clean with the family about the whole thing."

"I can imagine how Kohler took *that* news," Ross muttered.

"Yeah, Henry was less than happy when he spoke about it in the interview," Jackson replied. "Then again, he and Edmond weren't friends to begin with, and your uncle pulling out of the deal before Henry could get his hands on Elise's notes didn't go over well."

"So at what point in this meeting did Carlos hit Uncle Edmond, and what made him do it?" Elise asked.

"From what Carlos told us, after Edmond told Kohler he was reneging on the deal, a very heated argument ensued. Kohler was enraged and threatening all sorts of stuff. Carlos panicked," Jackson said with a shrug. "He was afraid Henry would take Edmond's withdrawal out on him by having Arturo sent back to Mexico. He says he picked up a rock and hit Edmond over the head before he even realized what he was doing."

"Then what? They just ran off and left Edmond there?" Caroline asked. "Henry had to know Edmond would spill everything the moment he came to."

Jackson shook his head. "Henry convinced Carlos that Edmond was bluffing when he'd said he was going to tell the family about any of it," Jackson replied and stood up. "In his mind, Edmond had just as much to fear from the scheme going public as he did. He says he and Carlos skedaddled at that point, leaving an unconscious but very much *alive* Edmond lying there on the riverbank."

"And what about Henry?" Elise asked. "How long do you intend to hold him?"

"We're not. I had Jim take him home after his interview. No formal charges will be brought against him — for now."

Caroline sat forward and bristled. "How is *that* fair? Why should Carlos be the only one in jail? Henry Kohler is in this mess up to his eyeballs."

"That very well may be, Caro, but I have no real evidence that he's done anything wrong. And Carlos has admitted to the assault."

"But what about the blackmail?" Caroline asked.

"Unfortunately, it's hearsay — Carlos's word against Henry's."

"When do you think you'll know if the rock was the murder weapon or not?" Elise asked. "Carlos must be so scared."

"I could hear anytime now, I'm just waiting on a call from the ME. Speaking of which, I need to get going. I just wanted to come out and tell y'all the news face to face and keep Sancia in the loop."

"Thank you, Señor Jackson. I know you'll take care of my Carlos."

Grabbing her purse and keys, Elise walked Jackson out to his cruiser. As she did, she thought about her uncle's journal again and wondered if Jackson had deciphered any of it yet. She knew she should tell him about what she and C.C. had discovered, but he'd probably blow up at her yet again.

Still, until she could decode more of the pages herself, giving him a gentle push in the right direction couldn't hurt.

"Jax," she began as they got to the cars. "Have you had any time to look at Uncle Edmond's journal?"

He turned and gave her a narrowed glance. "Some. Why do you ask?"

She hedged a bit, trying to find the best way to give him that nudge without blurting out what she'd been up to. "I was just wondering if you'd figured out the code yet."

"Elise —"

"No, Jax, come on, there could be some real clues about what happened in the days leading up to Uncle Edmond's murder! It might even reveal the killer's identity. I think you should take a closer look."

Jackson sighed. "I have been looking, El. I figured out that Edmond used a number code. It's pretty simple, but time consuming. And, as you may know, I haven't had much time to spare lately with all the other fires I've had to put out."

"I know, but this is important. I just know it. You should really dig into it — decipher some of the pages. I think there were more people involved in this scheme they were plotting than just Henry and Uncle Edmond."

Jackson leaned back on the door of the cruiser and folded his arms. "Spill it, pal. What aren't you telling me?"

She gave him the wide-eyed look of innocence. "What do you mean?"

"I know you, El. You know something, and you're trying very hard not to say it."

So much for a gentle push without confessing your sins.

"Oh, you think you're so smart," she said in a huff — then caved. "Okay, I've been looking at the pages that I photocopied, and I've decoded five or six of them."

"I knew it! You just can't help meddling, can you?"

She growled and mirrored his stance. "Nobody likes a wise-ass, Jackson."

He laughed out loud and shook his head. "And yet I like you just fine. Go figure."

She tried hard not to smile but lost the

battle. "You're such a dork, you know that?" Laughing, she shook her head. "I don't know why I even bother with you."

"Because I'm irresistible, that's why."

They stared at each other for a few moments. When Elise began to feel that familiar pull, she stepped back. "At one point, Uncle Edmond wrote that he wondered who was actually pulling the strings on the deal, and he didn't think it was Henry."

"I know. I've gotten quite a bit farther than that."

"Really? Anything interesting pop out?"

"A few things. And no," he said before she could ask, "I'm not going to discuss it with you. I have a little more to decipher before I'm ready to talk about what I may or may not have found."

When the pout she gave him didn't make a dent, she rolled her eyes. "Whatever. Anyway, I just wanted to make sure you weren't forgetting about the notebook."

"I haven't. Don't worry. I'm still working on it."

Feeling awkward and oddly shy, she searched for something to say. Failing, she jingled her keys in the air. "Well, I should get to the greenhouse. I still haven't completely cleaned up the mess Stuart made of my files."

"Yeah, I need to get back to the office."

She started to turn away and then swung back around. "And Jax?"

He opened the car door and turned to look at her over the frame of the window. "Yeah?"

"Thanks for coming out to give us the news in person, rather than calling. Sancia is wrecked over this whole thing. Sounds like they've been living in fear of Henry Kohler for quite awhile. But your coming out here like this . . . it made a difference, you know?"

"Just doing the job the only way I know how, darlin'." He smiled and climbed into the cruiser.

She watched him back out and then went to her car. Sliding in behind the wheel, she closed the door and then sat staring out the windshield.

Henry Kohler.

The more Elise thought about the man and his conniving, the angrier she got. And that he would blackmail a River Bend employee that way — over something as heartless as possible deportation — disgusted her.

Perhaps it was time someone from River Bend confronted the man good and proper.

By the time she parked in front of her greenhouse, she arrived at the conclusion that she was just the one to do it.

She would clean up her filing system and then maybe take a trip over to Kohler Winery and have a come-to-Jesus meeting with the man. She'd see what else she could learn from him, too, but she was determined to give him a piece of her mind before she left.

When she got inside the greenhouse and really looked at the mess Stuart had made, Elise realized it wasn't as bad as she'd originally thought, which helped calm her temper a bit. He'd mixed up several files and scattered a few others on the floor, but by the looks of things, she didn't think he'd found what he'd been looking for — her notes on the hybridization process.

As she worked, she couldn't get Henry and his schemes out of her head. It seemed like everywhere she turned, someone was trying to get their hands on her work.

It only took forty-five minutes or so to put her files back together, by which time she'd worked herself up all over again thinking about Henry Kohler's deception and black-mail. Grabbing her purse, she headed for the car. She was going over to the nearby winery before she changed her mind.

As she sped away from the greenhouse,

however, she decided to have a word with her grandmother. Abigail had known Henry longer than any of them and might have some tips on how to proceed.

Unfortunately, when she got to the Wine Barrel, she found that Abigail had gone into Austin with some friends, leaving Madison to mind the store.

"Why are you going over to Kohler's?" her sister asked when Elise told her of her plans.

Elise explained everything Jackson had told them. "I want to have a chat with Henry. He was trying to steal my work, and I'm going to tell him how angry it makes me. Plus, I want him to know that I know what an underhanded sleazeball he is."

Madison leaned on the counter and gave Elise a look full of reproach. "I don't think you should go over there — at least, not by yourself. Why don't you take Ross with you, or better yet, wait for Jackson?"

"Because Henry might speak more freely to me, say something he might not with one of the 'men' present," said Elise, using air quotes to denote her understanding of Henry Kohler's likely sexism when it came to business matters.

"True, but I still don't like you going over there without backup."

"I'll be fine, sweetie. This is hardly Miami Vice. I'll be back in a jiff."

Her sister gave her another doubtful look, but she ignored it. Back in the car and on the road, it didn't take but fifteen minutes before she was turning off the highway onto the long drive up to the Kohler winery residence.

Pulling up to Henry's two-story home, she parked between his Mercedes and a rental car and climbed from her vehicle, leaving her purse in the car. This wasn't going to take long.

She stormed up to the front door and rang the bell. When she got no response, she rang again. By the third ring, she was starting to get irritated, and just when she was contemplating banging on the door with her fist, it opened.

By the look on his face, finding her on his doorstep had taken Henry by surprise. He obviously didn't expect to see someone from River Bend so soon after his confession of espionage. "Elise. What are you doing here?" He looked around, as if suspecting that she was not alone.

"I'm here, Henry, because we need to talk."

"This really isn't a good time, my dear.

Why don't you come back later — or tomorrow?"

"Actually, right now works best for me," she said as she slipped past him and stalked toward the living room.

"Elise, wait —"

She heard the fear in his voice but kept going.

Good, a little taste of your own medicine, she thought. After all, the man had been terrorizing Carlos and Arturo for months.

On the heels of that thought, she rounded the corner and stepped down into the sunken living room.

And realized that Henry already had a visitor — a very familiar visitor.

Twenty-Two

"Elise, how nice of you to drop by," Stuart said with a congenial smile. "Inconvenient as it may be."

Henry stepped into the living room behind her and took her by the arm. "We're in the middle of something here, Elise. Why don't you go home and come back later? We can discuss whatever you want then."

The nervous quality to Henry's voice and the hard look in Stuart's eyes — despite his pleasant attitude — sent a shiver of apprehension down Elise's spine. Something unsavory was going on here; the atmosphere in the room was thick with it.

"Now, Henry," Stuart said with a chuckle. "I think it's a little late for that, don't you? I'm guessing our dear Elise has all sorts of questions swirling around in that pretty little head of hers. Knowing her as I do, she won't be put off that easily. I think we should bring her up to speed."

"Stuart —" Kohler began, but her ex cut him off with a look.

"Let me handle this." Stuart gestured toward the sofa. "Have a seat, darling. It *is* time to clear the air. I don't know about you, but I didn't like the way we left things last weekend after that unfortunate incident in the greenhouse."

Dropping down on the sofa, Elise raised her eyebrows. "Uh . . . if by *unfortunate incident* you mean me catching you trying to steal from me, then I have to agree. It *was* unfortunate and left a decidedly bad taste in my mouth."

Stuart went on as if she hadn't spoken. "You hurt my feelings with your allegations, and I was angry. But we've shared so much and can still have a bright future together. I had planned to contact you later to apologize for the misunderstanding and talk it all out — perhaps when you were feeling a bit more reasonable."

"I'm sorry, did you say *misunderstanding?*" She scoffed. "I don't think there was any confusion in my mind about what you were up to. Therefore, I have no interest in talking anything out with you, Stuart. And reasonable? Seriously? I thought asking you to leave was incredibly reasonable."

Stuart frowned and waved a finger at her.

"You wouldn't even let me explain, and that's not like you, sweetie." He tilted his head and pursed his lips in thought. "I blame it on Deputy Landry," he said at length. "I think he's turned your head, and not in a good way."

"What the hell are you yammering about? Jackson had nothing to do with my decision to break it off with you. That was entirely my choice. And don't try to change the subject. What's going on here, anyway?" Even as she asked the question she was starting to get somewhat of an idea.

Stuart had nagged her about her hybridization process on several occasions before she'd found him rifling through her files during Deana's wedding reception. Though she didn't want to believe it, thinking back, it was starting to make perfect sense finding him here now: he was working with Kohler. But how long it had been going on was the million-dollar question.

What she was thinking must have shown quite clearly on her face, because Stuart nodded. "Yes, I can see that you're beginning to understand."

"You and Henry are in business together, aren't you?"

"In a matter of speaking, yes." He took a sip from the wineglass in his hand and gave her another disturbing smile. "We've been . . . *collaborating* for some time now."

Lord love a goose, as her grandmother was fond of saying. How had she not seen this coming? She'd dated Stuart for over six months. Yet in all that time, she never would have dreamed he would involve himself in something as underhanded as stealing her work and giving it to the competition.

Elise turned to Henry, disbelief and sadness coloring her words. "What happened to you, Henry? Espionage, theft, blackmail? You and my grandfather built your vineyards at the same time. You were friends, for God's sake! How could you do this?"

Anger flared briefly in Kohler's rheumy eyes. "Don't you dare think to judge me, little girl. You of all people know how hard the last few years have been in this industry. I've lost crops, had to cut corners, sell vital equipment — and I'm still running in the red. I had to do something proactive or lose the vineyard." He scowled at her. "I did what I had to do."

Elise felt pity rise up inside her for the man who'd once been a good friend to her family — and then she squashed it like a bug. That man was gone, replaced by a greedy, unrecognizable stranger. Others had suffered — dealt with loss and struggled to survive — without stooping to theft or blackmail.

She glared at him. "That's a pathetic excuse for what you've done, and I think deep down you know it."

Stuart had remained silent throughout the exchange, but now he tsked. "Elise, sweetheart, where's your compassion? Henry's family isn't as invested in his vineyard as yours is. He simply wanted to save a piece of his personal history. I helped him do that."

She aimed a furious look at her ex. "Really, Stuart? And how did you help him? By attempting to steal my work for him?"

"No, darling — at least, not in the beginning. I infused his operation with cash," he said with pride.

Elise's jaw dropped. "You did what?"

"Of course, it will continue to operate under Henry's family name, but I bought the controlling interest in Kohler Winery. Although it would have been much better to have your hybridization notes, even without them I'm going to build this vineyard into the moneymaker it was meant to be. You'll see."

"Don't you mean *we're* going to do that?" Henry asked.

"Of course, Henry." Stuart smiled again.

"Forgive me. I misspoke. We're most definitely in this together."

They might be in business together, but by the look on Henry's face, he wasn't all that happy about it. Which made the next question on her mind a bit dodgier, but she had to ask.

"So, how did Uncle Edmond fit into the plan?" She glanced over at Kohler. "You told Jax he gave you a down payment in cash and was going to buy in with River Bend property."

Henry gave a short nod. "Yes, but then Laura wouldn't give him the land he wanted."

"So he was going to give you my hybridization process in place of the property?"

Again, the man nodded.

"But you took out insurance, didn't you, Henry? You tried to blackmail Carlos into stealing it as well."

She thought he would deny it, as he had with Jackson, but Kohler only shrugged. "Just hedging my bets. I wouldn't have turned his brother into Immigration, but fear can be a strong motivator."

Again, he gave Stuart a meaningful glance, and Elise got the feeling he was talking about more than blackmailing the Madera brothers. Then after a moment he looked away, and the sensation disappeared. "I figured one way or another, we'd get our hands on your notes."

"Wow. You guys were working it from all angles, weren't you? Just stringing along everyone involved." She looked back and forth between the two men. "You didn't expect Carlos to refuse to cooperate, but he did. Uncle Edmond thought he was buying into the scheme, but he was just being used to get access to my research. When he realized that, he backed out too." She glanced up at Stuart. "But in the end, you were the ace in the hole." Stuart didn't confirm or refute the allegation, but she figured she had her answer. "You thought you could eventually sweet-talk me into handing my notes over. Must have really pissed you off when I kept saying no."

Stuart heaved a sigh. "Yes, the whole thing would have gone so much smoother had you just played along like a good little girl."

"I should have suspected something was off when you kept at me to have a peek at my work. I guess when that tactic failed, you decided to take your shot during the wedding reception."

Stuart pouted and shook his head. "I don't understand how you can be so ungrateful, Elise."

"Ungrateful? What are you talking about?"

"Darling, I did this all for us and the life we were working to build! Think of it," he said as a dreamy look crossed his face. "Working at the foundation together, living the high-life in Dallas — the parties, the accolades. We would've had all that as well as a large interest in not one but *two* lucrative vineyards. It would have been such fun. We wouldn't have wanted for anything, but you had to go and ruin it."

Elise burst into laughter. "Oh my God! What a load of crap," she said when she could contain herself. "You didn't do any of this for *us,* Stuart. Face it. Everything you've done here, you've done out of greed and the pursuit of power. You're despicable. And I'm thinking a little bit crazy. I don't know how I didn't see it before."

Stuart drew himself up as his features turned to stone. "Do not call me that. Do you hear me? I am *not* crazy."

"Yeah, you keep telling yourself that." She turned and leveled a cool look in Kohler's direction. "So, Henry, when Uncle Edmond told you he was backing out of the deal, was it really Carlos who hit him with that rock? Or was murder something else you just *had to do*?"

The older man shook his head and wiped

his mouth with the back of his hand as a terrified look crossed his face. "I didn't have any part in your uncle's murder," he stammered.

"Now, that's not entirely true, Henry," Stuart said and giggled like a little girl.

Kohler's hands shook as he put them out to her in a plea for understanding. "Elise, Carlos hit him in a panic, but neither one of us killed him. Eddy was alive when we left him there. I swear it. Please. You have to let this go."

"What do you mean by *not entirely true*?" she asked, ignoring Henry and turning to Stuart. "What part could Henry have played if Carlos was the one to hit Uncle Edmond with that rock?"

It was Stuart's turn to laugh out loud, and the odd sound of it sent a chill coursing through her. "What did I tell you, Henry? She's as curious as she is stubborn! You know, Elise, that's always been your problem. You just don't know when to quit."

"Stuart, answer me. What part did Henry play?" She looked over at Kohler. "Did you come back and finish the job — use that rock to set Carlos up?"

"No!" Henry shouted.

"Oh, I think Deputy Landry is going to find that it wasn't that rock that killed your uncle at all."

The look in Stuart's eyes when he spoke had Elise's stomach doing a slow roll. "How do you know that?" she asked him.

"Elise, please stop," Henry begged. "What's done is done. You don't understand what you've stumbled into here."

This time when Stuart laughed it was low and evil-sounding, but he was clearly enjoying himself. "Where's your cane, Henry? That fabulous oak cane you always use? I haven't seen it for . . . several weeks now."

Lord, I think he really might be crazy, she thought. Stuart's creepy attitude was starting to scare her, and with his comment, a frightening notion exploded in her head.

If Stuart was the mastermind behind the theft scheme, was it possible he was capable of murder? A month ago — hell, a week ago — she wouldn't have even entertained the idea. But seeing him now, the strange look in his eyes . . .

"You know, I think you're right, Henry," she said and stood. She needed to get away from both of these men, and fast. "Maybe I should go back to River Bend and let you two conclude your business. We can finish this conversation later."

Preferably with the police present and a straight-jacket on hand.

Stuart turned and set his wineglass on the mantel behind him. "No. I don't think so," he said. When he swung back to them, he pulled a small, lethal-looking pistol out of his jacket pocket and pointed it in her direction.

Terror like she'd never felt in her life sprung up and grabbed her by the throat. "Stuart! What are you doing?"

"Elise, come on now. You've figured it out, you know you have, whether you want to acknowledge it or not. It's written all over your face."

She swallowed hard and struggled to find her voice through her fear. "I don't know what you mean."

"Oh, sweetie, you've never been a good liar."

"Stuart, please, no!" Henry said.

"Shut up, Kohler," Stuart snarled.

"Henry?" Elise put out her hand to the man, but he clammed up and turned away from her, visibly trembling with fear.

"You see, darling, I watched Henry and Carlos meet with your uncle that evening from the trees along the river. They didn't even know I was there. Henry had left his cane behind at the house, which was fortuitous. When Carlos knocked Edmond out and they left, I realized I had a perfect opportunity. I beat your uncle to death with Henry's oak cane."

"No," she whispered, shaking her head.

"Oh yes. I've put it safely away, as insurance. My original plan was to eventually leave it where Deputy Do-Right would find it, and Henry would be charged with the crime. But I found that the fear was, as Henry put it earlier, a strong motivator."

"You're insane," she replied, trying to get a breath around the constriction in her chest. She couldn't believe this was happening. Her ex-boyfriend had killed her uncle in cold blood.

Stuart frowned and gave her a steely look. "I told you not to call me that. You know, we could have had it all. Up until a few minutes ago, I was willing to give you a second chance. However, now I realize that it was just my nostalgic side speaking."

"Stuart, this has to stop," Henry wheezed. "I won't be a party to a third murder. Do you hear me?"

Elise gasped and felt her blood run cold. "*Third* murder? What are you saying, Henry?" The moment the question was out of her mouth her brain seized on the answer. "Oh God. Are you talking about Harmony Gates?"

Stuart sighed. "Poor, pathetic Harmony.

She was a faithful little soldier in the beginning. She gathered and passed on all sorts of useful information to me when I couldn't be here."

"You mean she spied for you," Henry muttered.

"She was my eyes and ears, yes," Stuart replied. "But then she got a bit too pushy, started making impossible demands."

Her ex-boyfriend was a murderer. That fact and a myriad of terrible questions collided in Elise's mind, though she wasn't sure she wanted to learn the answers that went with them.

On the flip side, she had very few alternatives. With her cell phone in her purse in the car, her best option seemed to be to keep Stuart talking and wait for an opportunity to flee.

She wished now that she hadn't been so hasty in wanting to confront Henry. Following that impulse had gotten her into this mess in the first place, but at least Madison knew where she'd gone. If she could only keep Stuart distracted long enough, hopefully, help would arrive or she would get an opening to run.

"What kind of demands did Harmony make?" she made herself ask.

Stuart waved his free hand in dismissal.

"She began to harass me for more and more attention. It was annoying and tedious."

"How did you two hook up in the first place? I mean, it's not like you ran in the same circles or had friends in common."

"No, of course not." He grinned. "Actually, you were responsible for our 'hookup', darling."

Elise gaped at him. "I beg your pardon? How was *I* responsible?"

"Remember my first visit here, when we went out to your artist friend's Harvest party? We ran into her and that clod of a boyfriend she was with, and you introduced us. Later in the evening, she approached me and was quite flirtatious. I gave her my card, and, as they say, the rest is history."

"So *you* were the new fiancé she'd been talking about after her breakup with Bud?"

Stuart barked out a harsh laugh. "Oh Lord, no! I was very clear about our relationship parameters from the beginning."

"Then where did she get the idea that you two were engaged?"

Henry grunted. "Strung her along just like the rest of us."

Stuart bristled. "I can't be responsible for what others take into their heads to believe," he replied. Then he addressed Elise: "I told Harmony on several occasions that you were my future. On that point, I was firm."

Elise nodded. "But she wasn't taking no for an answer, was she? What happened, Stuart? Did she give you an ultimatum — threaten to expose your scheme?"

"She caught me alone down by the Wine Barrel at the wedding reception. You remember — when I went to make that call to the office? Anyway, she demanded that I meet her later; said if I didn't, she'd tell you about my plans here with Kohler. Then that stupid ex-boyfriend of hers showed up whining like a sap, and I was able to slip away."

"But she didn't give up?"

He shook his head, explaining as though this were simple logic. "You have to understand, I couldn't have her jeopardize the entire operation. She'd become a liability that I had to remove. When she called later, I told her where and when I would meet her. Though I have to say, I didn't count on her being found so quickly."

Even though she really didn't want to know any more, Elise asked the next question on her mind. If she got out of this situation alive, she wanted to be able to explain everything. "What did you strangle Harmony with, Stuart? There was nothing found at the scene."

Stuart fairly beamed with pride. "I went to the meeting prepared. I took some rope out of your brother's tool shed."

Dear God, he'd killed Harmony right under their noses — and he'd stolen the murder weapon from her brother to do it.

The horror she felt at his admission must have been mirrored on her face because he chuckled. "Don't worry, darling. I put it back where I found it."

Sick to her stomach, she blurted out what she was feeling before she remembered her goal of keeping him talking. "You're as crazy as an outhouse rat!"

Stuart narrowed his eyes at that word and waved the pistol at her. "And you, my dear, are now just another liability I need to remove."

Before she could reply, Elise was taken by surprise as Henry grabbed her by the arm and pulled her behind him, shielding her with his body. "That's enough, Stuart. I'm putting an end to this whole fiasco right now. I won't let you harm another innocent person."

Stuart's mouth dropped open and his eyebrows shot up. "Excuse me? You aren't the one holding the gun, so I don't believe that's your call."

"Be that as it may, I'm done being afraid

of you. I'll turn myself in before I'll kowtow to you any further."

"You know, I should have gotten rid of you right after I killed Edmond," Stuart said matter-of-factly. "It would have been cleaner that way. Still, you were very useful for a time. But if you no longer want to play by my rules, that's fine. Fortunately, I can remedy that problem as well. A two-for-one deal."

"You'll never get away with this, Stuart," Elise spoke up from behind Henry. "My family knows where I am."

It was a bluff, and they all knew it, but she wasn't ready to die.

Stuart just laughed. "Even if that were true, it won't be an issue with what I have in mind, darling. Now, why don't we all take a walk out to the winery?"

TWENTY-THREE

Jackson hadn't been back at the office even ten minutes when the call came in from the Travis County medical examiner confirming what his gut had already told him. Carlos Madera was off the hook: the rock that he'd assaulted Edmond with was not the murder weapon.

Although it was a bit of a disappointment, it wasn't exactly back to square one. He'd been truthful with Elise earlier about deciphering Edmond's journal. He just hadn't related how *much* of it he'd decoded — or what he'd learned from the pages. But if his suspicions were on the mark, she wasn't going to like the outcome.

Once he'd figured out the code Edmond had used, unraveling the man's narrative had gone pretty fast. By the sound of it, Jackson figured he'd gotten a bit further along than Elise had before deciding to go to the end of the journal and work his way backward. That had proved to be much more illuminating; with what he'd learned so far, he was sure he was close to breaking the case wide open.

In the two weeks before he was killed, Edmond Beckett had discovered not only that Henry's vineyard was in financial trouble but also the identity of the money-man bailing Kohler out. That discovery had probably started the ball rolling and had ultimately led to the man's murder.

Though Edmond hadn't mentioned the mysterious benefactor by name, from the clues he'd left in the journal, Jackson suspected he'd known who was involved. And if his own theory was correct, it would also answer the question of how Harmony Gates's death was connected to all this.

His thoughts were interrupted by a knock at his office door. Looking up from the journal, he found Jim Stockton standing in his doorway.

"You talk to the ME?" Jim asked.

Jackson nodded. "Just a few minutes ago."

"And? What's the verdict, boss?"

"Not the murder weapon. There was some soil trace in the area behind Beckett's right ear where Carlos indicated he'd hit him. That lines up with the statements from both Carlos and Henry. According to the ME, whatever was used to bash in Edmond Beckett's skull was cylindrical in nature and left no trace evidence in the wounds."

"Huh?" Jim considered for a moment. "Like a piece of pipe?"

"No tool marks, and again, no trace."

"Maybe a bat or a club of some kind?"

Jackson leaned back in his chair. "Could be. But from the dimensions of the wounds, the ME thought it would have to be something small in diameter, but with enough length to swing with full force."

"Pool cue? Denny Rodriguez has several pool tables out at El Diablo. He'd have plenty of cues to choose from."

"True." Jackson flipped through the journal on the desk and thought for a moment. "But from what I've been able to put together from Edmond's notes, Denny didn't have anything to do with the scheme he and Kohler were involved in. He was just the guy's bookie."

Jim sauntered over to the desk and sat down in the visitor's chair. "What else have you found in there?"

"Well, I think I've found the link between Edmond and Harmony Gates — or at least the way their murders were connected."

"Really?" Jim sat forward, and his brown eyes lit up with interest. "How's that?"

Jackson turned a few more pages. "It seems the key to this whole mess was Edmond finding out that Henry was having money trouble — and about the double-cross."

"How so?"

"Well, Edmond started doing some reconnaissance. He says here that one evening he was snooping around Kohler Winery's processing room, and he heard someone enter the building. He tucks back behind the tanks and listens in on a meeting between Kohler and another guy. Evidently, Henry was thanking the man for the financial bail-out and promised to get his hands on Elise Beckett's hybridization process. They were going to cut Edmond out of the deal as soon as that happened."

"Does it say who this guy was?"

"No, but he does call him by the nickname Fancy Pants."

"Fancy Pants? What the hell does that mean?"

"I don't know what to tell you. Edmond liked nicknames. Once he met someone, he'd hang one on them and never call them by their given name again. Used to call Ross Boy-O and me Sidekick. Then when I joined the force, he changed mine to Deputy Dog."

Jim laughed and shook his head. "Takes all kinds."

"I guess. Anyway, I remember hearing him call someone Fancy Pants a few months back — and I don't think it's a coincidence finding it here in the journal."

"You think it's the same guy?"

"Yes, I do."

"Who was it?"

Jackson rubbed his forehead where a headache was beginning to brew and then looked over at the other deputy. "Stuart Jenkins, Elise's former boyfriend."

"Uh-oh." Jim whistled through his teeth. "That's not good. No wonder Edmond was so peeved."

"Yeah. An outsider horning in on his scheme to put the screws to his family wouldn't go over well."

"But it was okay for him to do it, right?" Chuckling, Jim shook his head.

"Something like that. Edmond wasn't the most stand-up guy I've ever met. However, this same guy dating his niece would have been salt in the wound."

"So, you like this Stuart guy for the murder?"

"I don't know. I hope not, for Elise's sake, but my gut is telling me that's where this is leading."

"Okay. I can see motive there. Edmond starts making waves and says he's going to tell the family all about it. This Stuart guy can't have that. It would jeopardize his operation on several fronts. But how do you figure a connection to Harmony Gates?"

"Edmond told me," he said, tapping on the journal. "In here he talks about witnessing another meeting outside Kohler's residence one night, between Harmony and Fancy Pants." Jackson flipped back in his decoded notes to the page he was looking for. "He says they were arguing about something, but he couldn't hear what was being said. Then the guy grabs her and kisses her. After that, the guy says something else, and she nods. Then she gets into a car and leaves."

"Oh man. If you're right and this Stuart Jenkins is Fancy Pants, then Edmond would've considered it a three-strike deal. The guy's horning in on the scheme, dating his niece, *and* getting a little on the side from Harmony behind Elise's back."

"Yeah. I'm thinking that would be a pretty volatile mix."

"And you think this guy not only killed Beckett but did Harmony too?"

"It's a premise that works for me. Edmond's stirring the pot, threatening to tell the world what he's discovered. He ends up with his head caved in for his troubles. Maybe Harmony was starting to cause him grief as well."

"Assuming she knew what was going on," Jim said.

"Or maybe it was something as simple as jealousy — not wanting to share him with anyone else. She starts hinting about letting Elise in on their secret, and he gets rid of the problem there too."

"It's a good theory," Jim agreed, "and it would explain why Harmony's house was ransacked; Jenkins would have had to make sure there wasn't anything there to connect him to her. And he could have been at Edmond's house for the same reason when Pam showed up looking for her money. So he knocks her out and makes a quick getaway." Then Jim frowned. "But if Edmond doesn't call him anything but Fancy Pants in the journal, how do you prove it?"

"I've asked Bud Thornton to come in and take a look at some pictures."

"Bud? What does Harmony's ex have to do with this?"

Jackson leaned forward and shook his head. "Nothing directly. But last Saturday there was an incident between him and Harmony at Deana Wilkinson's wedding reception."

"Yeah, I heard about it. So?"

"Well, when we broke up the argument, Darrell took Bud aside to hear his side of the quarrel. Last night, I went back over Darrell's report; Bud said something that caught my interest."

"What was that?"

"He said he went looking for Harmony to ask her to reconsider their break-up, and he found her down by the Wine Barrel talking to some guy. He said the exchange looked *intimate* at first but then turned ugly."

"You think the guy was Stuart Jenkins."

"Maybe. He attended the wedding as Elise's date, and I personally saw him head toward the Wine Barrel to make a call just before Harmony and Bud had their argument."

"I don't know, Jackson. Even if Bud can identify Jenkins from a group of photos, it's still all circumstantial," Jim pointed out. "It doesn't prove that he's the man Edmond called Fancy Pants, nor does it prove he killed either of them."

Jackson pulled a bottle of aspirin out of his desk drawer and dry swallowed a couple of tablets. "No, it doesn't, but I've got a strong feeling about this. It'll give me a reason to bring him in for questioning, and he'd better have an explanation that I can buy."

As he dropped the aspirin bottle back into the drawer, there was another knock at the door.

"Hey, Jackson," Darrell Yancy spoke from the doorway. "Bud's here. Where do you want him?"

"Put him in Interview One. We'll be right there."

"All right," Jim said with a smile. "Let the games begin."

"Damn straight."

Pulling out a file of photos from the bin on his desk, Jackson inserted Stuart's into the mix. He really hoped he was wrong about all this, but deep down, he knew he wasn't. He wondered how Elise would take the news. Unfortunately, he couldn't think about that now. He had a job to do, and like he'd told her on several occasions, he had to follow the evidence wherever it led — whether he liked it or not.

Down the hall in Interview One, Jackson found a haggard-looking Bud Thornton waiting and thanked him for coming in.

"Oh, hey, no problem, Jackson. If it will help catch the bastard that did this terrible thing to my Harmony, I'll do whatever I can."

Jim patted the man on the shoulder as he sat down next to him. "We understand how hard this is, Bud. We appreciate your help."

"Bud, tell us about Deana's wedding reception, particularly when you went to find Harmony. You told Deputy Yancy that you found her down by the Wine Barrel having a conversation with a man."

Bud's head bobbed up and down. "Yeah. They were talking real close, you know? I thought for a minute that maybe he was the guy she dumped me for."

"Why did you think that?" Jim asked.

"I don't know. I guess the way she was touching his arm and the soft look on her face. She used to look at me that way . . . back when we were together."

"You said you thought that for a minute," Jackson prodded. "Did something make you change your mind?"

Bud pressed his lips together and his brows lowered. "They started to argue. She poked him in the chest a couple of times, and he slapped her hand away. That's when I moved in. Nobody was gonna treat my girl that way."

"Did you ask Harmony who he was?"

"I did," Bud replied. "But she just said it

was none of my business anymore who she talked to. I followed her up the driveway trying to get her to talk to me, but, well, you were there, Jackson. You saw how that turned out."

Jackson felt for the guy. He was obviously torn up over losing Harmony, even though she'd dumped him and tried to leave him behind. "I'm sorry for your loss, Bud. I truly am."

Tears welled up in the man's eyes and leaked down his face. "Thanks, Jackson. She was my whole world, you know? Hell, we'd been together since junior high. I was gonna marry her."

"I know." Jackson handed him the box of tissues from the end of the table. "Bud, there is one more thing I need you to do."

"Sure. What's that?"

Jackson spread ten photos out on the table facing the man. "I need you to look at these and see if the man you saw Harmony with that day is here."

Bud started at one end of the line of photos and began scrutinizing each. When he got to the picture of Jenkins, he stopped and tapped the image. "That's him. That's the guy."

"You're sure?"

Again, Bud's head bobbed up and down.

"Yeah. Is this the guy who killed Harmony, Jackson?"

"To be honest, I don't know. But I'm going to find out."

As Jackson started to gather the photos, Bud stopped him. "Wait — let me look at that again."

Jackson slid Stuart's photo back across the table. "Is there a problem, Bud? Having second thoughts?"

"No, this is definitely the guy I saw with Harmony. I thought he looked familiar that day, but I couldn't place him. Then I got sidetracked with Harmony and what happened, and I forgot about it. But I just remembered where I've seen him before."

Jim sat forward. "Yeah? And where was that?"

Bud looked over at Jim and blinked. "Well, this can't be the guy that killed Harmony, can it?"

"Why do you say that, Bud?"

"Because Elise introduced us to him at the Harvest party awhile back. I don't remember his name, but this is her boyfriend." He gave Jackson a perplexed look. "Why would Elise's boyfriend be arguing with my Harmony? They would hardly even know each other."

Jackson glanced over at Jim before answering. "We don't know anything for sure yet, Bud. We're just following all the threads and trying to make some connections. But you've been a big help. Thanks again for coming in."

Back in his office, Jackson tried Elise's cell phone. He wanted to see if she'd talked to Stuart since giving him the boot on Saturday afternoon. When it went to voicemail, he left a message in frustration as a wave of apprehension washed over him.

It was probably nothing. She was always leaving her phone at home or in the greenhouse, so there was no reason to jump to conclusions. Still, this could be really important. He thought he'd better take a run out to River Bend and talk to her in person.

Grabbing his keys, he tagged Jim in the hallway and asked him to ride along.

Twenty minutes later they were pulling up in front of Ross's house.

"You weren't gone long." Ross said when he met them at the door. "I hope you have good news."

"I do. We'll be releasing Carlos shortly. The ME ruled out the rock as the murder weapon."

"That's not good news, its *great* news.

Sancia will be so relieved."

"I'm sure she will. But that's actually not the reason we're here."

Ross frowned. "Geez, what now? You've got your 'I've got more bad news to share' face on. What's happened?"

"Maybe nothing. I just need to talk to Elise. Do you know where she is?"

"El? Isn't she at the greenhouse? She said she was going to clean up the mess that jerk she was dating made of her files. When she walked you out and didn't come back, I just assumed that's where she went."

"Her car's not there or at the main house. We'll stop in and ask Laura and Miss Abby if they've seen her. Maybe she left word with them as to where she was going."

Ross shook his head. "Won't do you any good. Gram went to Austin with some friends and won't be back until tonight, and Mom went to Giddings with Neil."

"Well, hell." Jackson rubbed his forehead again, wishing the damn aspirin would take effect.

"What's going on, Jax? Why do you need to talk to Elise so bad?"

Jackson exchanged looks with Jim. "I need to ask her some questions about Stuart."

"Stuart?" Ross made a face. "What for? The guy's a douche."

Jim smiled at Ross's description. "We've found evidence possibly linking him to the scheme your uncle and Henry Kohler were hatching."

"You're kidding." Ross stared at them with his mouth hanging open. "What kind of evidence?"

"Look, Ross, we can't go into that. It's an ongoing investigation," Jackson said. "We're going to pull him in for questioning, but I wanted to talk to El first."

Ross studied his face for a moment, and then suddenly grabbed his arm. "Is she in trouble? I mean, you don't think her safety is at risk, do you?"

"Whoa. Calm down, buddy," Jackson said, trying not to think about that possibility himself. "I'm sure she's fine. I just want to talk to her, that's all."

"Okay. Then let's go find her."

Jackson shook his head. "Again, what part of 'this is police business' don't you get? Let us handle it, Ross."

"Screw your police business, Jax. She's my sister. I'm going with you."

Jackson sighed, but before he could argue further, Jim spoke up. "Would you two quit your damn squabbling? Let's just go, for God's sake. I've got dinner plans."

Jackson and Ross stared at each other a

few seconds and then both turned and headed toward the door. They piled into the cruiser and started up the driveway toward the highway.

Jackson was searching his mind trying to think of where Elise might have gone when Ross spoke up. "Stop in at the Wine Barrel. Maybe Maddy knows something."

"Good idea," Jackson replied as he pulled the cruiser into the parking lot.

The three climbed out and went inside. Madison was helping a couple with their wine selection and waved when she noticed them. Speaking briefly to the couple to excuse herself, she came over to where he, Ross, and Jim stood waiting.

"Wow, what a nice surprise. Are you three looking to buy some really good wine?" she asked with a curious smile. But that smile slowly faded as she took in their faces. "What's wrong? Has something else happened?"

Jackson spoke up first. "No, darlin', nothing's wrong. We're just looking for El. She's not on the property, and we hoped you might know where she went."

Madison made a *pfft* sound and wrinkled her nose. "Is she in trouble again? I told her she should wait, but you know El. When she gets something into her head, there's no talking her out of it."

"So you've seen her?" Ross asked.

"Sure. She was in here about forty-five minutes ago."

Jackson clung desperately to the little scrap of patience he had left. "Where'd she go, Maddy?"

"She went over to Kohler's Winery. She was hell-bent on having it out with Henry about his scheme to steal her work."

Twenty-Four

Elise tried to stay calm and concentrate on putting one foot in front of the other as Stuart directed her and Henry from the living room to the back of the house. When they got to the kitchen, he instructed Henry to find some duct tape.

"I don't have any," Henry stated, crossing his arms and giving Stuart a mutinous look.

"Really? But it's such a handy thing to have around the house. Would you rather I disabled Elise here in the kitchen with a round to her kneecap?"

Stuart lowered his weapon, pointing the barrel at Elise's left knee, and panic coursed through her body.

"Since you're going to kill her later anyway and then kill yourself, it doesn't make much difference to me. But this way would mean more work for you, as you'd have to carry her to the winery."

Henry's eyes widened as he put up his

hands. "Okay, okay, hang on a minute. I might have some around here somewhere."

Elise's legs went weak with relief when Henry pulled a roll from a drawer.

"Now, bind her hands together nice and tight. My sweetie is smart and can be very resourceful; I wouldn't want her slipping out of it. Once you've finished with her, we'll get your hands secured as well."

Elise looked up at Henry as he began to tape her wrists together, and the fear she saw in his eyes had her heart pounding a bit faster. Dying at the hands of a lunatic on Kohler property with no family in sight was not the way she wanted to go out.

She knew Stuart intended to take them to the winery's processing room. If he killed them there and hid their bodies, it could be days before they were found. The thought of her body crammed behind a row of tanks, bloating and decomposing, made her stomach roll.

No way! Don't think about that, you idiot. You have to hold on and keep your eyes open for any available opportunity. Jackson will come for you.

But short of him having telepathy, she knew the chance of that happening was slim to nil. With the exception of Madison, nobody even knew where she was.

Once Henry had finished taping her hands, Stuart held the gun on him with one hand and taped Henry's hands together with the other before shoving them both out the back door. Distracted by the wild thoughts rioting in her head, Elise stumbled as she went down the deck stairs. She would have fallen had Henry not turned at the opportune time and stopped her plunge.

"Nice job, Henry," Stuart said, beaming at him. "Very spry for an old goat."

"Oh, shut up, you evil little ass."

Surprise flashed across Stuart's face at the older man's remark. "Henry, I seriously don't think you understand how this works." He spoke as if he were talking to a small child. "Let me explain. The one holding the gun makes the rules and gives the orders. And let me also mention that name-calling is not going to help your situation."

"What difference does it make? You're going to kill us anyway," Henry grumbled.

"That's true. Still, it's how we carry ourselves in times of stress that shows our character." Stuart waved the pistol in the general direction of the winery. "Now get moving."

As they started up the long driveway, Elise searched the surrounding area for any means of escape but found nothing helpful.

There was no cover, nowhere to run. Stuart would shoot them before they could get clear. Even if there was something to hide behind, he would just hunt them down.

Knowing the winery's processing room was the end of the line — and most probably the end of her life — Elise decided to try reasoning with him. It couldn't hurt, and it might give her the time to think of something else. She stopped and turned to face him. "Stuart, please, this isn't like you. You're not this cold-blooded. You don't want to do this. I know you don't."

He tilted his head and seemed to consider his options. For a moment she thought she saw regret in his gaze. "You're right, darling," he said at length. "I don't."

But just when hope was beginning to bloom, the look in his eyes changed, and he shook his head. She realized then that it had been a wasted effort.

"Unfortunately, I have no choice," he said. "Don't you see? You know all my secrets now. So that makes you another loose end, and I can't have that, can I? It's nothing personal."

"But Stuart —"

He cut her off with a heartless laugh. "Oh, I know what you're going to say. You won't tell anyone what you know, right? But, sweetie, how can I trust you now, after all that's been said?" He gestured to Kohler with the gun in his hand. "Henry here has been easy to keep in line up until now because I held all the cards. His prints are all over your uncle's murder weapon, and I have that stashed away in a safe place. But what guarantee do I have that *you* won't blab?" He shook his head, his eyes never leaving hers. "This is much cleaner. It really is the best way."

She could see now that there was nothing more she could say that would make any difference. The Stuart she thought she knew was gone, replaced by this homicidal maniac who'd obviously lost his grip on reality.

As if confirming that point, he gave her a too-bright smile and motioned for them to start walking again with a sweep of his arm, as if they were about to take a walk in the park together.

Turning to follow Henry, hysteria began to build in her chest, but she worked hard to push it back. Freaking out wouldn't get her out of this mess. What she needed was some kind of logical plan. This whole nightmare was like a scene out of a spy thriller or an action film. There must be something she could do.

And with that, an idea popped into her head.

It was crazy and probably wouldn't work. But a good defense always involved having a kick-ass offense. And she and Henry were running out of time.

Okay, here goes nothing, she thought before saying a quick prayer. With her next few steps she pretended to trip, dropping to her hands and knees in the gravel driveway.

"Oh, for God's sake," Stuart muttered, coming up behind her. "Dragging your feet isn't going to get you anywhere, Elise. You're being childish. Now get up."

As he reached down to grab her, she scooped up as much gravel as her taped hands would allow and hoped it would be enough. Swinging around, she flung the whole of it into his face.

Stuart cried out and shouted several expletives as he lurched backward. And when he did she screamed, "Run, Henry!"

The older man took off up the road toward the vineyard with the speed of a much younger fellow. Scrambling to her feet, Elise ran for the winery instead. It wasn't the best choice, considering it was the place where Stuart intended to kill them both, but she had few options. Plus, with them running in different directions, it would split Stuart's focus. He couldn't go after both of them. If she could get inside and find a hiding spot before he could follow, it would at least buy her some time.

A shot rang out as she threw open the door. She heard it ricochet off the building somewhere close by but didn't stop to look back.

The moment Elise was inside the winery she heard a second shot, and she quickly closed and locked the door. She knew it was a futile measure but hoped it would slow him down and give her a chance to think. He'd eventually find a way in — and he might still kill her — but she was going to make him work to accomplish the task.

Pausing to get her bearings, she looked to her right. The hall opened up onto the processing room with its rows of large tanks and labyrinth of pipes and valves.

Nope, she thought, *definitely not going in there.*

At the end of the hall to the left was an office, and she raced in that direction hoping to find something to use to free her hands.

Throwing open the door, she dashed inside and immediately began searching the desk drawers. Though there were no scissors to be found, she did run across a small

Swiss Army knife. Figuring it would do the trick, she fumbled to open it.

With her hands shaking, she dropped it once. It took several tries, but she finally got it open. Turning it around so that the point faced her chest, she began to see-saw back and forth against the duct tape at her wrists. Within moments her diminutive tool had sliced through her bonds, and she was free of them.

Unfortunately, there was no time to celebrate her good fortune. Even as she rejoiced in her clever escape, a banging at the front door reminded her that she wasn't out of the woods just yet. She could hear Stuart yelling and knew it wouldn't be long before he gained access to the building. She had to find a place to hide. But where?

It was then that she noticed the slim window above the credenza on the opposing wall. Although it was a crank-out style, she hoped it would open far enough for her to shimmy up and out.

Climbing up onto the console, she tried to turn the window's lever, but it was frozen in place and wouldn't budge. She stared at it with annoyance. *Just my lousy luck!* she thought.

Breaking the glass was an option if she could find something heavy enough, but she worried that Stuart would hear the sound. That's all she needed — to crawl out of the window over broken glass only to find him waiting for her on the other side. So she dismissed that idea and concentrated on getting the lever to rotate.

With great effort, she worked it back and forth until it finally started to move and the window began to lift outward.

It was slow going — too slow — and the lever was getting more difficult to turn. Then it stopped altogether and no matter how hard she tried, she couldn't get it to move any farther. Ripping off the screen in frustration and tossing it over her shoulder, she eyed the opening. She could probably wiggle through, but it was going to be a tight squeeze.

Looking over her shoulder, she forced herself to be still and listen. Worrying her bottom lip with her teeth, her anxiety skyrocketed when she realized the banging had stopped. Where had Stuart gone? At least when he was pounding on the door she knew his location. Now he could be anywhere. He could pop up when she least expected him, like some crazed jack-in-the-box. It was a frightening thought.

Then she heard the sound that had her breath backing up in her chest.

The front door of the building was thrown open, the sound reverberating through the space like a gunshot as it hit the opposite wall.

"El-*ise*?" Stuart called out in a sing-song voice. "Where have you gone, darling?"

"Elise, don't move!" Henry yelled. Then she heard a sickening thud and the sound of something heavy hitting the floor; she could only assume it was Henry.

Looking back at the window, her heart sank. The opening appeared to be big enough, but what if she tried to climb out and got stuck? Stuart would find her, and her bid for freedom would be over before it had begun. She had to make a quick decision.

Climbing down off the credenza as quietly as she could, she looked around the room for a hiding place. She briefly considered the two large storage cabinets along the adjacent wall but figured Stuart would check them both first thing.

Tip-toeing over to the old wooden desk, she eased the chair out and looked into the knee-hole. It was a solid piece of furniture that went clear to the floor on all sides.

It was a gamble. If he found her, she would be trapped with nowhere to go, but she was out of options. It would have to do.

Scooting into the tiny space, she pulled the chair back in toward her body as far as she could. If she was lucky, Stuart would see the screen on the floor with the window halfway open and think that she'd escaped.

Hearing his footsteps coming down the hall, she clapped her hand over her mouth to stifle the scream that threatened to burst from between her clenched teeth. Moments later, her terror grew when he paused just outside the office. Holding her breath, she sent up a prayer as she heard him enter the room.

"Darling? Are you in here?" he asked as if he thought she would actually answer him. "What the —"

When she heard the surprise and then anger in his voice, she figured he'd spotted the screen on the floor and the open window.

"Oh no, you didn't," he said.

She listened as he threw open the doors on both of the cabinets, just as she'd feared he would. She did a short happy dance inside her head that she'd decided against hiding there. It was followed up with another prayer that he wouldn't think to check under the desk.

Then there was silence for what seemed like an eternity.

What is he doing?

Her heartbeat was so loud in her own ears that she was certain he would hear it too. In her mind's eye she envisioned him staring at her hiding place, convinced that any moment now he would jerk the chair away and discover her there.

As the seconds ticked by, she could tell he was still in the room but had just stopped moving. When she heard the sound of gravel crunching outside, she knew why.

A car was coming up the driveway.

And her hope soared.

"Dammit! What now?" he muttered to himself. She heard him climb up onto the credenza to look out the window. "Well, well, Deputy Do-Right, and his trusty sidekick. And Ross too. Why, it's just a party, isn't it?"

Oh, thank you, Jesus, she thought, as relief poured through her.

Jackson and Ross were here. They had come for her, and this nightmare would soon be over. But the happiness she felt at their arrival was short-lived. With Stuart's next words, it became clear to her that he had no intention of giving up or running away.

"Come on in, boys," he said then giggled like the lunatic he'd become. "I've got enough ammo for everyone."

In that moment she knew with certainty that the decent man she'd once known had completely lost his mind.

She heard him climb down then, his footsteps getting softer as he left the room and headed down the hall toward the front door.

Dear God, they had no idea what they were walking into. He would kill them all.

Twenty-Five

She had to warn them. That one thought kept circling Elise's brain. Jackson, Ross, and whoever was with them had no idea they were walking into a trap. She had to do something and fast.

But that meant leaving her hiding spot, which she was terrified to do. She had no idea how far away Stuart had gone, and if she revealed herself too soon, they would all be done for. Unfortunately, she had no choice; if she did nothing, the guys wouldn't stand a chance.

Slipping off her sandals, she set them on the seat of the chair in front of her. Whatever plan she came up with would need to be executed with the utmost silence.

Drawing her threadbare courage around her like a shield, Elise held her breath and pushed the chair far enough away from the desk to slither out of the knee-hole. Peeking up over the lip of the desk, she listened for any sound or movement.

Nothing.

Hoping Stuart wasn't doing the same thing and just waiting for her to emerge, she stood up and skirted the desk, tip-toeing her way to the door. Holding her breath, she took a quick look into the hall.

She spotted Henry, lying on the floor along the wall just outside the processing room. He appeared to be unconscious, but she had no way of knowing how badly he was injured. She couldn't worry about that now. Warning her loved ones and thwarting her evil ex-boyfriend was her top priority right now.

Stuart was nowhere to be seen, but she wasn't taking any chances. He might have been distracted by Jackson's unexpected arrival, but Elise suspected he hadn't gone far. She didn't know if he actually believed she'd escaped, though she was sure he wouldn't have forgotten about her either way.

Just as she was working up the nerve to move into the hallway, Stuart came out of a room on her side of the corridor. She ducked back into the office and held her breath. She could hear him muttering to himself, but from where she stood, she couldn't understand what he was saying.

Sneaking another quick look, she watched him open the front door a sliver and peer through the crack. He was obviously checking Jackson's location, planning to get the drop on him and the others when they found the residence empty and came this way.

She'd be damned if she would allow that.

Pulling her head back out of Stuart's sightline, she turned and went to the open cabinets. She was going to need a weapon, or at least something she could use as one. But after a brief search of the shelves, she found nothing that would work.

Then an idea struck her. She remembered seeing something here in the office that would fit the bill quite well. Whipping around, she stared across the room and zeroed in on a lone golf club standing in the corner behind the desk.

Hurrying to its location, she snatched it up with a satisfied grin spreading across her face. It was a driver with a good-sized head and sturdy shaft. Perfect. Now all she had to do was get close enough to Stuart to use it. She flexed her fingers on the handle and tried a few practice swings, imagining his head as a target.

Get ready, you homicidal lunatic. Mama's lookin' for a hole-in-one!

Going back to the door, she peeked around the corner and saw Stuart leaning over Henry. She figured he was checking to see if the man was lucid enough to fight back anymore. When he was satisfied, Stuart got up and went back into the room she'd seen him come out of moments before.

She assumed he was going back and forth between the door and the window in that room to keep tabs on the progress of their visitors. She only hoped he would be in there long enough for her to make it closer to the front door.

The problem was cover. She wasn't sure she was stealthy enough to sneak up the long hallway and surprise Stuart without getting caught mid-stream. She'd have to do it in increments.

There was another door between where she was currently holed up and the room he'd gone into. Although it was only a fifteen- or twenty-foot dash from the office, if that door was locked she would be screwed. She had no way to check and time was ticking away.

It was a chance she'd have to take.

Elise left the relative safety of the office before she could change her mind and scurried up the hallway, holding the club at the ready and keeping a close eye on the front of the building. When she got to the door at the halfway point, she held her breath. Taking pains to make no sound, she turned the knob to the right. To her relief, the door opened without so much as a squeak. She quickly slipped inside and let out a shuddering breath.

The room turned out to be a small storage closet. Though it would provide good shelter for the moment, she was only halfway there. The last twenty feet would be the hardest — and, she suspected, the longest — sprint of her life.

While she listened for Stuart's return, Elise closed her eyes and tried to imagine her approach. With any luck, she would be on him before he knew what was happening, but even the best laid plans could fall apart in a heartbeat. Her timing would have to be impeccable.

Just as she was fantasizing about bashing him with the golf club, she heard movement in the hallway. She opened her eyes, and after counting to ten, peeked around the doorjamb.

Stuart had moved back to the front door. With it cracked, he was peeping through the opening with his face plastered against the jamb.

"Come on, boys," he said and then giggled to himself. "That's right; nobody's at the house, so come down and check the winery. Uncle Stu's got a surprise for y'all."

Dear Lord, Jackson and Ross must be leaving the residence and heading this direction, she thought. It was now or never. With her pulse racing, she stepped out into the hallway, feeling exposed and vulnerable. Her eyes were glued to Stuart's back as she began to carefully close the distance between them.

Twenty feet. Fifteen feet. Ten feet . . .

She was as silent as a prayer, certain she was going to make it. Unfortunately for her, Henry picked an inopportune time to come around. When the older man moaned, Stuart turned toward the sound.

And caught sight of her in his peripheral vision.

Time shifted into slow motion as she watched Stuart's head begin to swivel toward her. They each raised their respective weapons simultaneously. Terrified she would be a split second too late, she swung the club with all her might like Babe Ruth swinging for the outfield.

Maybe it was fate — or maybe it was just dumb luck coupled with a system pumped full of adrenaline — but the golf club connected full force with the side of Stuart's head before he could get off a shot. The pistol flew out of his hand, and his body did a neat spin before crashing face first into the metal door.

She raised the club for another shot but then realized it wasn't necessary. Just like that, Stuart had crumpled to the floor and looked to be out cold. Frozen in place, Elise stared down at him watching for any sign of movement, amazed that her plan had actually worked.

"I hope that was as good for you as it was for me, you homicidal douche bag," Elise told his unconscious form after a moment. " 'Cause let me tell you, it felt mighty fine from this end."

Wanting to keep her distance — just in case he was faking — she eyed him carefully as she stepped around his inert body to retrieve the gun.

"Is it over?" Henry asked. Although his voice was barely audible, it held a note of rebellion she had to admire. "Did you take that crazy bastard out?"

When she was confident Stuart was no longer a threat, she moved to Henry's side. With an incredible rush of energy still flowing through her system, Elise dropped down next to the vintner. "So it would seem."

"Good job, little girl."

Though the man had made some terrible choices and would soon have to pay the price for them, she couldn't find it within herself to condemn him. It wasn't her place to judge his part in this mess. That would be a job for someone else. For the moment, she was just so glad they were both still alive.

"How are you feeling, Henry?" she asked, trying to put the distressing thoughts out of her mind.

"I've been better." Henry cleared his throat and when he spoke his voice sounded rusty. "SOB clocked me with the butt of his gun a couple times before I lost consciousness. My head's poundin' and my vision's fuzzy, but I s'pose I'll live."

"That's good to know," she replied with a gentle smile. "Hang on. Help is on the way. We'll get you to the hospital and all patched up before you know it."

When she made to get up, the older man grabbed her arm. "Elise. I'm so sorry about . . . everything. Please believe me when I say that this was never my intent."

"I know, Henry," she replied with a nod. "I know."

"Everything just seemed to spiral out of control before I knew what was happening."

Elise felt pity for him. He was a decent

man who'd lost his way. "Don't worry about that now, okay? Let's concentrate on getting you some medical treatment."

In the next moment, she was startled as someone tried to open the door, only to smack an unconscious Stuart in the head. Though she knew it was probably Jackson or Ross, she jumped up, gripping both the gun and her club a bit tighter.

"El?" It was Jackson's voice, and she'd never been happier to hear it than she was in that moment.

"I'm here," she said, leaving the weapons with Henry and scrambling over to Stuart's body. "Hang on a minute."

She grabbed him by one foot and dragged him away from the door. "Okay, it's clear."

Jackson entered the building first, followed by Ross and Jim Stockton. "What the hell is going on in here?" Jackson asked, taking in the scene. "Are you okay?"

"I'm fine, but Henry needs an ambulance." With adrenaline still coursing through her veins, she couldn't hold back the hysterical laughter that bubbled out of her. "Stuart could probably use one as well. He killed Harmony and Uncle Edmond and was going to kill me and Henry as well. I put a stop to his plan with a golf club." At Jackson's dumbfounded look, she shook her head and added, "It's a long story, and I'll be happy to give you a detailed statement. But could we do it somewhere else? I have got to get out of this building."

While Jim went back to the cruiser to call for an ambulance, Jackson zip-tied Stuart's hands and feet together before pulling out his cell phone. "Ross, take your sister out to the cruiser. I'll be along as soon as backup arrives."

Thirty minutes later, Elise had completed her statement of the afternoon's harrowing events and stood watching as two ambulances left the property. One carried Henry, and the other carried Stuart with an armed officer on board. Her high-energy rush was nearly gone, replaced by an incredible exhaustion, chills, and a heart full of grief.

The worst part was that she couldn't get the idea out of her mind that she'd brought this mess down on her family. She'd been the one to introduce Stuart to River Bend.

As she and Jackson walked toward the cars to finally leave, a horrible guilt over everything that had happened began to build inside her. When she stopped walking and tugged on his arm, Jackson turned to face her with a perplexed look.

"El?" His eyes were full of concern as he

searched her face. "What's wrong?"

The compassion in his voice tore at her, making the remorse she felt seem a hundred times worse. Tears welled up in her eyes as everything hit her at once, and she put her free hand to her lips to stifle the sob that rose up in her chest.

"Oh, hey now. Don't cry, baby. It's all over and we're okay. Everything's gonna be fine."

"No. It's not that. It's . . . I'm so sorry." She blurted it out as tears began to trail down her cheeks. How could he be so kind to her when the entire thing had been her fault?

"Sorry? About what, darlin'?"

Swiping at her tears and working to rein in her rioting emotions, she gave him a miserable look. "I did this, Jax. I brought a madman into our lives, and I can't tell you how horrible it makes me feel. How am I going to make this up to everyone?"

"For crying out loud, El, that's not even good conversation," he murmured, tucking a strand of her hair behind her ear. "And it doesn't merit a response, because you've done nothing wrong. You're in shock, that's all. It's to be expected after what you've gone through. None of this is your fault."

"Yes, it is," she insisted. "This would never have happened if I hadn't hooked up with

Stuart. Uncle Edmond, Harmony — they'd both still be alive. And Henry wouldn't be on his way to Austin with a skull fracture as we speak."

"Stop it, right now. Do you hear me?" Taking her by the shoulders, he gave her a gentle shake. "You're not responsible for Stuart's rampage. That's just bullshit."

"But he wouldn't have been here in the first place if I hadn't been dating him!"

"You don't know that. And besides, since when does dating someone make you responsible for their actions?"

"Jax —"

"No, El." He cut her off with another quick shake. "You said yourself that the man you saw today wasn't the one you knew. Something just went haywire in Stuart's head. Who knows what set it off, but I do know you couldn't have predicted it; no one could have."

She heaved a sigh as Jackson gathered her into his arms and held her tight.

"I'm just thankful that it's over and no one else was killed," he murmured. After a moment he pulled back and tipped her chin up with a finger. "I think you were incredibly brave today, pal."

"You do?" She gazed up at him thinking how lucky she was to have him in her corner. And wondering why they'd wasted so much time.

"Yes, I do. You did good."

She sniffed and choked out a laugh. "I was so scared. All I could think about was the three of you walking into Stuart's trap — not knowing he was waiting with a gun. I was terrified he would —"

Jackson put a finger to her lips before she could finish her sentence. "But he didn't because of your quick thinking." He gave her a wry smile. "Now come on, let's get you home."

TWENTY-SIX

That evening after dinner, with the entire family gathered around the dining room table, Elise gave an account of the afternoon's events. She began with the outrageous story of Stuart's gradual meltdown and how it was tied to the scheme to steal her hybridization process. She ended with her luck in finding the golf club and her cockeyed plan to save them all.

Abigail gave a bloodthirsty cackle when she got to the part about bashing Stuart in the head with the club. "Ha! Serves the little pissant right."

"Mom!" Laura said in a disapproving tone.

"What? He killed two people and could very well have added another *five* to the list had it not been for Elise's quick thinking. I say he got what he deserved."

"And I'm not disagreeing with that," Laura said. "But you don't have to sound so pleased about it."

Abigail crossed her arms and lifted an eyebrow. "Well, it does please me, and I'll show it however I want, thank you very much. I'm proud of Elise."

Madison giggled. "I'm with you, Gram. I only wish I could have seen Elise in action."

"Yes." Abigail gave a satisfied nod. "She was very brave."

"That's what Jax said, Gram." Elise glanced over at him and grinned.

"Well, he's right," Abigail said and got up to get more coffee from the sideboard.

Jackson smiled. "Brave, yes, but don't ever do that to me again, do you hear? You scared the crap out of me."

Laughing, she shook her head. "I won't. I scared the crap out of myself."

He sobered then and gave her a stern look. "I mean it, Elise. No more poking around in police business. Promise me you'll stay out of trouble from now on."

She sighed and crossed her heart then held up her hand in a solemn oath. "I promise, Deputy Landry. Besides, I have too much work to do. Maddy, C.C., and I are helping Gram with our booth for the next Lost Pines Food & Wine Festival. I doubt there'll be much mischief there to speak of."

"That's a fact," Abigail confirmed as she sat back down. "We have a boatload of work to do and less than two months to do it. Our booth is going to be the best one at the festival, or I'll know the reason why. So there won't be time for that kind of nonsense."

"Good wine and good friends." Madison smiled. "It's gonna be a party for sure. I have so many ideas. Now that the wedding from Hades is over, I can't wait to get started."

"From your mouth to God's ears, Maddy. I just hope Third-Rate Winery doesn't show," Abigail grumbled.

"Third-Rate? Never heard of it," Jackson said.

"Third *Coast* Winery. It's a small vineyard down toward the coast," Ross explained. "It's run by Gram's high school sweetheart and his trophy wife."

"Uh-oh. Bad memories, Miss Abby?" Jackson asked. "Or was he the one that got away?"

Ross burst out laughing. "Gram doesn't approve of his choice in spouses, that's all."

Abigail made a *pfft* sound and rolled her eyes. "Divia Larson is a brainless twit. Always trying to one-up everyone with her designer clothes and snooty ways. I don't know what Garrett sees in her."

"Be that as it may, we're going to have the best booth with or without Third Coast's entry." Elise glanced over at Jackson. "And there'll be no mischief. I promise."

"That's good news," Jackson replied with a smile.

"Speaking of good news," Ross said as he stood and raised his wine glass. "I have some awesome news for us all. I spoke with the bank yesterday afternoon, but with everything coming to a head at once, I didn't have time to get the family together to discuss it."

"Is this about the balloon payment that's coming due?" Madison asked.

"Yes." Ross nodded. "After the success of the Adams/Wilkinson wedding, and with subsequent referrals for several more events, they've agreed to take half the payment now and the other half in ninety days."

"And we have enough to cover the first half now?" Elise asked.

"Yep. And, we have a couple CDs maturing next month as well. So, it looks like things are smoothing out."

"Oh, Ross, that's wonderful!" Laura said. "We always get good numbers before the holidays. By the time the second half is due, our cash flow should be under control and we can stop worrying. That is, until the next crisis," she finished with a laugh.

"So, a toast," Ross said, holding up his glass. "To family, good wine, and a bountiful future. *Salut!*"

"*Salut!*" They all responded lifting their glasses high, and Elise couldn't help but grin. They may have had a rough summer, but things were definitely looking up. The vineyard was out of the woods financially, at least for the time-being, she and Jackson finally seemed to be finding their footing, and the future looked bright. She sent Jackson a wink just before putting the glass to her lips.

Salut, indeed!

ACKNOWLEDGMENTS

There are also a few folks to thank, so I hope you'll indulge me, dear reader. First and foremost, I must start with my agent, the amazing Christine Witthohn. Thanks for taking a chance on me, girlfriend. You are the most amazing partner, cheerleader, task master, and friend. I can't express how grateful I am for your hard work, advice, and support. And for being my bulletproof vest.

A shout-out goes to my beta-readers: Diane Nelson, Recca Maze, Penny Jensen, Robin Pearsall, and longtime buddy Natalie Bellissimo. Thank you all for your encouragement . . . and for cleaning up my grammar. I am grateful.

A special thanks goes to Liz Lipperman, my critique partner extraordinaire. Thank you for going first and blazing the trail. You keep me honest and are a tireless sounding board, a continuous source of support, and truly a valued friend. I couldn't have done this without you . . . and wouldn't have wanted to.

Last but not least, to my family and friends who've stood behind me throughout this mad endeavor: I love you.

ABOUT THE AUTHOR

A native of Oregon, **Joni Folger** spent twenty-two years with an airline, traveling and moving around the country before settling down near the beautiful Pacific Ocean with her three very spoiled cats. When she's not spending quality time with the characters she creates, she enjoys gardening, crafting, and working in local theater.

The employees of Thorndike Press hope you have enjoyed this Large Print book. All our Thorndike, Wheeler, and Kennebec Large Print titles are designed for easy reading, and all our books are made to last. Other Thorndike Press Large Print books are available at your library, through selected bookstores, or directly from us.

For information about titles, please call:
 (800) 223-1244

or visit our Web site at:
 http://gale.cengage.com/thorndike

To share your comments, please write:
 Publisher
 Thorndike Press
 10 Water St., Suite 310
 Waterville, ME 04901